Incident, CA

Also by Celeste White

The Resistance Factor

Summer of Fire: A Memoir

Crazy Good Fortune: A Year of Adventures in Costa Rica

Altar of Fire

The Last Good Fairy

The Legend of the Flying Hotdog

Incident, CA

by

Celeste White

Keswick House Publishers

ISBN No. 978-1-7345044-0-8

Keswick House Publishers
Redding, CA

ACKNOWLEDGEMENTS

I would like to thank my first readers, who gave me such excellent notes for getting *Incident, CA* in good shape: Susannah Hardaway, Jim Dowling, and Caryn McVoy, as well as, of course, my husband, Richard Hardie. I would like to express my deep appreciation to Susannah as well for her help in getting my front cover finalized.

I also want to thank Rupert Sheldrake, Ph.D., for graciously allowing me to use his name and research for one of the characters in this book. I have never had the pleasure of meeting Dr. Sheldrake, nor his lovely wife, Jill Purce, so the characters that grace these pages are from my imagination. Dr. Sheldrake's research, however, is represented to the best of my ability from the books of his that I've read. If you've never read any of his works, I highly recommend them. I mention two of them in this book, *Dogs That Know When Their Owners Are Coming Home: And Other Unexplained Powers of Animals*, and *The Sense of Being Stared At*, but he has an impressive oeuvre that is well worth exploring.

Olivia's research is based on my own research in graduate school and beyond.

With gratitude to Robert D. Hare

CHAPTER 1

Piper stepped out her back door and paused, breathing in the crisp autumn air. She let her eyes travel over the garden, as she usually did first thing in the morning, to see how everyone was doing. She noticed that the vibe was off right away but didn't spot the problem until she left the stoop and rounded a corner. Where a stand of insanely flourishing snapdragons normally stood, nothing remained except for one crushed plant, its wilting yellow blossom mashed into the dirt. She suspected deer as the most likely culprit, but as she sought out the devas that tended this stand of snapdragons, they had disappeared, too. That was odd. Even after getting preyed upon, most plants' devas continued to hang around, at least until they realized whatever it was they inhabited wasn't coming back.

She sought out the neighboring pansies' devas, but they peeped out from between the blossoms and foliage, unwilling to leave the shelter of their plants.

What happened? she asked them.

They didn't answer right away, but after a beat she received an image of something large, dark, and menacing. A bear? Did bears eat snapdragons? She supposed they could. Seemed like they ate pretty much anything and everything, and they were a regular presence in this part of town. Her home, and those belonging to a handful of neighbors, backed up against old-growth northern California forest. When food became scarce in the forest, bears made raids in town. Garbage was their favorite meal, but they also loved berries and fruit, sometimes taking down entire limbs to get what they wanted.

Piper loved living in a wild place, and she pretty much loved all nature; but there were certain animals that were a pain in the ass and bears were one. Deer and ground squirrels occupied that category, too. And some bears could be dangerous. Bear attacks were extremely rare, but Piper shuddered as she remembered a news item she had read recently about a woman back East who was killed by the bears she was feeding. An extremely unwise thing to do, but for all Piper knew, bears in her neck of the woods thought she was feeding them with her compost pile and berry bushes and fruit trees.

Distracted, she headed towards her potting benches to find something to replace the snapdragons with, veering too close to one of her raised beds and sending herself sprawling. She sat up, checking for bruises. A sharp pain in her left wrist let her know that she had at least strained it, if not sprained it. Sighing, she went back into the house where she applied some Helichrysum and Arnica, then wound an Ace bandage around her wrist. She didn't have classes to teach until the afternoon and now that she had sprained her wrist, her gardening plans would need to wait. She had just picked up her phone to see if her friend Marion could meet her for brunch, when it buzzed. Delighted to see that she had a text from her boyfriend, she hurried to open it.

"I'm afraid we're not working, Piper. It's not you, it's me," it said. "You're the perfect girl for someone, just not me."

"What?" she texted back. She sank into the nearest chair, her knees and elbows trembling. She hadn't seen this coming at all. She decided to call him. She was afraid he might not pick up but he did. "Have you met someone else?" she asked.

"No, not really," he said.

Not really? she thought. Either he had or he hadn't. "Well, look, do we have to decide right now? I mean, if there's a problem, can't we work it out? Can't we talk?"

"Piper," Jared sighed. "There's nothing to talk about. You're a great person. I just don't have … you're just not the kind of woman that I … listen, I don't want to be cruel, but I—I've met someone who's really hot."

"I'm not hot," she said quietly. Frankly, she had never aspired to hotness. Hotness, she always felt, was overrated.

Jared didn't reply. And Piper didn't have the heart to pursue the topic any further. She hadn't realized that everyone had to be hot. Or at least, she had hoped. Everyone always told her how pretty she was, and how sweet, and she thought that there must be guys out there who appreciated that, who didn't need her to be sexy, too. But some subtle change seemed to have taken place in the world of dating, where hotness had become some kind of baseline requirement for attractiveness.

She hung up without saying goodbye, tears stinging her eyes. Her morning was turning out so awful, she considered not calling Marion after all. The way things were going, she'd probably have an accident on the way. But she decided that seeing Marion was probably the most comforting thing she could do. She tried to sound normal when Marion answered and accepted her invitation, but her voice was breaking as she said goodbye.

Piper arrived first at Buffington's, and one of the waitresses seated her. Piper felt so droopy she was considering laying her head on the table when she heard Marion call her name. Looking up, Piper observed with a pang how hot her friend looked in her skinny jeans, ultra-high-heeled shoes with straps that buckled around her ankles, expertly applied makeup, and tight-fitting T shirt that hugged her generous bosom as well as her toned abs. Piper glanced down at her peasant blouse and skirt, thinking maybe they weren't as nice as she thought they were when she put them on.

Marion swooped on Piper and grabbed her up in a fragrant embrace. "What's the matter, sweetie?" she asked. "You sounded heartbroken over the phone."

Fresh tears started into Piper's eyes. "I am," she croaked, then bent her head and began shredding her napkin.

"Aww, honey," Marion said, patting one of her hands as she took her seat. "Tell me."

Piper opened her mouth to begin when their server stopped by to get their drink orders. Marion ordered for both of them, iced basil tea.

"You were saying." Marion nudged her foot under the table.

"Jared broke up with me," she blurted, biting her lip as her tears spilled over.

"Oh, for God's sake," Marion said. "That jerk! You're better off without him, believe me."

Piper looked up from her napkin, which had begun to resemble hamster bedding. "Why do you say that?"

"Piper, honey, only you would have been blind to what an egomaniac he is. He's a complete narcissist!"

"No, he's not!"

"Whatever." Marion rolled her eyes. "I stand by my statement. And now you're free to find someone decent."

Piper didn't know what to say, so she propped her cheek on her hand and sighed.

"Anything else?" asked Marion. "I see you sprained your wrist."

Clearly, she had come to the wrong person for sympathy, Piper thought. But she told Marion about the snapdragons and their devas anyway. At this news, her eyebrows bunched together in concern. Piper knew that Marion couldn't see devas, but she believed her, for which Piper was grateful. At least in Incident, there were more people who believed in these kinds of things than a lot of places.

"What do you think could have upset them so badly?" Marion asked.

Piper shook her head. "I don't know. All I got was impressions and feelings, some mental images from the ones nearby who didn't disappear."

"What were those?"

The server appeared and set their iced teas down on the table. Piper smiled up at him and thanked him. "Just something dark and big," she said as he left. "And frightening."

"A bear?"

"Well, that's all I can think." Piper drummed her fingers on the side of her glass. "But the whole thing just felt … odd."

Marion shuddered visibly. "You're kind of giving me the creeps, Piper."

"I'm giving myself the creeps!"

"Well, if you live right next to the forest, you're going to have some odd shit happening. I mean, wild animals do some odd stuff, when you think about it. Anyway, keep me posted." Marion reached over and squeezed Piper's forearm. "And forget about Jared. His loss."

"Right." Piper forced a smile. The problem was, she didn't seem to be all that well suited for relationships. None of them seemed to last. She had been with Jared longer than anyone else and that had only lasted two years. Marion's husband absolutely adored her and she adored him, and they had been together since high school. Piper had barely dated in high school, she felt so shy and different.

She had thought that the university at Incident, with its notorious—or famous, however you wanted to look at it—departments of parapsychology and fringe biology, not to mention theoretical physics, would create a more accepting environment than where she grew up in San Francisco. Her father was an internist, her brother an oncologist. Her mother had been a nurse. So her desire to study botany and become an herbalist was not met with great enthusiasm. And in fact, she had found a more welcoming attitude here. But her luck with men hadn't fared any better.

They spent the rest of the meal on lighter topics. Marion worked as an interior designer, and she cultivated eccentric people as clients. Her current client was a man who had spent his professional life studying fresh water turtles, and he wanted his home to resemble turtle habitat as much as possible.

"So I'm like, perhaps you would like to wainscot with mud, sir," Marion giggled, Piper joining in. She was about to tell Marion a story about an interaction she had with a turtle the week before when she noticed a handsome, smartly dressed man approaching their table.

"Excuse me, ladies," he said, smiling first at Marion, then Piper, where his gaze lingered. "I'm Axel, the manager here, and I just wanted to ensure that your meal was meeting all your expectations."

Marion batted her eyelashes at him. She flirted with everyone. "It is now," she said.

He laughed, showing perfect, gleaming white teeth. Piper made a mental note that perhaps it wouldn't be a bad idea to buy some teeth-whitening strips. All the teas she drank tended to stain enamel. He turned to Piper. "And for you, miss?" he said.

"Oh! Absolutely," she said, flustered. Extremely good-looking people always flustered her.

"I'm glad to hear it," he said, giving her a warm smile before moving on to another table.

"Ooh, he thinks you're cute," Marion teased.

"I'm sure he's like that with everyone."

"I don't know, girl. Seems to me he had eyes specially for you."

"Well, whatever," Piper said, swiping the air dismissively. "I'm not interested in anybody right now. I need to think about things. And anyway, I'm hardly the type for somebody like that."

Marion shook her head. "Piper, how many times do I have to tell you—I think you'd be anyone's type. You have no idea."

"I guess not," Piper said.

"You just have terrible taste in men. What's that all about?"

"Can we change the subject? Let me tell you about this turtle I met last week …" As she told her story, Piper's gaze roamed around the room and she spotted a woman sitting at a table who was wearing a set of clear plastic nasal prongs, a small oxygen tank at her feet next to her chair. *I wish good health for you,* Piper thought; *whatever your problem is, I hope you have a happy outcome.* As she continued to scan, she noticed a nice-looking guy about her age sitting alone at a table in a dejected slump. Probably the same energy I have right now, she mused, as she sent him a wish, too: *I wish happiness for you,* she thought; *I hope that whatever is causing you sadness turns around to bring you something unexpectedly wonderful.*

She had borrowed this habit from her grandmother, who was religious though Piper was not. When Piper was young, she had shared that she liked to bless people whenever she saw someone who was suffering. "It's the best antidote I've found to my own disappointments," she said; "and why not put some goodness out into the world? Maybe it doesn't do anything, but it certainly can't hurt. And it always makes me feel better."

It was true. It always made Piper feel better. Maybe it was corny, maybe she was old-fashioned, maybe it didn't do anything at all for the person she blessed, maybe she was naïve. She didn't care. The practice honored her grandmother, it made her feel good, and it couldn't hurt.

The handsome, well-dressed manager caught her eye as he talked to one of the servers and pointed at a table where two elderly ladies sat. His apparent concern for their service warmed her heart, and she found herself wishing that she could be the kind of person to catch his eye. But that person, she had no doubt, would be extremely hot.

CHAPTER 2

Mom?" Carson called; "your toast is ready." The mechanical pop from the toaster spurred a jangle of sparkly bluish-white triangles in his vision. He plucked both pieces from the toaster and laid them each on a plate, then grabbed the apple butter from the fridge. Merilee shuffled into the kitchen, still in her bathrobe, her dog Jessie padding behind her.

"Thanks, sweetie," she said, stretching up to give him a peck on the cheek. She smelled like her face cream. "What's on your schedule today?"

"Oh, I've got a recording session this morning and a rehearsal this afternoon."

"Will you be home for dinner?"

He nodded. "I will. Want me to pick something up on my way home from my rehearsal?"

"Oh, no thanks, honey. I'm working today. I'll pick something up before I leave."

"See if they have any Fuyu persimmons and pomegranates. I'll make that salad you like so much."

She smiled, which was what Carson was after. His father had died fourteen years ago, when Carson was a sophomore in high school. They both had a hard time for a couple of years, but when Carson went to Santa Cruz for college, he managed to find his footing once again and enjoy life. His mother never recovered, it seemed. He had hoped for a while that she might find someone else, but though she dated half-heartedly, she had never found anyone who really captured her heart. And to be honest, Carson had never really liked anyone she had brought home.

Carson slathered his toast with apple butter and wolfed it down, gulping the rest of his coffee. He reached down to give Jessie a quick scratch behind the ears. She was a particularly fortunate mix, with the markings of a Malamute and the body shape, soulful brown eyes, and soft, pettable ears of a Lab. "I'll see you later tonight, Mom," he said, slinging his arm around her for a quick hug before grabbing his guitar and heading out the door. The sound that the screen door made banging behind him stimulated an image of a rapidly swelling reddish-orange sphere surrounded by a dark, russet brown halo.

One of the things he missed most about his dad was their shared synesthesia. His mom was always interested in what he saw, but she couldn't relate. He didn't know any other synesthetes in Incident, though he had known two friends in Santa Cruz who had different forms of it. One saw the days of the week and months in color, and another perceived both colors and personalities in letters and numbers. "Six is a happy-go-lucky kind of guy," she told him once; "rotund and outgoing, a snappy dresser. He's always dressed in navy blue and brown. Whereas two is yellow and white, wispy, shy, and languid."

He hopped into his aged Toyota Corolla and placed his guitar in the passenger's seat. His friend Zach had a small recording studio near the University; Carson was working on his second solo album. His first had been released by a small independent label in Santa Cruz after his band broke up, but that label collapsed when the business manager absconded with all the money. He was now recording and producing his own music, and doing as many gigs as he could book on the West Coast. He was barely able to cover his expenses with what he made, though. He taught private classes at the junior college in town, but as adjunct faculty, he didn't get paid much. He occasionally taught a few individual students at home as well, but again, it was pocket change. He sometimes felt embarrassed by the fact that he was living with his mother, but he told himself that she needed him. Besides, it was comfortable and they got along great. His girlfriend du jour loved to make snarky comments about it, and he knew she thought he should move in with her. But he didn't feel committed enough to do that. Maybe one of these days.

Zach's studio wasn't far from the university, located in a small storefront on what used to be the old main street of town, before it grew to its present size of 150,000. When he drove up, he found a small group of people milling around in front of it, the large front window shattered. He parked and got out, leaving his guitar in the Corolla. He spotted Zach, talking to two policemen.

Zach saw him as he approached and held up his finger, letting Carson know he'd be with him as soon as possible. Carson took a seat on one of the public benches nearby, squinting into the darkened interior of Sounds True.

After twenty minutes or so, Zach came over and flopped down on the bench beside Carson.

"What happened, man?" Carson asked.

"Tweakers, probably," Zach sighed. "Who knows? Thieves, at any rate. They stole all my equipment."

Carsons's heart sank. "God, that's terrible! Are—are you insured?"

"Oh, yeah. Thank God. But it's going to be a while before I'm operational again. And no one's going to pay me for the lost business."

Carson nodded morosely. He had really hoped to have

his next album out before Christmas, but with this delay, he probably wouldn't. And he wouldn't have his new album for sale at any of his holiday gigs.

"I'm really sorry, man," said Zach, throwing Carson an apologetic look.

"Hey, it's not your fault!" As bad as Carson felt, he knew that Zach was feeling a hundred times worse. He just hoped that this setback wouldn't put his friend out of business. He operated the only decent recording studio north of Sacramento. Carson didn't relish the idea of having to drive three hours or more to record his music. He wondered, though, if he should try to book some time in Sacramento. If he could, he might be able to produce his album in time for the holidays.

He said goodbye to Zach, told him to call if there was anything he could do to help out while he got things back together. Then he locked his car and walked down to the nearest coffee shop. He bought an espresso and took it outside. Even though it was October, the weather was still warm and pleasant, a few clouds passing overhead. He got on his phone and started calling recording studios in Sacramento, but it was as he feared: Everyone wanted to get an album out by Christmas. They were booked solid.

He went back to his car and drove to a nearby park, took his guitar out and played for an hour or more, trying to raise his spirits. His favorite band was Radiohead, though now he was entranced with Atoms for Peace, which featured the lead singer for Radiohead. He played acoustic, but also electric guitar, and keyboards as well. Music created the most magnificent visuals for him, and he sometimes thought about taking up painting so that he could paint what his music produced for him visually. One of the most fantastic things about synesthesia was the incandescence of the colors produced. They glowed and pulsed and the various shapes and lines moved and shifted their perceived planes like the aurora borealis, which he had been fortunate to see once when a solar flare created a light show as far south as Incident a number of years ago. For the first time, he felt like his mom could get a small glimpse of what he and his dad saw on a regular basis.

With his form of synesthesia, the shapes and colors appeared to be projected on a screen in front of him. If he wanted to, he could look through them, or dampen them down so that he could do whatever task was required. But most of the time, he enjoyed focusing on them. He felt sorry for anyone who didn't have this ability, actually.

But today, even this wonderful gift didn't raise his spirits. He felt that he was falling further and further behind in his career goal to be a successful, self-supporting musician. Most record labels wanted music far slicker than what he produced, and even though there were exceptions, like Radiohead, the kind of music he composed and performed was considered fringe. He honestly didn't understand it. The music he created was designed to evoke deep and powerful emotions, positive emotions, though some of them were hard to put a name to, and some of them felt melancholy and filled with yearning. But his fans—all three of them, he thought wryly—loved his music. They played it to feel better, more hopeful, more alive, they told him. So much of the music he heard on commercial channels was irritating, in his opinion. And the visuals they prompted were ugly. Ugly colors, ugly patterns. Why was it so popular?

He didn't feel like going home before his rehearsal, so he headed over to Buffington's Bistro for a light lunch. He couldn't really afford eating out, but he needed something to raise his spirits and Buffington's had terrific food. He got there before the lunch crowd hit, so he was able to get a small table at the booth that ran along one wall. Normally, he would enjoy people-watching while he waited to get served, but today, he felt so disheartened that he kept his gaze on first, the menu, and then his sesame noodles, hunched over the table like a capo fastened around the neck of a guitar. The noodles were very good, but they weren't doing much to lift his spirits, he observed dejectedly.

Then he felt something tickle his consciousness. He looked up and scanned the room. A pair of cute, elderly women shared a table nearby, one of them wearing a purple hat that had a feather coming off it. The slick, sleazy manager was slinking around. He was new. A table of four college girls was full of giggles, which, when he focused on them, produced the most wonderful spray of twinkling, orange-pink blossoms in his field of vision. He saw an old man with a young man, probably his grandson. Then there was a table where two women in their late-twenties/early thirties sat. One woman had her back to him; she looked like a character with her wild hair and crazy shoes. And the woman opposite—Carson took in a sharp breath. She couldn't have looked more different than her friend. He would love to know their history. She was quite pretty in an innocent, unaffected way, which he liked, although usually that wasn't what floated his romance boat. But something about her touched him deeply. He rarely experienced the obverse of sound –> vision, that is, vision –> sound, but in her case, he heard the shimmer of a set of concert chimes when he looked at her. She looked as though she had been crying. He already wanted to beat up whomever it was who made her cry, she had such a sweet, vulnerable look about her.

Should he go over and introduce himself to her? No. They were getting up to leave and if he tried to intercept her now, it might seem like he was accosting her. He watched her walk out the door, her honey blond hair rippling down her back like a fairy princess. Who was she? Why hadn't he ever seen her before?

But most importantly, how could he see her again?

CHAPTER 3

Checking her phone for the time, Olivia saw that she had arrived early for her appointment. She decided to wander around the campus for a few minutes. It was the most recent addition to the University of California system, and the architecture was both modern in design and constructed with environmental sustainability in mind. The mild winters meant that most of the buildings had covered walkways that were open to the elements, and solar panels covered some of the roofs, while others were living roofs, maintained by students in the Biology Department. The vast bulk of California's population lay to the south, much farther south, whereas the northern third, where Incident was located, was sparsely populated, checkered with national forests, parks, and wilderness areas. It was that wildness that had attracted the bulk of Incident U's students.

Despite its contemporary look, the place had a whimsical, eccentric quality, the grounds dotted with fanciful landscaping, sculpture, and various structures on which students could climb, swing, slide, and skateboard. Incident University had a reputation for thinking outside of the box, which was why she was applying for a position here. Her own studies in biology had led her to some unorthodox thinking and was alienating her from not only her colleagues at U. Mass., where she had just earned her doctorate, but also her boyfriend, Lance. She had never realized how scathing and contemptuous he could be. But then, she had never disagreed with him before.

Remembering their last argument pricked her eyes with tears; she blinked them back with a fierce resolve. He had quoted that stupid old saw about people whose minds are so open their brains fall out, which proved nothing whatsoever except that he was an asshole. She had been charmed by her phone interview with the head of the Biology Department, Rupert Sheldrake, one of the pioneers in research that involved such things as telepathy and other unexplained powers of biological creatures. Dr. Sheldrake was not exactly some airy-fairy thinker—he had obtained his degrees from Cambridge and Harvard. All of his research studies were rigorously designed, controlled, and analyzed. Lance could learn a thing or two from his methods, she thought. His cancer research was lazy, in her opinion, and broke no new ground; it was only because his field was so generously funded that he was doing so well.

She gazed at students making their way to various classes, some of them stopping to play on the structures, some of them grouped on the lawn here and there, chatting or reading. Her eyes rested on a pretty young woman dressed in some kind of garb that seemed vaguely medieval as she stopped and talked to a couple of students, gesturing over toward a gate. Olivia wondered what lay behind the gate. Oddly, she felt a frisson of a connection with the woman, but she couldn't imagine what it would be, and in any case, she should probably be on her way. She didn't want to be late.

She found the office to the Biology Department and checked in with the assistant who manned the front desk. She was ushered to a small conference room and invited to sit in a comfy upholstered chair that gave her a breathtaking view of the southern Cascades, craggy from a history of volcanic eruptions, frosted with snow on the higher elevations. She accepted a cup of coffee from the assistant and then settled in to wait. One by one, the three faculty who were interviewing her came in, introducing themselves and shaking her hand as she stood to greet them: Rupert Sheldrake, Frances Ligurian, and César Perez.

"Dr. Harper, welcome to Incident University." Dr. Sheldrake smiled warmly at her; his eyes contained a nice sparkle.

"Please call me Olivia," she said, hoping that wouldn't be too informal. But everyone responded in kind and put her at ease.

Frances opened the folder that contained Olivia's application and glanced at it before addressing Olivia. "I see that your doctoral research was in epigenetics."

"That's right. I was interested in the ways in which the three-dimensional structure of the interphase genome affected how genes were read."

"Some outstanding work," César commented.

"Thank you."

"But you told me on the phone that you've started to expand your ideas regarding gene regulation," Rupert said.

Olivia cleared her throat. It was now or never. And frankly, this was probably the only biology department in the country where she could share these thoughts and still have a reasonable expectation of being offered a job. "That's correct. I believe that consciousness is involved. I just couldn't figure out any other way that such a complex system could be regulated so quickly and responsively." Rupert had already heard this from her when they spoke on the phone. She cautiously observed Frances's and César's reactions; they both looked surprised.

Frances turned to Rupert with a grin. "This should be right up your alley," she said.

An ongoing area of interest for Sheldrakee, Olivia knew, was how people often knew when they were being stared at. His theories of how this might work involved a concept he called a "morphic field," a phenomenon whose existence he had inferred from various kinds of evidence and whose properties he was still defining and describing. He felt that it was based on neither matter nor energy, that these fields comprised a different kind of force. Neither time nor space seemed to limit these fields; the connection often seemed to transcend both.

Yet despite being somewhat unencumbered by the usual four dimensions, Sheldrake felt that these fields did not fall into the category of parapsychology. Instead, he believed that they were intrinsic abilities possessed by all creatures, ones that conferred a selective advantage in survival. Sheldrake's reputation was what first drew her attention to Incident. At first, she had assumed that the properties of consciousness involved in gene regulation would be based on minute electromagnetic fields generated by biophysical aspects of the body. And she still hadn't rejected this idea, for a number of reasons. But after reviewing Sheldrake's work, she thought it possible that morphic fields could also be involved, either alone or in combination.

Sheldrake laughed, saying that was certainly true. All three of them quizzed her for a good half-hour on her plans for future research and her interest in the University. She would be giving a seminar later this afternoon for anyone in the department who was interested. As they wound up the interview, César asked her if there were any questions she might have for them. Because she had so thoroughly researched the department and all its faculty, she had only one: "How did the town of Incident get its name?" she asked. That was the kind of information she assumed would be readily available on the Internet, but she hadn't found anything, oddly enough.

The three biologist exchanged glances. "Well, there are several tales," Rupert said. "One story is that in the mid-1800s, two miners were visited by a space ship one night. They were invited to take a ride and they said they rode to Mars and back."

"Another story," said Frances, "is that trappers around the same time came across a man dressed in robes that looked biblical to them. He was nine feet tall and seemed to glow. The next thing they knew, they were miles away from where they had been trapping, with no knowledge of how they got there."

"But my favorite is the story involving Sasquatch," said César. "When two explorers were first charting the territory around here, they came across a bigfoot village. At first the explorers were welcomed and treated well, but something happened and the Sasquatch went on the attack. The explorers had guns, so they were able to kill them. Though some say a few escaped."

"I see," said Olivia. No wonder the town wasn't eager to advertise any of these legends. Especially if they were wooing a state university back in the Eighties. Rupert stood then, and they all followed, shaking Olivia's hand as she thanked them for the interview. They would all no doubt be attending her seminar later.

She had a little more time on her hands at that point, so she decided that she would head over to the student center and grab a pastry and a cup of coffee while she reviewed her notes for her seminar. She had agonized over whether to simply give a summary of her doctoral research involving the three-dimensional genome, or whether to outline her evidence for her new area of interest. She decided on the latter. It was a risky move, she knew, but somehow she didn't think that she was going to get the position here by playing it safe. Frances's area of expertise involved regeneration in mammals, and César's involved homing instincts and migration. Incident did also have a robust and well-respected parapsychology department, and she knew that professors in both departments often collaborated.

As she sat nibbling on her pastry, she tried to get a feeling for what it would be like to live here. She had grown up on the East Coast and all her family and friends lived there. She had enjoyed the department at U. Mass., and her doctoral research had gone extremely well; she had studied her last two years on a fellowship while the National Science Foundation funded her research. It had been a wonderful feeling to have her work so well regarded and to be considered such a bright young scientific talent. She could have—perhaps should have, she reflected somewhat regretfully—squelched her growing belief in the role that consciousness played in turning genes off and on. But something inside her just wouldn't let her do that.

It had been painful, though, to have so many former supporters turn on her and even make fun of her. Scientists, for all their vaunted objectivity, had preconceptions and sacred cows just like everyone else. She had been impressed by the story of how much scorn had been heaped on the first brave scientist to suggest that some viruses' genetic material was comprised of RNA rather than DNA. Today, knowledge of retroviruses was commonplace.

You would think they would learn, she thought, taking a swallow of coffee to wash down the last bit of her apricot Danish. Her cell phone buzzed then and she fished it out of her purse to see who was calling. It was Lance. She dropped her phone back into her purse.

It would be nice to have a whole country between them, she mused. She was realizing that their relationship wasn't going to survive, and it would be hard to watch him take up with someone else. Making a fresh start was appealing quite a lot to her right now.

But there was also the worry that Lance had brought up before she flew out to the West Coast for this interview:

"Who's going to fund your New Agey research?" he had sneered.

"Oh, for God's sake, it's not New Agey, Lance!" she had retorted. "Why do you have to be so insulting?"

He had one good point, though. Pharmaceutical and agricultural companies were funding most of the research in the biological and medical sciences these days. No one was interested in investing in something that wouldn't eventually pay off. In many ways, she couldn't blame them. It only made sense.

But what about research to benefit mankind? she thought; Have we really become so mercenary as a species?

She didn't like to think so. And if there were any way, any way at all that she could make a contribution to all humanity, she wanted to do it. In her opinion, the long-term survival of humans depended on it.

CHAPTER 4

Axel parked in the front lot of the Golden Oaks assisted living facility, checking his teeth and straightening his tie in the rearview mirror before exiting his Mercedes. After marching in the front door, he stopped at the front desk manned by a plump, bored-looking young woman.

"Can I help you?" she sighed.

"I hope so," he said, giving her his most winning smile. "By the way, I love that necklace you're wearing."

Her hands went to her throat as she fingered her turquoise pendant, and she sat up straighter. "Thanks," she said, brightening. "So what can I do for you today?"

"Well, it might sound a little wacky," he said, shaking his head with a self-deprecating roll of his eyes. "I just moved into town a little while ago. My grandmother died last year, and she lived in an assisted living facility. The people there were so nice, and they told me that I was welcome there any time, that a lot of the residents didn't have family and that they loved to get visitors. My company moved me here, so I wasn't able to take them up on their offer, but the fact is … I don't have any family and haven't had a chance to make friends yet. And I have to tell you, I miss my grandmother like crazy. She raised me when my parents died."

"I'm so sorry." The young woman smoothed her hair back and lifted her bust just a little.

"Oh, thanks." He smiled ruefully. "It's been over fifteen years, but I still miss them, you know?"

"I can imagine," she said, nodding vigorously.

"So, I was wondering if you knew of anyone here who might like the occasional visitor. It's an age group that I find comforting, as nutty as that might sound."

"Oh, not at all! We have several residents that I'm sure would love to have the occasional visitor. Let me check with my supervisor."

"Thank you so much," he said. He scrutinized her nametag. "Crystal, is it? What a pretty name."

"Thanks," she said, flashing her dimples.

Axel checked out the environs while Crystal disappeared into an office whose door opened behind her desk. The lobby was tastefully furnished and even had a big fireplace with a stone hearth—probably cultured stone. One old man in a wheelchair seemed to be sleeping, his head drooping towards his chest; an elderly woman was chatting with her middle-aged daughter.

"Sir?" Crystal called.

"Oh, for Pete's sake, I'm not as old as all that, am I?" he laughed. "Call me Axel."

"That's a very cool name," she said.

He grinned. "Thanks. My parents were very cool people."

She gestured to the office she had just exited. "Mr. Mandel would be happy to talk to you."

Axel adjusted his tie, thanked Crystal, and strode briskly into the office. Mandel, an older man with thinning hair combed back and the craggy complexion of a smoker, half-rose to shake his hand and offered Axel a seat in a faux-leather upholstered chair.

Mandel gave him an appraising stare. "So you want to hang out with old people, huh?"

Axel gave a wry chuckle. "Well, if you want to put it that way, sir. I'm just new to the community, and my last job was with a nursing home in Fresno. I—"

"Really?" Mandel interrupted. "Which one?"

"Well, I worked at several. Actually, I was more of a consultant."

"Oh yeah? As what?"

Axel shifted in his seat. "I was an auditor. At any rate, the point is, I ended up making some wonderful friendships with some of the residents. Plus, I was very close to my grandmother, who died recently, and I've always just found this age group to be one I felt at home with. And I know that so many of our elderly are either forgotten, or all their family have passed before them. The Christian Men's group I belonged to in Fresno was very active in helping seniors." He shrugged. "But if you're concerned about your residents' privacy or safety … I can certainly understand. I can try some other places to see if they might have more need of what I have to offer."

Mandel gazed at him for several more moments before apparently making up his mind. "We do have several residents without family here," he said with a sigh. "I don't see any harm in visiting with them. As you're not family, though, we couldn't let you take anyone off the premises."

"Goodness, no. I totally understand."

"Ask Crystal to bring Mrs. Bainbridge to the lobby. There's a nice little alcove where you can chat."

"Wonderful." Axel stood and offered his hand, taking Mandel's in a firm grip as he looked him in the eye. "I'll look forward to seeing more of you, sir."

"Oh, call me Glenn," he said.

"Glenn," Axel repeated.

Crystal had evidently been listening to the conversation

because as soon as Axel reappeared, she jumped up from her desk and said, "I'll fetch Mrs. Bainbridge right away."

Axel thanked her, giving her a winsome smile and waited. Soon, Crystal came down the hall pushing a sparrow of a woman in a wheelchair.

"You've got a visitor, Ethel," she said, coming to a halt in front of Axel.

Ethel glanced up with undisguised hopefulness, her expression changing to confusion when she took in Axel.

"But I … don't know you," she said.

"Mr. …" Crystal turned to Axel.

"Smith," he said, giving Ethel a wink.

"Mr. Smith is … is …"

"I'm here making a nuisance of myself, I'm afraid. I lost my grandmother last year and I guess I'm looking for a surrogate grandmother."

Ethel's hopeful look returned. "Well, I don't know how much use I'll be to you—I'm not as sharp as I once was …"

Axel sat down in a nearby chair and took her hand. "I can tell from your face that you're a nice lady," he told her. "That's good enough, don't you think?"

Ethel beamed at him.

Crystal coughed. "So I guess I'll just let you two get acquainted?"

"Absolutely," Axel replied. "Thanks so much, Crystal."

A half-hour later, Axel left with a promise to return next week. He checked his watch, noting that he had an hour to kill before his evening shift at the restaurant. He decided to run by the address he had gotten on Craig's List for some bedroom furniture. He yanked off his tie as he called the number listed and talked to the seller, who was at home and eager to show him the set. The address was on the other side of town, in a middle-class suburban neighborhood built in the 1970s, if he were to guess. Ranch-style homes with trimless windows and neat, sterile lawns.

The woman met him outside and took him to the garage where she had the set stored. It was a fairly tacky set, but Axel didn't have a lot of money, and he hadn't found anything else any more promising. He bargained her down, telling her that he had had a lot of medical expenses lately, to which she was very sympathetic. He then talked her into having the set delivered to his place for free.

After that, he went home to get ready for his evening shift. His wardrobe was a combination of expensive clothes that he bought when he was flush, and meticulously scouted-for items from thrift and consignment stores. Right now, all he had in his bedroom was a mattress and box springs on the floor; the clothes that weren't hanging in his closet were still stored in boxes. The apartment was in a brand new Mediterranean-style complex that cost a little more than he could afford on his salary, but he planned on getting ahead quickly, and anyway, once he got settled, he would work on ancillary means of income.

He shaved for the second time that day, admiring his dense five o'clock shadow in the mirror, as well as his thick, dark head of hair. His parents might not have given him much, but at least they gave him good, strong, masculine looks. As he shaved, he thought about the young woman he had introduced himself to at lunch. Just his type—pretty, innocent, and completely unaware of her effect on men. Vulnerable, too, that much was clear. He had a pretty strong hunch that she had just gotten dumped.

At work, he made himself useful, bussing tables when the wait and bussing staff got behind, making sure well-heeled diners were tended-to and that he made them feel special. The occasional high roller would slip him a bill and the occasional older woman who had seen better days gave him her phone number. He made sure they knew how much he appreciated a mature woman who had drunk deeply from life, instead of silly, empty-headed coeds.

He stayed till the end of the shift, past everyone else, even the bartender. It was his responsibility to close up shop and reconcile the cash register. He pocketed a few twenties, making sure to cover his tracks—if anyone was suspect, it would be one of the wait staff. Then he selected a couple of bottles of wine from the wine cave as well as a steak from cold storage, all carefully accounted for as breakage or spoilage. Of course, if the owners didn't pay such shit wages, he wouldn't have to resort to such tactics.

When he got home, he put the steak under the broiler and opened one of the bottles of wine, a nice Sonoma cabernet. He cooked some frozen peas in the microwave and when everything was ready, sat down to eat. No sooner had he taken his first bite than his cell phone rang. He started to switch it off when he saw it was from his old man. Better take the call.

"Hey," he said.

"Hi, how's it going in that crap town?"

"Fine."

"Remind me again what name you're going by these days?"

"Axel."

His dad laughed so hard he started coughing. He was a heavy smoker and Axel fully expected him to keel over from lung cancer any day. "Axl, huh? As in, Axl Rose?"

"Spelled differently, Dad." Actually, he had been inspired by Jules Verne's protagonist in Journey to the Center of the Earth. It held some sort of poetic appeal.

"Yeah, whatever, you little shit."

Axel made a mental note to refrain from giving his parents his next cell phone number. "So what's up?"

"Hey, I just wondered if you knew what happened to that girlfriend of yours."

Axel tensed. "Which one?"

His dad chortled. "Which one … what a player."

Axel didn't reply, just waited with a fake smile on his face, though he knew his dad couldn't see it. "Always stay in character, son," was one of his dad's famous pieces of advice when he was teaching him how to hustle.

"You know, that little strawberry blond. Cute little thing."

"I have no idea, Dad. We broke up."

"Right, right. Well, she's officially missing."

"Is she."

"Yeah, I thought you might like to know."

"Well, that's a shame, but we broke up a couple of months ago. You know that."

"Oh yeah, that's right. They're casting quite a drag net."

"That's good. I hope they find her."

"I'll bet you do."

"And just what is that supposed to mean?"

"Nothing. Just giving you a heads up is all."

Axel expelled an impatient breath. "I don't need a heads up."

"No. No, I'm sure you don't."

Axel waited a beat. "Anything else?"

"Not at the moment."

"Bye, then. Thanks for calling and brightening my day." Axel hung up before he heard his father's reply. Old fuck. What the hell was he up to?

He didn't have the same appetite as he had before, but he finished the steak, dumped the uneaten peas into the garbage disposal, and took his glass of wine into the living room. He had a couch and one end table. That was the extent of his furnishings in that room. He should have brought his television from his last apartment in Sacramento, but it was cheap, and he had his eye on a big screen TV. Soon.

He emptied his pockets onto the cushion next to him. A hundred and forty bucks and two phone numbers. He'd pursue those phone numbers in time.

But for now, he was most interested in that pretty young woman crying into her beer with that slutty-looking friend of hers. He saw a lot of possibilities there. A lot. And the next time she came in, he'd be ready.

CHAPTER 5

usk was falling, Piper's favorite time of day. She even loved the word that referred to both dawn and dusk: crepuscular. A magical word for a magical time. She wasn't alone in her fondness for this hour. A lot of animals were deemed crepuscular, active at dawn and dusk, and the devas loved it, too. It seemed to be the time that they most liked tending to their plants.

Not everyone perceived devas the same way. Some saw them as orbs of light; others didn't see them but felt or sensed them instead. Perhaps her perception came from her own imagination or tendency to anthropomorphize, and perhaps they came from her grandmother's succulent collection of illustrated fairy tales; but to her, they appeared as miniature, incandescent children clothed in flowers, leaves, fruit, and graceful tendrils. The deva for foxglove might wear a blossom as a cap, for example, while a deva for a sugar snap pea plant might wear pea pod shoes. The deva for an apple tree might have an apple blossom skirt while the deva for a raspberry might wear a plump berry for a hat. It was possible that they appeared to her in guises that they knew she would enjoy—they were generous like that, at least the ones in her garden.

But whatever the case, she found their whimsical, botanical appearances utterly charming and a source of great joy.

The devas for the ravaged snapdragons hadn't reappeared. The other devas were still loathe to communicate anything about the visitor who plundered the snapdragons, so she decided to let it go for now and simply tend to her garden as best she could with her sprained wrist. Fortunately, it had turned out to be a mild sprain. The other devas seemed to want to make up for their brethren's absence, and the deva for her dogwood, which was resplendent in scarlet leaves, outdid himself in a fanciful outfit of a roseate, leafy jacket and trousers buttoned with crimson berries and silver seed husks, his jaunty cap borrowed from a nearby oak tree's acorn. When they wanted to express their affection for her, the devas glowed more brightly than usual, and they were so bright tonight, her garden looked as if it were filled with fireflies—which had recently been successfully introduced from the east, much to everyone's delight.

She was renting her house from a sweet older couple who lived closer to town. This had been their first home when they were newly married, and it contained many happy memories for them. She felt that energy the minute she viewed the place, and was thrilled that she had been chosen as their tenant. They wouldn't rent to just anyone, they told her; they could tell that she would take good care of the place. She had gotten their permission to extend and develop the gardens, and just recently, she had made arrangements to have her rent payments start to count as a down payment on the house, should she choose to buy it. Every single bit of extra money she made was going into a savings account for the house, added to the modest inheritance she had received from her grandmother. Not only did she love the house—a cottage built with stucco walls and slate roof, numerous, well-placed windows, and a cozy hearth—she also loved the fact that it backed onto an old-growth forest.

In addition to providing her with the lovely grounded feeling that she received from unmolested nature, the forest served as a wonderful resource for some of the wild herbs she used in her practice. She was careful never to harvest more than the plants could easily replenish, and because she had harmonious relationships with their devas, they were happy to give her as much as she could use. She made a good living as an herbalist, and she taught two classes a semester on herbology at the university, which she greatly enjoyed. Her faculty status there gave her access to their gardens and greenhouses, another rich resource.

If not for the yearning she felt to share her life with a good man, her life was pretty close to perfect, she had to admit. She was stewing a bit over Marion's remark that she had terrible taste in men and wondered if that were true. If it were, what did that say about her? Marion said Jared was a narcissist and that everyone else could see it but her. Was that true as well? He did seem very keen to do the things that were important to him, but she hadn't minded. Her boyfriend before Jared had been pretty focused on his career, but he was an artist. Didn't artists need to be focused? It was a tough business.

Well, if it were true, it was all the more important that she wait before getting involved with another man until she figured out the lack in her own character. All these break-ups were hard on her heart, which she knew was more tender than most. She wasn't sure she could handle another one.

As she wandered around her garden, snipping off a dead blossom here and a yellow leaf there, she thought about the interesting-looking woman about her age she had spotted at the university after her lunch with Marion. She had looked very sad, and if Piper were to bet, she would bet that it was love that was making her so sad. Why did love often seem to be so difficult and painful? It didn't make a lot of sense, quite frankly. At any rate, she had sent a wish to the woman that she would find happiness and something to soothe her and lift her spirits.

Before long, the light dwindled as the twilight faded and the devas bedded down for the night. Piper put her clippers away in the garden shed, then stood still in the yard for a moment, closing her eyes and breathing in the rich, autumnal scent of her garden. An old apple tree stood in one corner and although Piper harvested a good deal of them, she left some windfalls on the ground for the animals. She loved the brandy-like scent that they gave off, and combined with the scent of musty leaves and marigolds, she found it a heady fragrance. As she breathed in the cool air of twilight, she caught a whiff of something not nearly so pleasant and wondered if an animal had died in the forest. She opened her eyes and glanced up at the sky to see if any buzzards might be circling, but didn't see any. It was late in the day for vultures, so it wasn't surprising.

Shrugging, she started to head inside when she heard several loud knocks coming from the forest. She froze. It was an unfamiliar sound. It didn't sound like a woodpecker. It was deeper than that and had a different rhythm. It sounded like someone hitting the trunk of a tree with a stout pole. She supposed kids could be playing in the forest—maybe they had a game that involved a special code of knocks. Her place wasn't the only one to back up on the forest, and several houses in the neighborhood had children. But as she hesitated, trying to make sense of the knocks, she became overwhelmed with the sense that someone was watching her.

This filled her with a blind panic, and she dashed inside as quickly as she could. She locked all the doors, something she rarely did, and pulled the blinds. Taking a deep breath to calm herself, she busied herself with making dinner—parsnip-cinnamon soup with popovers on the side—and told herself she was being silly. It was probably just a raccoon or a deer. But the missing devas nagged at her. Something large, dark, and unknown was out there. She regretted not having a dog. She loved dogs, but since she rented, she didn't think it was right to have pets. But when she bought the place, she promised herself, she would get a dog—a sweet, loving, protective dog. Maybe if she had a dog, she wouldn't feel so bereft without a man in her life.

She ate her soup and popovers at the kitchen table, leafing through a beautiful book of botanical etchings that she had found at the library. She usually read until it was time to turn in, but she was feeling restless this evening, whether it was because of the fright she had experience earlier, or she was missing Jared, she didn't know. But she grabbed her jacket and drove over to the university. She could see if there was a lecture or a movie going on that she wanted to attend. If nothing else, she could hang out at the student center and maybe run into someone she knew. She was friendly with a number of the faculty as well as her former students.

It turned out that she was too late for everything scheduled, so she went to the student center café and picked out a chocolate croissant at the pastry bar. Her gaze roaming the tables as she looked for a place to sit, she once again saw the sad woman she had noticed earlier today, sitting alone. Piper decided that she would see if she would like some company. She figured it couldn't hurt and she didn't see anyone she knew.

She approached the table and cleared her throat, smiled at the woman as she looked up. A flicker of confused recognition crossed her face.

"Hello," said Piper. "I don't want to intrude, but would you like some company?"

"Actually," said the woman, smiling and gesturing to the empty chair opposite, "I'd love some. Please join me."

"Thank you," said Piper, noticing how pretty the woman looked when she smiled. Her hair was a dark auburn and she had beautiful skin. "I'm Piper."

"And I'm Olivia. Pleased to meet you, Piper." Olivia extended her hand for a shake, which Piper took.

"Are you faculty here?" Piper asked.

"Not yet. I'm hopeful, though. I'm applying for a position in the Biology Department."

"Well, we might end up colleagues, then! I teach classes in herbology. What's your field of specialization?"

Olivia hesitated, then filled her in briefly. Piper could see that she felt self-conscious about her new area of interest. Not surprising, since she came from a hard science background.

"You've certainly come to the right place," Piper reassured her. "This is one of the most ground-breaking, cutting-edge departments in the country." She giggled. "Of course, sometimes we get called Incense University, which, in my opinion, is pretty dorky as insults go. For Pete's sake, what does it mean? We're all Buddhists or something? Although, I suppose that's not all that far-fetched … hmm …" She propped her chin on her hand as she thought about it.

"I've been called worse lately," Olivia muttered. And once again, sadness flitted across her face.

Maybe her sadness wasn't love-related, Piper reflected. Maybe it was something else. "I'm a huge fan of Rupert Sheldrake's work," she said.

Olivia nodded. "I am, too. He's the reason I applied here."

Piper quizzed her a little on her background, where she had traveled from, where she obtained her degrees. She liked Olivia, and hoped that she would get the position she was applying for. For one thing, she found her interest in the ways in which consciousness might affect gene regulation to be fascinating. Her knowledge didn't usually go to that level—she was more focused on whole plants and whole people—but given the consciousness that she felt certain dwelled inside plants, with their devas and innate botanical wisdom, she felt sure that Olivia was onto something.

And there was something else, too. Sheldrake had written a book called *The Sense of Being Stared At*, which she had read a few years ago. She had certainly found it to be the case that when she made a wish for someone, they often glanced up and looked around the room. And sometimes, she had felt the subtle brush of someone's regard and when she turned, caught someone's eye just as they looked away.

That sense she had had earlier of being stared at by something in the woods, stronger than any other time … maybe she wasn't being silly. And in fact, normally she wouldn't discount something like that. She just didn't want to be afraid. Especially at her own house and in her own gardens. And she really didn't like the idea of being too scared to collect herbs in the forest.

"So what do you think about Rupert's work with people being able to feel when they're being stared at?" Piper asked.

"Oh, I definitely think there's something to it," Olivia said. "Don't you?"

"I do," said Piper, with a sigh.

"It makes sense," Olivia said. "If prey wants to elude a predator."

"A predator," Piper murmured. "Oh dear."

Olivia gave her a close look. "Oh dear?"

"Oh, no worries!" Piper waggled both hands in front of her, palms out. "It's nothing. Although … well … of course you know we have cougars here, right?"

Olivia laughed, a pleasing, deep laugh. "In the abstract, yes. I guess I just hadn't thought that they'd come close to a town."

"They're not prowling main street," Piper said. "But they do like easy access to prey, and with so many people having pets …"

Olivia blinked as the implication sank in. "Right, that makes sense. We don't have cougars where I live."

"And where is that?" Piper asked.

"Massachusetts."

"I've heard it's beautiful."

"It is." Olivia glanced at her watch. "In fact, I'm flying back tomorrow and I've got an early flight, so I should probably head for my hotel."

"Do you need a ride?"

"No, I've got a rental car, thanks." Olivia stood and smiled warmly at Piper, offering her hand. "I hope we meet again," she said.

"I hope so, too." Piper rummaged around in her bag and handed Olivia a card before taking her leave. "Good luck with the position you've applied for." On impulse, she stood and gave Olivia a brief hug. She felt her stiffen momentarily, then relax. Piper suspected that cougars weren't the only thing that weren't common in Massachusetts. Well, if Olivia got the position here at Incident, she'd just have to get used to it. Residents were a huggy bunch.

"Thanks." Olivia grinned at her, then headed for the door.

Piper sat back down to finish her croissant, gazing thoughtfully at Olivia's back as she left. She had a good feeling about both Olivia's prospects and Olivia herself. But the discussion about predators nagged at her. She supposed there could be a cougar in the forest. It would be surprising if there weren't a cougar, as a matter of fact. But this felt different, though she couldn't say how.

Thinking about it carefully, she decided to appeal to the devas to warn her and protect her, any way they could. That thought comforted her. So the first thing she did when she got home was to linger in the garden and make her request, the moon casting mysterious shadows, transforming familiar plants and objects into enigmatic forms. Then an owl replied, reassuring her even more.

"Hoo hoo!" it called, causing the most delicious shiver to scramble over her scalp.

"Hoo hoo!" she echoed, waiting for the owl to respond. But it had fallen silent.

CHAPTER 6

Carson ambled along the trail, his knee buckling when Jessie came trotting past him with a big stick in her mouth and caught him on the back of the leg with one end of it.

"Jessie, damn it, watch your stick!" he scolded, grabbing at the nearest tree trunk to keep from going down.

Jessie paused, looked momentarily chastened, then pranced on up the trail. Carson wasn't really all that annoyed. Jessie could pretty much do no wrong as far as he was concerned. He had picked out Jessie as a puppy for his mom four years ago when he was home from Santa Cruz, for what he thought was going to be a short visit. But it turned into a move when his record label went out of business. He hoped that a puppy, especially one as winsome and cute and smart as Jessie, might coax Merilee out of her depression. And in fact, it had helped considerably. Of course, Jessie belonged to both of them now, given how his life had turned out since then, but it was his mom that Jessie had bonded with most deeply. It was as if she could sense that Merilee needed love and solace, and the two of them were pretty much inseparable. The days that Merilee worked at her job as a cashier at the local health food store,

Jessie stationed herself next to the door twenty minutes before she came home and waited. Unfailingly. But Carson was more active than his mom, and Jessie loved going for walks in the woods and fetching sticks, so he and Jessie had a nice bond, too.

Jessie's favorite way to hike was to run ahead and scout, then run back and check on her human, then lollygag behind while smelling everything that needed smelling, then lope to catch up. Often, she found a stick that she occasionally wanted thrown, although sometimes playing keep-away or tug-of-war was her preferred game. Carson had noticed that lately she had been presenting bigger and bigger sticks for him to throw, as if engaged in some private joke or experiment. They had recently become so large that he couldn't help but laugh when she showed up with them; this seemed to gratify her immensely. She showed back up now with an even stouter stick than the one she had nailed Carson with, dropped it at his feet and froze into her fetch pose, one paw lifted, ears pricked up, her brown eyes riveted to his throwing arm.

"You are one silly dog," Carson said, shaking his head as he reared back and gave her stick—more of a tree limb, actually—a mighty heave up the trail ahead. "That should keep you busy for a half a minute, anyway," he shouted, as she rocketed up the trail in pursuit.

Lost in thought, mulling over yesterday's rehearsal with his band, Tachyon Fundicle, he didn't notice that Jessie didn't come back right away with her stick. He wasn't certain, but it seemed that Evan, the bass player, was thinking about backing out of the band. Carson wasn't sure what the problem was, whether he felt that Tachyon wasn't going anywhere—a concern that Carson himself harbored—or whether Evan was more interested in playing jazz, whether he wanted to start his own band, or what. He wasn't very communicative. And not very enthusiastic. Carson reflected that maybe he should just focus on his solo efforts. By using a synthesizer, he could provide his own bass and percussion. But he liked playing with other musicians. And percussion on a synthesizer never sounded as good as a real drummer.

When several minutes had passed, Carson began to wonder what had happened to Jessie. As he stopped to call her, he heard a sharp bark that ended with a yelp, a sound that produced an upwardly swooping, elongated indigo comma shape with yellow-green spikes in his vision. Soon he spotted Jessie, running toward him in a funny slinking fashion that he had never seen before, and no stick.

"What's wrong, girl?" he asked. Did she get sprayed by a skunk? He sniffed gingerly. Not a skunk, evidently.

He crouched down to pet her and noticed that she was trembling as she tucked her tail and sat next to him. "What is it?" he asked. Jessie had always seemed fearless, one time chasing a full-grown bear out of the back yard. Carson had spotted a makeshift shelter in the woods the other day when they went off the trail, but he didn't think a homeless person would spook Jessie. She whined and licked his hand, crowded closer to him. "Maybe it's time to go home, huh, girl."

At the mention of the word "home," Jessie sprang to all fours and turned around to face the direction they had just come. She looked back over her shoulder at Carson.

"I'm coming," he said. He himself wasn't necessarily keen to encounter whatever it was that had troubled her. Maybe a cougar. They had made quite a comeback in the past couple of decades.

When they got back to the house, Carson noticed his mom's car in the driveway. Jessie made the same observation, too, evidently, because she bolted from him and danced at the door, waiting to be let in. Carson opened the door for her, then followed her to the kitchen where his mom was making herself a snack at the counter.

"Hi, honey," she said, smiling at him while she bent down to stroke Jessie's ears. "Hey, girl," she crooned. "Hey, Jessie."

Jessie wagged her tail enthusiastically.

Merilee straightened up. "Guess what I did today?" she asked.

"Got a tattoo?"

"Ha. Ha."

"Sorry. I have no clue." Carson opened the refrigerator and grabbed an apple.

"I signed us up for an experiment."

"You what?" Carson whirled around to stare at his mother. Had she lost her mind? "What kind of experiment? Jesus, Mom."

"A really fun one. You'll like it, I promise."

Carson seriously doubted that, but he listened as Merilee described the experiment. Rupert Sheldrake, a researcher in the biology department at the university, was conducting a long term study of animals who knew when their owners—or "people," as Sheldrake preferred to call them—were coming home. He had already published a book on the subject, which Carson knew about but hadn't read. His mom had, though, and she had been fascinated by it. He had to admit, he had been impressed with Jessie's faithfulness in waiting by the door for Merilee when she was due home from work. He always assumed that she knew what time Merilee was due home, but his mom had pointed out more than once that she didn't always come home at the same time. At any rate, one of the researchers was coming by the house in a couple of days to install a video camera by the door.

"Your job," she said, pointing a finger at him, "should you choose to accept it, is to keep a log of Jessie's movements when you're home and I'm not. Just write down the times that she heads over to the door."

She explained that Sheldrake's theory, based on some rigorous yet mind-blowing experiments, was that pets headed to the door to wait when their person formed the intention to come home. Sheldrake had ruled out timing: Some owners had erratic schedules and he had even conducted some experiments that involved calling subjects on their cell phones at random times and telling them to head home; their pet invariably headed over to the door during the call. He had also ruled out the sound of the owner's car: Some owners came home via all kinds of means—bus, bike, foot, taxi, car pool.

"It has to do with morphic fields," she said, then paused. "Whatever they are. I don't really understand them. But we'll get a little money for participating. And doesn't it sound like fun?"

Carson actually didn't think it sounded all that fun, but he knew they could use the money and he didn't want to squelch his mother's excitement. He only had himself to blame, anyway. He was the one who had gotten Jessie in the first place.

He knelt down and rumpled her ruff. "What do you think, Jess? You want to be part of an experiment?" She had sat down during their conversation and she thumped her tail loudly on the floor in response.

"See? She thinks it's a great idea," said Merilee.

Carson just shook his head, though, truth be told, Jessie's ability to understand human speech sometimes blew his mind. He was certain she had at least a seventy-five-word vocabulary, and she even, on occasion, seemed to understand entire sentences.

"Just tell me what to do and I'll do it," he said. "But I'm going to be away for some gigs."

"That's okay, sweetie. We'll have the camera as back-up. Are you home for dinner tonight?"

"No, I'm having dinner over at Heather's."

"That's nice. Tell her hi for me, okay?"

Carson said he would and headed out to the shed that he had turned into his music studio. If he could ever make enough money, he could maybe turn the shed into his own recording studio; but he would need to soundproof it and he needed much better recording equipment. He had acquired some decent instruments over the years, including a synthesizer, but that was when he had a label. Now he was lucky to have enough money for gas for his car and strings for his guitar.

As he played, he thought about the pretty young woman he had seen at Buffington's Bistro the other day. The fact that he was fantasizing about her made him think that he should probably break up with Heather. He wasn't exactly being unfaithful by fantasizing, and he didn't even know this mystery woman, but he wanted to be in a comfortable position to ask her out if and when he did. He couldn't stop thinking about that bewitching shimmery sound that he had heard when he first saw her, like what he imagined elfin music might sound like. He wondered if maybe it was the sound of love at first sight. He wasn't sure if he believed in love at first sight—what did it mean, anyway? But now that he had experienced this, he was reevaluating his stance on the subject.

Along with his synesthesia, Carson possessed a plastic sense of time. He sometimes felt that he could grasp all time all at once, that past, present, and future were all fused together in some vast, spacious realm. He knew, from the one physics class he had taken in college, that time was a dimension, and that in the bigger picture, time didn't really exist, at least, not in the way that humans thought about it. Contemporary western humans, anyway. So he sometimes wondered if things like premonitions or hunches came not from peering into the future, but from dabbling in the pool of timelessness, where probabilities swam about like fish.

Was it possible the feeling this young woman gave him was some sort of splash back from the future into the present? That they were destined to be together and in the future, they were already together? So that, what he was experiencing now was almost more akin to memory than prescience?

Ah well, idle speculation. But he decided that he would try to capture this feeling in a new composition. And as he worked, the visuals—undulating ribbons of lucent green and rich, deep plum spangled with fuchsia and ivory orbs that glided along the ribbons as they shifted from one plane to another—filled him with deep joy and satisfaction. And when he felt his cell phone vibrating in his pocket, he ignored it.

CHAPTER 7

livia deposited a stack of empty boxes in her living room, then went back to her Honda for another one. She was still so elated from the phone call she had received from Rupert this morning that she could barely focus on getting ready for her move. She was glad, now, that she hadn't taken either of the job offers she had received last spring. They were not particularly exciting, but any offer for a teaching position was considered a good thing, and Lance took great pains to remind her that if she didn't take one of them, she could consider her career over.

"Who's going to hire an out-of-work academic?" he pointed out more than once. He himself had nabbed a prestigious post-doc at Harvard. She had been very pleased for him until it became clear that he was pleased enough for both of them.

She knew that it didn't help that she had started waffling on her own research direction while she was job-hunting. At first, she had simply started to downplay her doctoral research in mapping the 3D organization of the interphase genome. Not a good idea, given how hot the area had become during the course of her studies. Her advisor, initially skeptical and more interested in what was now known as two-dimensional mapping—the location of genes along the individual chromosome—had become thrilled with her choice when the research money started pouring in. Pharmaceutical companies were interested in anything that might help them target their drugs better and it was becoming clear that, during interphase, when the chromosomes unraveled from their characteristic, tightly coiled shapes during cell division and were available for transcribing genes, the 3D structure played a role in gene regulation. Researchers had often been puzzled by the fact that related genes and even regulatory portions of genes lay on different chromosomes. Now they were learning that these genes and portions of genes were actually located near one another when the chromosomes uncoiled and assumed a new organization.

Failing to follow through aggressively on her accomplishments in this area had been undermining enough. But then she had had the bad taste to actually float her ideas about consciousness having a regulatory role in epigenetics. She might as well have said she believed a tiny homunculus dwelled inside the nucleus of each cell to personally direct which genes were read and which were not.

She had started to despair, in fact. And she had begun to wonder if there would be any place for her at all in biology or research science or whether she would have to back down and return to carrying out research that didn't excite her just to be able to make a living. But now she had a position as close to a dream job as she could hope for. She was taking over for a professor who had left unexpectedly when her husband was awarded a senior management position with the World Health Organization, so she would have classes to teach as soon as she arrived. That would be a bit of a scramble. But she knew the subjects well, so it shouldn't be too bad.

Outside her windows, the fall color was just starting to fade. The sweet gum in the front yard of her apartment had dropped a number of leaves overnight, leaving a pool of crimson around its base while the maples and birches across the road still held on to some brilliant orange and yellow leaves. She would miss Massachusetts. She had grown up here, spent her entire life here. She felt glad that she was moving to some place equally beautiful, and in many ways, far more grand. One of the offers she had received was in southern Illinois, which, when she visited, was flatter and more bereft of forests than she had imagined Kansas to be. "Yep, you can watch your dog run away for three days," an old-timer had told her at the diner where she took her breakfast.

She glanced at her wall clock, one made out of kitchen utensils—loaf pan, splayed measuring spoons, a lid to a canning jar—to resemble a moose, and saw that it was time to go over to her parents' house for lunch. They would not be happy about her news, as much as they would want to be, and she dreaded telling them. She would miss them terribly, and she knew that they depended on her in a lot of ways. And just recently, her father had developed a worrisome health problem, which she was hoping was simply an aging issue and one that wasn't too serious. But she couldn't let this opportunity go; she couldn't. It was just too exciting on so many levels. And she knew that her parents wouldn't want to hold her back.

She drove over to their house in neighboring Sunderland, where more leaves in riotous shades daubed the landscape in rich color. As she got out, she sniffed appreciatively, enjoying the umami scent of fallen leaves and the contrasting crisp, clean autumn air. She had grown up in this house and she loved it, a classic New England white clapboard house with black shutters and a gracious side porch where she and her family had shared many meals, cozy reading sessions, and ultra-competitive games of Scrabble. She was glad that her younger sister, Emily, lived not too far away in Boston and had no doubt settled there permanently, with a lawyer husband, a baby, and a toddler, all of whom her parents adored. Olivia loved her sister and her kids were cute as far as kids went, but her husband Grant wasn't really one of her favorite people. She would miss them, too, though not as much.

She entered without ringing the bell, calling out for her mom and dad, whom she found in the kitchen. Her mother, still pretty at age sixty, tall and slender with shoulder-length silver hair, was slicing bread on a cutting board while her father, also tall but more solidly built with thick auburn hair that hadn't a single gray strand in it, sat on a tall kitchen stool stirring something in a large pot—butternut squash soup, from the smell of it.

She gave them both a kiss on the cheek, her dad commenting on the lovely fragrance of outside air that she brought in with her. Her mother asked her to fill the water glasses on the table, adding that they were ready to serve. Olivia complied, then held soup bowls for her father to fill and set them at each place. Her mother brought the bread and butter with her to the table; her dad winced as he collapsed heavily into his chair.

"Not doing any better, Dad?" He had recently begun to suffer from a muscle pain and tendon problems. At her urging, he had recently undergone a series of tests but nothing much had come out of them.

He shook his head. "Hard to know what's going on," he said. "At least they've ruled out ALS. So that's good."

Olivia felt frustrated that she couldn't help him out, despite her background in biological sciences. Her work was abstract as far as immediate applications went; although, if she actually made some progress with her new area of interest, her work might lend itself to more pragmatic uses. If he were taking statins, she might suspect them as the culprit; their connection to muscle wasting and pain was becoming well-known. But he wasn't. His cholesterol ran naturally low, though his blood pressure ran somewhat high, so he was taking blood pressure medication.

"Well, I'll do some research on your medications and see if I find anything," she said. "You never know." She had no reason to think his hypertension meds might be causing problems, but one thing her work in gene regulation had made abundantly clear was the inevitable connection between pharmaceutical drugs and side-effects. It was always worth considering, especially if nothing else was turning up. For one thing, different genes had different jobs in different cells. If you targeted one aspect of a metabolic pathway with medication, there was presently no way to avoid having some other, undesirable effect on another one where the same enzyme was involved. You just had to hope that you could tolerate whatever the side-effects were.

"Sure, honey," he said. "Whatever you say."

She cleared her throat. "So … I have some news to share," she said, smiling to soften the blow that was coming.

"Good news, I hope," said her mother.

"It is, it's really pretty fantastic news. I was just offered a university position this morning."

Both of her parents set their spoons down and beamed at her. "Why, honey, that's terrific!" exclaimed her mother.

"Well done!" said her father. "Where is the position?"

Olivia could feel her smile taking on a more plastered quality. "Well, it's at the University of California at Incident."

Though they tried heroically to keep from letting their faces fall, they didn't manage. "California?" her mother squeaked.

Olivia bit her lip. "Yes, I'm afraid so."

"That's wonderful, Olivia," her father said heartily, making Olivia feel even worse.

"I know it's a long way away," she said. "But you know—you can come visit me there! And I'll come home for Christmas. I'll probably have some symposia and meetings to attend back here, things like that."

"Oh, don't worry, sweetheart." Her mother reached across the table to clasp her hand. "We always knew that you might have to move away to get a good position. How do you think we ended up here?"

Olivia's father, David, taught comparative religion at a nearby private college, while her mother Leigh had a job as a social worker. They were originally from Michigan; Olivia and Emily had enjoyed their visits to their grandparents in the summers. But Michigan wasn't nearly as far away as California.

"But we did hope you might be able to find something close by. How could we not?" Her dad smiled at her so fondly that Olivia teared up.

"Well, I'm going to miss being so close," she said, blinking hard. "I absolutely won the parent lottery."

"And we won the child lottery, honey. We are so proud of you." David winked at her and squeezed her free hand.

If they had an inkling of Incident's reputation, they didn't give any indication of it. They no doubt felt, as most people would, that a position at any of the U.C. campuses was a feather in her cap. She hadn't told Lance yet and was thinking about moving first and telling him later. She didn't want him spoiling her good mood.

When she got home, she decided that she didn't have time to call Lance. He was probably in the lab in the middle of an experiment, anyway. She meant to put some time into researching her dad's symptoms, but she ended up so exhausted by the end of the day that she fell asleep on the floor next to a box she was packing. And when she woke up the next morning with a painful crick in her neck, it was all she could do to get the apartment cleared out and her Honda packed for her cross-country drive.

She drove by her parents' house for a final goodbye, then took back roads until she reached the interstate. The day was clear and fine, one of those sumptuously beautiful autumn afternoons of azure skies, fleecy clouds, and Trix-colored hillsides—a good omen, she thought. She had new horizons ahead of her, and she was feeling happier and more optimistic than she had in months and months.

CHAPTER 8

xel parked his Mercedes well away from the thrift store he intended to scout out in the nearby town of Mt. Shasta City. It probably didn't matter here, but it was a habit that had become ingrained. He took his time getting there, ducking into a coffee bar for an espresso, idly perusing listings in the window of a real estate office while he drank it. Then he took a quick look around to see if anyone was paying any attention to him before he sauntered inside New 2 U. It just wouldn't fit his image for anyone to know he shopped at places like this; he thought it too risky to shop in Incident, where he was building his reputation.

Mt. Shasta City was a hippie town, a lot like Incident, but there was money here, too, and that usually meant for good pickings at thrift stores. Plus, in a hippie town like this, there was usually less competition for the kinds of clothes he was looking for—dress shirts, nice slacks, and sport coats. He didn't really need anything at the moment, but a few of his thrift store purchases from the past were starting to look a little worn. He saw only two other people in the store, a stooped old man and a young woman who looked like a refugee from a Phish tour.

He hadn't been in the store long, expertly rummaging through the racks, when he heard the bell jingle as someone else came into the store. He kept his back to whomever it was, focused on his task, flinching when a woman's voice exclaimed, "Eric! Is that you?" He tensed. Eric was the last name he used. Hoping that perhaps the old man's name was Eric, he glanced at him. But the man made no sign. Axel turned, then, to see who might have recognized him, wondering if he could pretend he wasn't the person she thought he was. Unfortunately, it was one of his old girlfriend Kristy's roommates, coming right for him. What the hell was she doing here?

"Amanda?" he ventured.

"Yes!" She threw her arms around him. "This is crazy! What are you doing here?"

"I might ask you the same thing," he said, flinging his arms out in comic bafflement.

"I moved here! Can you believe it?"

"You're kidding."

"No, I got a job running a spa."

"Oh yeah? Is the pay good?"

She shook her head. "Not really. But the cost of living here is so much cheaper. And it's so beautiful. What about you?"

"Oh, I'm still in the restaurant business." He hesitated, trying to decide whether to tell her he had moved to Incident or not. He decided it would probably be a good idea. Who knew whether he might run into her again? "Hoping to start my own one of these days. But right now, I'm managing a restaurant in Incident."

"Well, hey, you're practically right down the street! We should get together!"

"Absolutely." Axel had always found Amanda a little irritating, she was such a Rah Rah, but she was good-looking and had a great body. He wouldn't mind fucking her if nothing else came along any time soon.

"By the way," Amanda leaned close and lowered her voice. "Did you hear what happened to Kristy?"

"No, we've been out of touch since we broke up."

"They … they think she was murdered."

Axel's jaw dropped. "God, no! How horrible!"

Amanda nodded, her face both grim and sad. "A fisherman found her body snagged in the American River. It took a while to identify her, she'd been in the water so long, poor thing."

"My God." Axel wiped his face with his hand. "Listen, do you mind if we go somewhere I can sit down? This is just—I just—"

"Oh, sure!" Amanda twisted around, looking out the storefront window. "Let's see … well, you want to get a cup of coffee?"

"That sounds great, thanks," Axel said, cradling Amanda's elbow as he ushered her out the door.

Seated at the place where he had just bought his espresso, another one steaming in front of him, Axel rubbed the bridge of his nose, then focused a soulful stare on Amanda. "This is just so hard to comprehend, you know?" He allowed tears to well into his eyes as he mashed his lips together hard. "She was so sweet and so pretty. Who on Earth would want to murder her?"

Amanda lifted one hand, then dropped it heavily on the table. "I can't even imagine." Tears brimmed her eyes, too. "She was such a good friend. I mean, I know you guys broke up and everything …"

"Well, it was my fault," Axel replied firmly. "I was just too full of myself. A girl like Kristy deserved a lot better than me."

Amanda reached over and squeezed his wrist. "Don't be too hard on yourself."

"Well, it's true." Axel hung his head briefly, then glanced up, his eyes full of pain and regret. "Do they … have any suspects?"

Amanda shook her head. "Not yet. The news just broke.

She might have been jogging along the trail there. We've run across some dicey characters along there when we've been bike riding. I told her she shouldn't ever run there alone, but, you know how she could be."

Axel let out a deep, shuddering sigh. "I do." Suddenly, he smashed his fist into his hand. "I can't help thinking if we hadn't broken up, maybe she'd still be alive today!"

"Oh, Axel," Amanda said, giving his wrist a caress this time. "You can't think like that. These things just … happen sometimes, you know? I understand how you're feeling, though. I keep thinking if I'd … I don't know, taken her out for lunch that day or insisted she go for a bike ride with me instead …" Amanda fell quiet, spooling a strand of hair around one finger. Her tears fell onto the table.

Axel took her hand. "Now you're being too hard on yourself," he said softly.

Amanda kept her hand in his, shaking her head sorrowfully. "Yeah."

Axel raised his espresso cup. "Here's to Kristy. May she rest in peace."

Amanda lifted her cup of cappuccino. "Here's to Kristy." Her eyes welled up once more as she took a trembling sip.

By the time they had finished their coffee, Axel had taken her phone number and promised to call. "My job at the restaurant is pretty demanding—crazy, long hours," he told her, "so I might not be able to get up here any time soon."

"I could come down!" said Amanda.

"That would be great! But I can't expect you to do that. I'll find some time." He winked at her. And when they parted, he gave her a chaste but lingering kiss on the cheek.

Starting up his Mercedes, he felt annoyed that he hadn't had a chance to buy anything at the thrift store. And now that he knew Amanda lived here, shopping here had become more problematic. He didn't have any problem with Amanda knowing he shopped at thrift stores—she probably thought it was cute—but he didn't want her blowing his image should the issue come up with anyone else. She wouldn't do it intentionally, but she was almost as ditzy as Kristy. He would have to find time, now, to drive up here see her, or she probably would come looking for him in Incident. And that didn't suit his plans.

When he got back to Incident, he logged on to his laptop and checked out *The Sacramento Bee* for news about Kristy. It was just as Amanda had said; they didn't really know much. They had just identified the body and were starting to compile a list of suspects. Axel knew, however, that most murders were solved in the first twenty-four hours of a crime. If they weren't solved then, the chances that they would ever be solved dropped dramatically.

His stomach started growling, so he grabbed a prepackaged dinner out of the freezer and shoved it in the microwave. He poured himself a glass of wine and sat down at the kitchen table, muttering an expletive when his cell phone rang. He pulled it out of his pocket and saw that his dad was calling. He punched the reject button, then took another swallow of wine. When his dinner was ready, he ate half of it and dumped the rest into the garbage.

After his meal, he felt restless. He wasn't working this evening and he still didn't have a television. Maybe he should check out Craigslist, see if someone needed to get rid of one fast. But this evening, he wanted to go out. He needed to go out. He went into his bedroom and rummaged through the scraps of paper he kept in the top drawer of his dresser, phone numbers that older women had given him. On the back of the note, to keep track of who was who, he gave them a star rating in terms of looks and some identifiers: "big hair, probably has extensions," "could use nose job but good body, "ass a little big but nice tits and expensive jewelry," etc.

He called three before anyone picked up. He didn't like to leave messages. But he finally got ahold of Big Ass Nice Tits.

She was thrilled to hear from him and suggested they meet for a drink at a bar near the University.

When he got there, it took a while for him to find her, the light was so dim, but she spotted him and gave him an enthusiastic wave. She was actually not as good-looking as he remembered, but that was okay. It wasn't really her face that he was interested in. And after three drinks, she was looking a lot better. He managed to manipulate her into inviting him to her place, upon which he was congratulating himself until he walked with her outside. There, strolling by the bar, was that ethereal young woman he had found so entrancing at the bistro. But he couldn't really hit on her while he was with Big Ass. Cursing his bad luck, trying to figure out if there was any way he could ditch his current date, he finally gave up and got into his car and followed his date to her house. And there he was able to forget his troubles, at least for a little while.

CHAPTER 9

iper led her class down the hall and out the door, heading for the potting benches of the university greenhouses. It was a glorious day, in the 60s and sunny, and the trees dotted about the campus stood ablaze in yellow, scarlet, and plum. This potting class was one of her favorite classes of the semester, part of Introductory Herbology. The students loved it, too. It got them out of the classroom and outside even if just for a few minutes while they made their way to the greenhouses. And the university had such beautiful facilities that they were a treat as well, even in the more mundane potting area. The rest of the greenhouses had gorgeous displays of various classifications of plants—the ferns and mosses room, the conifer room, the flowering plants room—that Piper often visited them, just for the fun of it.

As they entered the potting room, Piper inhaled appreciatively, delighting in the smell of damp, rich soil and fresh plants. She had asked the greenhouse manager to provide her with seedlings of lavender and oregano that the students would transplant from the germinating beds into individual clay pots, so the plant fragrances were particularly piquant today. Stacks of clay pots and mounds of soil, humus, sand, and gravel occupied the middle of the room; the glass walls were lined with wooden potting benches and germinating beds. When everyone stood in front of her, waiting, she began her lecture on basic horticulture.

"Plants have a few basic needs that are not hard to meet: water, light, and soil," she said. "But knowing how much and what kind of these basic needs a plant requires is where skill and experience comes in. Some plants love full sun while others prefer shade. Some plants need well-drained soil while others are more hydrophilic."

A movement over in one of the germinating beds caught her eye and she noticed a deva stepping out from behind one of the plants. As soon as she saw Piper's gaze on her, she curtsied and removed her hat, which resembled a miniature crocus blossom, only to reveal another hat underneath, a tiny tiger lily. Piper's speech faltered for a moment. Collecting her thoughts, she pressed on. "In fact," she said, "you can kill a plant by giving it too much water. If the roots can't drain, fungus and rot can set in …"

Curtsying once more, the deva removed the tiger lily to display yet another hat underneath, this one made from a cymbidium. Her expression was so droll that Piper giggled. Several of the students turned around to see what was making her laugh.

Stop that! Piper scolded the deva silently, unable to repress a snort of laughter when the deva snatched off the cymbidium to reveal a frog on her head that sat blinking in staid solemnity. Now everyone was turning around.

"I'm sorry," Piper said. "I—I was just remembering something funny that happened earlier today. At any rate, as I was saying …" The deva tossed her a mischievous grin as she disappeared behind her plant, the frog staying put, evidently liking his perch.

Piper didn't share the fact that she could see devas with anyone at the university. She had discovered that learning this information made some students or colleagues discount everything else she had to say. And she felt that she had a lot of good knowledge to offer. She had a special way with plants—she knew it, and so did everyone else—and her main goal in her position at the university was to optimize the interaction between plants and humans. Nothing made her sadder than visiting a friend and seeing neglected houseplants drooping in their pots, or plants that were woefully out of their sweet spot languishing away. If people could hear what she heard in these circumstances, the pitiful cries and heartbreaking moans, they wouldn't let those poor plants suffer like that, she felt certain. But in the absence of that sort of awareness, education was key. And she could educate people about plants without bringing in the devas. Although, to be honest, it would be nice to share this magical lore with everyone. She often wondered if there were students in her classes who could see the devas, too, but were afraid, like she was, to let people know.

Finishing up her instructions on how to prepare a pot for a freshly transplanted plant, she then demonstrated, selecting the plant with the mischievous deva, who couldn't resist one more trick. When Piper gently grasped the base of the plant in order to pull it up, the deva created the sound of air rapidly escaping a balloon. As Piper glanced around at the startled expressions on her students' faces, she deduced that she wasn't the only one to hear it.

Thanks a lot, Piper thought.

De nada, the deva giggled, blooming briefly with light before melting into the plant.

Piper spent the rest of the class walking around and giving tips to students as they worked. Since this was an elective, just about everyone who was in this class wanted to be here, so they worked diligently. The handful who took the class because they thought it would be easy usually came around by mid-semester. Most people, unless they were gardeners or liked flowers, didn't really think about plants, and they treated them like furniture that needed watering. If she could teach one extra thing in addition to responsible plant care, she wanted to help her students see plants as truly alive and responsive creatures, each possessing their own personality. Some plants were pushy, for example, while others were sneaky. Some were exuberant while others were shy. They were capable of communicating with each other as well as humans. And they had likes and dislikes, just like people.

Afterward, Piper spent a little time with a student who asked for some extra instruction, thinking that he might like to start a landscaping business when he graduated. She appreciated the thought that he was putting into his plans, in addition to his respect for the subject. She didn't have an office at the university, since she wasn't full-time faculty, so they walked to the arboretum and selected one of the park benches for their conversation. Piper stayed put after he left, having a half-hour to while away before meeting up with her women's group for their monthly get-together. The group had been started by a woman who worked as a shaman, so most of the women were pretty "woo-woo," as her dad would say. She supposed they were, but then, so was she. And what was wrong with that, anyway? Were they hurting anyone? Taking anything away from anyone?

An exquisitely colored bluebird came and perched briefly on a nearby bush, examining her closely with his bright black eyes before flitting off, filling her with awe. It must be bluebird season, she reflected. Just last night, an entire flock of them had visited her garden, feasting on the dogwood berries. The resulting sumptuous palette of color—cobalt blue birds, vermilion berries, incandescent yellow, orange, and crimson leaves—so dazzled her that she had had to sit down, she felt so overcome.

It had been several days, now, since she had heard the knocking in the woods behind her house, so she was starting to think it was nothing, just a one-off sort of thing. Probably kids playing. And as for the feeling of being stared at, she supposed it could have been a cougar. Cougars so rarely attacked people, though, that she didn't feel she should avoid the woods because of them. In fact, the last cougar attack in northern California was seven years ago, in 2007, and it had taken place on the coast. To her knowledge, there had never been an actual cougar attack on a person in this part of California—most of them had taken place to the south.

The time passed quickly and soon the sun dipped low enough in the sky that a chill breathed into the arboretum. Piper grabbed her purse and strolled to her car, which was parked in the nearest faculty lot. The group was meeting at Buffington's Bistro for drinks and appetizers. As she drove, she thought about the handsome manager who had introduced himself to her and Marion the last time she was there. She hoped he wouldn't be there tonight—or at least, if he were, that she wouldn't act like a complete idiot. Interestingly, she was finding that she wasn't missing Jared all that much, once the initial pain and shock of his rejection had worn off. What did that say?

Marion, of course, wouldn't be here tonight. She hated things like women's groups. "If Danny's not welcome, I don't want to come," she always said. Piper suspected that she found this group a little too woo-woo for her taste. Their friendship was an unlikely one, but they adored each other. Marion was the first person Piper had become friends with when she moved to Incident. They had met when Piper got a flat tire and she had left her cell phone charging at her new residence, forgetting to grab it before she left. She was trying to decide whether to hike to the nearest pay phone—if one even existed—or try to flag down a passing motorist, when Marion pulled over behind her.

At first, Piper thought she was going to offer her the use of her cell phone. But instead, she asked where the spare was and changed the tire herself. And she was wearing a tight, short skirt and extreme high heels. At first, Piper wondered if she was showing off for any men who might be driving by, but that was before she got to know her. Marion had grown up with four brothers, liked dressing this way, and possessed a big heart. When she found out that Piper was new to town, she insisted on having her over for dinner, where she met her husband Danny, a friendly, handsome Italian.

There, Piper found out that Marion had had several communications and prophetic dreams from dead relatives, so her tales of devas were readily accepted. But Marion's tolerance for the mystical stopped there. The moon was just an astronomical body orbiting the earth, she neither had nor wanted to have some freaking animal totem, and her style was not in any way, shape, or form compatible with that Earth Mother business. Piper sometimes wondered why Marion was so fond of her, given all that, but Marion always cooed over her like the little sister she never had, and found her adorable, like a Beatrix Potter character, she once said. Piper got the feeling that Marion thought she needed someone looking out for her.

When she got to Buffington's, Piper found a parking place practically right out front. Congratulating herself on her good luck, she wandered into the Bistro, looking for her friends. When she didn't see anyone, she checked her phone and saw that she was ten minutes early. She started to go back outside to wait when the manager appeared.

"Well, hello!" he greeted her, giving her a heart-melting smile. Piper immediately felt her knees go weak.

"H-hi," she stuttered. If at all possible, he looked even more handsome today than he did last week.

"Are you meeting someone?" he asked.

"Yes, my women's group."

"Ah, yes." He ran his finger down a piece of paper lying on the podium. "We have a table reserved for you. Would you like to be seated?"

"Um, sure."

"I'm Axel, by the way," he said over his shoulder as he led Piper to her table.

"Nice to meet you, Axel." Normally, she wouldn't reciprocate in such a circumstance but something compelled her to say, "I'm Piper."

"Piper, is it?" Axel smiled at her once more as he held a seat out for her. "How charming."

Piper sat down, trying to be as graceful and cool as she possibly could. "Thanks," she said. She willed for him to leave now, before she made a fool out of herself. But instead, he leaned against the table, resting his knuckles on the surface.

"Listen," he said. "You'll probably think I'm crazy, but I have to say, I've rarely been so affected by someone as you."

"Me?" she squeaked.

"Yes, you." He gazed at her seriously now. "I can only imagine you're seeing someone—"

"I—I'm not, actually."

"How is that even possible?" he exclaimed. He held up his hand. "Okay, let me first thank my lucky stars."

Piper giggled and he looked at her as if he had never heard anything so enchanting in all his life.

"And second, let me ask you now before I lose my nerve: Will you have dinner with me?"

"I'd like that," Piper said before she could even consider. She was feeling a powerful attraction herself. Of course, who wouldn't, to such a handsome guy, but even so, there was something magnetic about him. Could it really be possible that someone like him found her attractive?

"That is the best news I've had all week." Axel beamed down at her. "How can I get in touch with you?"

"Oh, here—let me give you my business card. It has my phone number on it." Piper fumbled in her purse, found a card, and handed it to him.

Just then, two of her friends showed up, engulfing her in hugs and filmy scarves and musky patchouli.

"Good evening, ladies," said Axel. "I'll send your waitress right over."

They thanked him and sat down, chattering to Piper about their latest news. When she had a chance to look up, she caught Axel's eye, who held up her card and mouthed, "I'll call you." Then he winked at her.

Piper flushed so deeply she was sure that her friends would comment on it, but then two more of the group showed up and everyone shared hugs all around.

So much for my resolution not to see anyone until I got my issues sorted out, Piper thought guiltily. But when she snuck another peek at Axel, all she felt was excitement that such a suave, good-looking man was interested in her. She couldn't wait to tell Marion!

CHAPTER 10

arson was flying high, higher than he had been in a long time. The phone call that he had ignored last week when he was composing turned out to be from a producer, Jim Forsythe, who needed a film score. His film editor was using Carson's CDs for reference music while editing the film and thought his music would make a good soundtrack. He had been a fan of Carson's band in Santa Cruz and had followed Carson's solo work when they disbanded. The director loved what he had heard, too, he said, and they wanted Carson to send them a demo. The movie was a documentary about climate change, portraying both the beauty and diversity of the planet as well as the destruction in places already impacted.

Forsythe sent him a DVD with some lightly edited footage and asked Carson to write some music to go along with it. Carson watched it the minute it arrived. He was deeply moved by it, and thought that he could, in fact, write a good score for the film, even though he had only written one, and that was for a class at UC Santa Cruz. He would need to purchase some new software for the job if he got it, which posed something of a problem. But when his mom found out what he needed, she offered to take some money out of savings to help him. He protested at first, but caved quickly, promising to pay her as soon as he got paid—assuming he got the job.

Of course, he would need to get up to speed on the software, too. Everything he had learned along those lines in college was now hopelessly out of date. But at least he had a grasp of the general concepts. He was pretty good with computers and software. And nothing could dim his excitement in having this unexpected opportunity come to him completely out of the blue. Maybe what he was doing wasn't hopeless after all.

Today, he was taking a break from his music to support his mom's latest project, the experiment involving Jessie. One of the researchers was arriving in just a few minutes to take notes, explain the setup, and install the video camera. Jessie seemed to know that something was up and had acted frisky all morning.

When the doorbell rang, Merilee and Jessie answered it together. Carson ambled into the hallway after their visitor had come inside. She was a tall, attractive woman around his age, he guessed, with dark auburn hair down to her shoulders. She looked serious but nice. And Jessie took to her right away.

"Mrs. Duran?" The woman offered her hand to Merilee. "I'm Olivia Harper."

"Call me Merilee." She smiled warmly at their visitor. "Oh, and this is Jessie."

"Hi, Jessie." Olivia crouched down and let Jessie give her a sniff before stroking her ruff. Jessie gave a little whine of friendly greeting, producing for Carson an image of something that resembled Silly String erupting out of a central source, the strands indigo, ochre, and rust.

"This is my son, Carson," Merilee said, reaching over to ruffle his hair. Carson had thick, unruly hair that Merilee had always loved to tousle, from the time he was a little kid. She had to reach up now, instead of down, a fact that seemed to both delight and dismay her.

Olivia stood up and shook hands with Carson. She had a firm grip, he noted; no nonsense. Merilee showed her around the house while Jessie and Carson followed. She told stories about Jessie waiting for her faithfully, even though her job required her to work sporadic hours and she sometimes carpooled with other employees.

"One time," Merilee said, "I had gone on a camping trip with some friends in the Sierra. A wildfire broke out where we were staying, and we came home early. This happened before Carson moved back, so Jessie was staying with some other friends. They told me that she became expectant of my return several hours before I even called to let them know I was on my way to get her. She kept going to the door, which at first, they thought meant she wanted to go out. But when they opened it to let her out, she just stood there and looked up at them."

Carson groaned inwardly when he heard his mom tell Olivia he had moved back home. Oh well. It was probably obvious. And anyway, he wasn't the only one. His whole generation was getting royally screwed.

Olivia took notes in a small notebook and when she had gotten the full tour, went out to her car to fetch the video camera. Carson offered to help her with the installation, which she accepted. It soon became clear that a stepstool would come in handy, so he got one for her, then hung around to hand her tools and hardware when she needed them.

"So did you grow up here?" she asked, marking the places she would need to drive screws. Jessie wandered in to check out the installation, tail wagging.

"I did."

"How did you like it?"

Carson shrugged. "Well, for a little kid, it was great. Even up to the age of sixteen it was great. There's lots of great places to ride bikes and explore, lots of wildlife, plenty of places to camp and go swimming. But it's kind of in the boondocks. You know, with Sacramento being a three-hour drive away … the Bay Area even farther … it's true the university helps a lot. But I was really enjoying living in Santa Cruz. Really great music scene there."

"Are you a musician?" Olivia asked, keeping her eyes on the mount for the camera as she installed the screws with a cordless drill. The "zzzz!" sound of the drill created a fuzzy purple-orange blob in Carson's mind's eye, which ballooned out, then shrank according to the volume.

"I am, yeah."

"What's your instrument?"

"Oh, guitar and keyboards, mainly. I sing, too."

Olivia finished installing the mount and stepped down from the stepstool to check out her handiwork. "I assume you play around town? Do you have a band?"

"Yeah, Tachyon Fundicle. I can give you a business card that's got the website on it and you can see when we're playing in town, if you want."

Olivia grinned. "Tachyon Fundicle, huh?"

Carson grinned back. "You have no idea how hard it is to come up with a name for a band. Every conceivable name had been taken."

"I can imagine! Actually, I think it's a great name. I know what 'tachyon' means. But I'm not familiar with 'fundicle.'"

"I made it up. I'm not sure what it means. I just liked the way it sounded." Which was certainly true. The word created a velvety tactile sensation, smooth and undulating. "What about you? Are you from around here?"

She shook her head. "No, I moved here from back East. Just arrived two days ago, in fact."

"Well, welcome," he said.

"Thanks." She smiled briefly, then her face clouded.

Carson debated about whether to invite her to do something together. She wasn't wearing a ring and she used the first person singular referring to her move. She probably didn't know many people here yet and would no doubt appreciate some company. But he also didn't want to give her the wrong idea, that he was asking her out. He had broken up with Heather, which didn't go well. Worse than he had anticipated, actually. But right now, the only person who interested him romantically was his mystery woman.

As if sensing his dilemma, Olivia climbed back onto the stepstool and asked Carson to hand her the video camera. Once it was secured, she peered through the viewfinder to make sure that she had the area where Jessie liked to wait for Merilee in the field. Obligingly, Jessie had plopped herself down in her usual spot, which Carson verified for Olivia. She fiddled with the settings, and when she was satisfied, she climbed back down.

Rummaging around in her briefcase, Olivia located the logbook and handed it to Carson. "Whenever you're here and your mother isn't, just note any times that Jessie goes to the door and waits, okay? All we need is the date, the time, and a brief note about her movements and behavior."

"That doesn't sound too hard."

"No, it's pretty straightforward."

"Well, hey, here's a card with my website on it," said Carson. He pulled out his wallet, extracted a card, and handed it to her.

She peered at it with interest. "Great, thanks," she said. "I'll check it out."

"Our next gig in town is three weeks from now. At The Contrarian."

"I hope to be there." She bent down and gave Jessie a pat. Jessie stood up, stretched, then nosed Olivia's hand, tail wagging once more. "Ohh, you're a sweetheart, aren't you, Jessie?" she said, scratching her behind the ears. Jessie thumped her tail against the door jamb with enthusiasm. Floating potato-shaped objects, the color and texture of buckskin. "Where did your mom go, do you know? I'd like to say goodbye."

"Let me get her for you." Carson figured she was in her crafts room, where she spent most of her free time. She was always hopeful that she might be able to get some kind of cottage business going with her sewing and crocheting, but the fact was, she wasn't a good businessperson. She didn't charge enough for her wares, and she didn't work very fast. Not to mention the fact that she hated marketing. He could certainly relate to that.

"Hey, Mom." He poked his head into the room. "Olivia's leaving and wanted to say goodbye."

Merilee set aside the pattern that she was cutting and got to her feet. "All set?"

"Looks like it."

In the entry, Merilee told Olivia how pleased they were to be able to participate in such fascinating research. "I've never done an experiment before!" she exclaimed.

Olivia told her how much she and the team appreciated their help. "You'll be getting a check from the university in a few weeks," she added. "And I'll be coming back weekly to retrieve the footage from the camera and make sure that it's working properly."

"That all sounds great," said Merilee. Carson felt glad that his mom was so excited about this whole thing. Which then made him feel guilty about being such a curmudgeon about it when she first brought it up.

After Olivia left, Merilee turned to him. "What a nice young woman," she said.

"She is."

"Attractive, too."

"Mom, don't start."

"What do you mean?"

"You know what I mean." She was aware that he had broken up with Heather. And even though she hadn't been especially close to her—Carson rarely brought her to the house—she thought Carson needed a girlfriend. She was probably wondering if she was ever going to get any grandchildren.

She threw her hands up and headed back to her workroom. Jessie followed her.

Carson thought about going to his studio, but he wasn't really in the mood to work, so he shouted to his mom that he was heading into town. If he was lucky, he might run into his mystery woman. He most definitely wasn't going to bump into her at his house.

He wished he knew more about her so that he could frequent some of her haunts. But he didn't know a thing. Still, Incident wasn't all that big, despite the university. Surely, if he spent some time out and about and kept his eyes open, he'd run into her sooner or later. On the other hand, he didn't want to be a stalker. He had never really felt this way about someone before, so he wasn't entirely clear about where being a romantic ended and becoming a stalker began. He definitely didn't want to be a stalker.

He also contemplated the fact that he was quite possibly projecting all kinds of fantasies onto her that she wouldn't be able to live up to. And who knew whether she would feel the same way about him? Not to mention the fact that she probably already had someone in her life. A beautiful girl like that? It was silly to even think about her at all. He just couldn't dismiss the effect she had had on him when he had seen her that day. That counted for something, didn't it?

He let his imagination roam as he drove into town, trying to think where someone who looked like her might hang out. She looked pretty crunchy granola, so she might attend some of the New Age-y stuff around town. Ordinarily, that kind of stuff annoyed Carson a little. But he was willing to be open-minded, and if anyone could present that kind of thinking in its best light, he felt certain that she—he decided to call her

Sky Blue—could do it. And maybe he was generalizing. Which was annoying on his part. Maybe someone who looked like her was into theater. Or maybe she was … well, hell, she could be a lawyer for all he knew. Though he seriously doubted it.

After giving it some careful thought, he decided to go to his mother's employer, the Incident Food Co-op. For a nanosecond, he pondered asking his mom if someone of Sky Blue's description ever came through her station, but then it occurred to him that she would get too interested and too involved and that wouldn't work at all. Now was the best time to go, when his mom was at home.

When he got to the co-op, he stood at the front of the store for a moment, ignoring the visual stimuli produced by the bleeps of cash registers, rattle of shopping carts and buzz of mingled voices. He pondered, wondering which section he should visit first. He decided that fresh produce and the chocolate section were his best bets. He went to the chocolate aisle, but no luck. And honestly, what could he expect? They'd have to be at the exact same place at the exact same time, neither one of them even knowing the other one … statistically speaking, this could take months if not years. He headed to the produce section nevertheless, trying not to feel too stupid.

He rounded the corner of the condiments aisle, letting his gaze travel over all the customers checking out squash, pears, eggplant, and lettuce. No Sky Blue. He sighed. He'd have to try again. He started to go when a flutter caught his attention out of the corner of his eye. He stopped, turned his head to get a closer look. And there she was, strolling into the produce section with a basket on her arm: radiant, happy, and even more beautiful than he remembered.

CHAPTER 11

They all started exactly the same way. She's driving across Pennsylvania, in a stretch of weathered mountains where the interstate dips and curves along the ancient, eroded topography. She has just stopped for gas, grabbed a Philly cheesesteak sandwich, and refilled her water bottle. The sun is shining and the pavement clear, with no hint of what will happen next: A deer dashes onto the freeway and the big rig in front of her brakes hard. The deer is reduced to a spray of blood and a carcass, and the truck jackknifes, sprawling across both lanes in magnificent slow motion. Time suspends, crystalizing into dust motes that sparkle in the sun, and she feels oddly weightless as she slams on her brakes, the juddering shock traveling up her leg to her teeth. Her instincts take over and aim her car towards the grassy swale that serves as the median. The car jounces, fishtails, then spins a few times before the air bag deploys with a loud bang and a whoosh. When the car comes to a stop and everything is still, she extricates herself from the car, feeling as though she's looking down at everything from above. Yet she can feel her left temple throbbing, for no reason she can ascertain; she will think later that she must have hit her head on the window when the car was spinning. Other than that, she feels perfectly fine. Oddly detached, but fine.

That part of the dream was always the same, exactly the way the accident happened as she was driving to Incident from Massachusetts. That day, as she stood on the median, collecting her wits, she watched as the truck driver emerged from his cab relatively unscathed. The car she was passing when the truck jackknifed wasn't so lucky, however. It had crashed into the trailer so hard that it had flipped into the air and landed on its roof. Looking at the mangled wreck, Olivia found it hard to believe that anyone could have survived. And in fact, she found out later that both the driver and the passenger died. They were alive when they were rushed to the hospital, but they died three days later.

All of this was bad enough—the accident, the nightmares, the wrecked car with people inside. But what made everything even worse was the fact that for the next three nights, she not only relived her own trauma, but she also relived theirs—at least, so it seemed. When she climbed out of her car in her dream, feeling as though she were looking down from the air, her point of view changed and she found herself in the doomed couple's car, the action rolled back to the point at which the truck lost control. She saw the truck jackknifing, sparks raking the asphalt. She watched with surreal, fatalistic horror as the trailer loomed closer and closer, a horrid blossoming of scale and mass. She observed but didn't feel the shock of the impact, yet she did experience the sickening, exhilarating sensation of becoming airborne. Then everything went black. She would wake up then, her pajamas drenched in sweat, tears on her cheeks that she hadn't even known she had shed.

When she read on the Internet that the couple had died, she no longer dreamed about their part of the accident. Instead, she began dreaming about other disasters—a ferry that capsized in a freak squall, a gunman bursting into a café, a terrible pile-up on an interstate in a dust storm … So far, none of these things had come true—at least, not to her knowledge—which was a relief. But why was she having these nightmares? She wasn't one to dream strongly in the first place; most of her dreams were of the mundane variety if she remembered them at all, which she usually didn't.

She wondered if the bump on her head had anything to do with it, and she stopped in at an Urgent Care clinic the first chance she got, but nothing had shown up. Apparently, she had sustained a bruise on her temple and that was all. She had way too many other things to take care of to spend much time trying to figure out what was going on in her dream life, though. In her real life, she was teaching, attending committee meetings, putting together a plan for her new research, dealing with an insane email load, and moving into a new place, an apartment over a storefront in downtown Incident not too far from the university. She had met with Rupert to talk about her research and was discouraged to find out that he had to hustle for grant money for his research. Because of that, he tried to keep his experiments as simple as possible. She also realized that, despite her hunches, she had so little experience in conducting the kind of research that someone like Rupert did, she was at a loss to know how to design her own new experiments. Her previous research was straightforward, if high tech and expensive.

Rupert offered to let her participate in some of his work so that she might get a better idea of how to approach research that involved consciousness—plus, he would put her name on some of the papers to boost her publication history while she was getting started. So she was now making the occasional visit to subjects' homes and setting things up for his experiments on animals who seemed to know when their owners were coming home. It was fun, if time-consuming, and the other day she had met a mother and son with a sweet malamute-lab mix whom she had liked very much. She was realizing just what a comforting network of friends, colleagues, and family she had left behind, and she was feeling lonely, wondering how she was going to make new friends with such a busy schedule. She had never moved very far from home, growing up in western Massachusetts, attending Wellesley College for her undergraduate work, then returning to western Massachusetts to get her PhD. There were so many universities and colleges in the Northeast, she had always assumed that she would be able to find a position close to home. But that was before she changed directions.

She had broken up with Lance via text shortly after the accident, which she knew was cowardly, but she just didn't have the energy for anything else. He had sent her a terse reply. So here she was, on the other side of the country in a part of the world where she had never spent any time, with no friends, no boyfriend, and no family. At least she had a job. But she knew that she was going to have to get some grant money and papers published if she was going to keep her job. She had never felt so vulnerable on just about every front. Maybe that's what the nightmares were about. And maybe, once she got her legs underneath her, they would stop.

This morning, a Saturday, she decided she had been driving herself too hard and she needed a break. On impulse, she located the card that Piper had given her when they chatted at the student center. She had noted earlier that Piper was an herbalist and wondered if she might be able to suggest something for nightmares. More than anything, though, she just wanted some friendly company. Someone like Piper no doubt had a full life, but she had given her a card so Olivia hoped that she would genuinely like to hear from her. Piper answered after the fourth ring, sounding a little out of breath.

"Piper? This is Olivia. We met at the student center a couple of weeks ago."

"Olivia! How lovely to hear from you!" Piper exclaimed, raising Olivia's spirits. "I take it you got the job?"

"I did."

"Well, congratulations!"

"Thank you." Olivia paused. She hadn't planned what to say next. "Listen, I'm thinking about going out for breakfast and wondered if you'd like to join me."

"That sounds like fun," Piper said. "I've got a couple of things to take care of here, but it shouldn't take me more than a half-hour. Where would you like to go?"

"I'm not sure. I thought maybe you could suggest a place."

Piper suggested they meet at The Morning Glory. "There could be a bit of a wait," she said, "but the food is so good it's worth it. It's not far from the University. You might have even noticed it."

Olivia had noticed it. It not only looked popular, it occupied a lovely old Craftsman-style house painted periwinkle, which made it distinctive. She thanked Piper and hung up, feeling glad that she had acted on her impulse.

A half-hour later, she parked behind the restaurant in the lot and met Piper on the front porch.

"I've put our name on the list. Only a fifteen minute wait, they said."

Piper looked as charming as she did before, like Titania out of *A Midsummer Night's Dream*, Olivia thought. And she seemed to be in great spirits, with a glow about her that Olivia associated with someone newly in love. She wondered who the lucky guy might be. They sat on the bench provided for those waiting for a table while Piper quizzed her about her new situation, wanting to know how she liked the university, how she liked Incident, and what it was like to work for Rupert. Olivia said it was all great, but she confessed to feeling a little lost, having moved so far from home.

Piper nodded. "I know how you feel. When I moved here from San Francisco, I was so ready to be out of the city, but it was still an adjustment. All my friends were in the Bay Area, and it took a year before I made any new real friends—except for Marion, whom you'll have to meet."

"I'd love to," Olivia said, smiling.

Piper wanted to know where she was living and ended up knowing the building where Olivia was renting. "Fun part of town," she said. A waitress stuck her head out the door at that moment and called Piper's name. They followed her into the noisy, crowded interior, fragrant with cinnamon rolls, bacon, and citrus.

"Speaking of which, what do you do for fun?" Piper asked, once they were seated, their menus in hand.

Olivia tore her gaze away from the tempting descriptions of brunch dishes and opened her mouth to reply when she realized she didn't really have an answer. She enjoyed her work so much and had such an early proclivity for it—not to mention the fact that her field was so highly competitive—that "fun" hadn't really entered into the equation. "Well, I—I guess work is what I do for fun," she stammered.

Piper gave her a close look, then dropped her gaze onto her menu. "That is incredibly lucky," she said. "In fact, I suppose I would say the same thing, to be honest. I love my work. I don't really have this distinct separation between work and play."

Olivia felt reassured. "Exactly! I feel sorry for people who hate what they do."

Piper nodded. "I do, too."

Soon the waitress came to take their order and they spent a lovely breakfast together. This was something she could certainly do more of that wasn't "work," Olivia mused, as they took their leave in the parking lot. Most of her friends were colleagues at this point in her life, the majority of her childhood friends having married and started families while she was in graduate school. Olivia had found that this created a psychosocial gap, particularly since she had never been strongly drawn to babies or small children. And it seemed easier and more satisfying for her friends who were parents to share the experience with other parents rather than singles.

She sat in her car after starting it up, trying to decide what she might like to do next with her day. Her admission that she actually didn't do anything for fun was making her want to have some. She settled on a walk through a nearby park, one that featured a healthy, well-tended rose garden whose creamy, vivid blossoms still bloomed furiously. Afterward, she decided to see if there were any good movies playing at the theater near her apartment. A comedy would be nice.

She parked on the street and walked to the theater, glancing idly at the newspaper vending machines that lined the sidewalk near the theater entrance. Incident had a number of local periodicals, she had noticed: one devoted to the arts and entertainment, one devoted to community service, and one to gardening and small farming, in addition to the main paper that covered mainstream news. She was thinking she might grab a copy of *Prospero* to see what else was going on in town when the headline on the *Incident Daily Gazette* snagged her attention. "Freak Storm Capsizes Ferry En Route to Catalina Island!" it blared in a giant font. She stared, then began to shake violently. She leaned against the closest vertical surface, swallowing hard.

It's a coincidence, she told herself; they happen.

Nevertheless, she decided not to go to a movie. She decided to go home. Once there, she plopped herself down on her loveseat and called her parents. She hadn't told them about the accident because everything had turned out okay and she didn't want them to worry. She told them now that everything was fine—in fact, it was great, because that was what she wanted and that was what would make them feel the most at ease.

"But I sure miss you," she said, choking up as she said it, feeling as if she were six years old.

"Ohh, honey, we miss you, too," her dad said. "You left a big hole in your wake. But we're just so proud of you, don't forget that."

"I won't," she whispered. "I'll call again soon."

"You do that. Love you, sweetheart."

She said that she loved them, too, and hung up, then drew her knees to her chest and wrapped her arms around herself. Maybe she should go to the movies after all. She needed to do something to get her mind off things. She didn't have a television and it was hard to avoid news on the Internet. A movie would take up a good two or three hours and then she could make something somewhat complicated for dinner. That would occupy her thoughts. Afterward, she could read a book. It had been a very long time since she had read a novel.

The only problem was night. She would have to go to sleep sometime.

She wasn't looking forward to it.

CHAPTER 12

xel stood on the front step to Piper's house and pushed the doorbell with his free hand. He could hear the melodious chimes through the door and was glad that he didn't hear barking. He didn't care for dogs. Actually, Piper seemed more like a cat person anyway, though she hadn't brought up any pets during their first date last Monday. Her thing was plants, not animals. In his other hand, he held a bouquet of a dozen pale pink roses. If she hadn't told him about her love for plants before, he would have guessed, seeing her home: Evergreen bushes with glossy leaves crowded the front stoop, marigolds thick with blossoms lined the sidewalk to the door. Hanging pots bloomed in profusion from their various perches, their colors vivid even in the fading light, and flower beds bordered the foundation. All the place lacked was a round door and it could have passed for a hobbit house.

The door opened, and before he could even step inside, Piper had wrapped her arms around him and given him a big hug. She smelled wonderful, like fresh shampoo and clean clothes dried outside in the sun, but some subtle floral fragrance clung to her as well. She looked a vision in a pretty lavender dress with a fitted bodice and gathered skirt that hung mid-calf; her luxuriant hair was partly pulled back with a barrette, but most of it cascaded about her shoulders.

"Welcome!" she said, grabbing his hand and pulling him inside.

"Wow," he said, giving her a slow smile. "You look gorgeous!"

She blushed. She actually blushed. How many women blushed any more? "Thanks," she murmured, clearly pleased. She gave his hand a squeeze before letting go, turning her attention to the roses. "Oh!" she exclaimed. "Those are beautiful!"

"Probably coals to Newcastle," he laughed.

"Absolutely not!" She accepted them from him with reverential care. "Let me put these in some water. And can I get you something to drink? Would you like a tour of the place?"

"How about both?"

"Sounds good to me," Piper said with a giggle. "I have wine, both white and red, I have beer …"

"Red wine would be perfect."

"Great." Piper beamed at him once more before turning to head into the kitchen. Axel followed.

"I already love what I've seen," he said, leaning against the kitchen island while Piper filled a crystal vase with water. She settled the roses in the vase, admired them once more, and took two red wine glasses down from a cupboard. He wasn't surprised to see a number of crystals hanging in the kitchen windows. He looked for signs of a cat but didn't see any. Truth was, he didn't like dogs or cats.

"Thank you!" Piper set the glasses on the counter, then picked up the wine opener. "I was so lucky to get this place."

"Do you own it?"

Piper shook her head ruefully. "Not yet. I'm renting from this dear older couple. But I hope to buy it someday. My grandmother left me a little money when she died, and I've been saving ever since Frank and Mary told me they would count my rent money toward a purchase if I was interested in buying."

"Here, let me do that," Axel offered, holding out his hand for the wine opener. "I'm a professional, you know." He winked at her.

"That's right, you are," she said, smiling.

He surreptitiously checked the bottle for the label and vintage as he expertly manipulated the bottle and opener, pulling the cork out with a satisfying pop. Okay, but not great. Drinkable, at least.

Piper suddenly looked anxious. "Oh dear, that's right—you are. I hope you like this wine. My friend Marion recommended it to me, said it was one of her favorites."

"Marion. Have I met Marion?"

"Well, sort of. She was the friend that I was having lunch with the first day we met."

"Ah, yes. October 9. A very auspicious day." Piper's face relaxed and she beamed at him. Women loved it when you remembered those kinds of things—the date of the first time you met, what she was wearing, what the setting was like. He poured Piper a small amount of wine to taste but she pushed it back at him.

"You do it," she said. "I'm sure your palate is more refined than mine."

He took a sip, being careful to keep his face neutral in case it was worse than he feared. Thankfully, it wasn't horrible. "Lovely," he said, holding Piper's gaze while he poured her a full glass. Then he poured himself a glass and held it up for a toast. "Here's to love at first sight." He gave her a smoldering look while she blushed, again. Setting his glass down, he leaned over and kissed her very gently on the lips. "Mmm," he said. "Delicious."

She seemed at a loss for what to say or do next so he

suggested she give him the tour. That she gladly did, taking him into the living room where she had a lot of colorful furniture that she had no doubt purchased at import-export stores. The art on the walls was composed of botanicals and prints by classic illustrators featuring fairies and the like, a Chinese dragon thrown in for good measure. Nothing particularly valuable, though her taste would suggest that she grew up with some money.

"So tell me more about you," he said. "Where did you grow up? What do your parents do? What about siblings?"

She told him that she grew up in San Francisco and that her dad was an internist, her mother a nurse. "I have one brother," she said, "who followed in my parents' footsteps, more or less."

"I take it that you did not follow in their footsteps."

Piper shook her head. "No, I preferred to become a quack. At least, that's what they think."

"I think what you do is wonderful. Drugs have so many side-effects. And isn't that where the original medicines came from?"

"They are! Pharmaceutical companies are still researching plants from all over the world to find new drugs."

They went from the living room to her study, a charming little nook with windows on two sides. She totally scored in finding this place, that's for sure. Then she led him outside to get a glimpse of her garden before the light completely faded. He could see her love of plants there as well. Several mature fruit trees graced the garden, along with artfully arranged plots that contained flowers, herbs, and fall vegetables. Beyond that he could see a thick woods. As they stood taking in the dusky scene, he put his arm around her and pulled her close. She shivered in the cooling air, so he tightened his grip and kissed her on the top of the head, breathing in the smell of her hair. As they turned to go back inside, Axel heard a series of knocks coming from the forest beyond Piper's garden. It had a definite rhythm. Two knocks, then a pause, then two more. Then it repeated. She tensed.

"What's that?" he asked.

"Oh, kids," she said. "Seems to be their new game. Let's just go in."

"You don't think they're a problem, do you?"

"Oh no, I doubt it." She closed the door firmly behind them. "I mean, that's all they seem to do—make those knocking sounds. And if they're trying to scare me, I don't want to give them the satisfaction."

"Do you have a gun in the house?"

She looked alarmed at the very suggestion. "No!" she exclaimed. "What would I do with a gun?"

He shrugged. "Protect yourself."

She set her jaw. Adorably. "I prefer other kinds of protection."

"Oh, really?" He lightly bobbed her nose with his cupped hand. "What kinds of protection?"

"Well …" she faltered. "Just … I don't know, not attracting people like that through negative energy."

"Oh, Piper." He swept her up in his arms and held her close. "Don't ever change. Promise me?"

She laughed and hugged him tight. Presumably her bedroom was up the flight of stairs he had noticed when he first came in. He released her and said, "Charming, beautiful home of a charming, beautiful lady. Can I help with dinner? Something smelled delicious in the kitchen." He hoped it wouldn't be vegetarian. She had ordered a vegetarian meal when they went out last week.

"It's a chicken stew," she said, "made from one of my neighbor's chickens." Axel blinked. He hadn't expected that. "I've got biscuits made, too." She gave a self-deprecating laugh. "Comfort food."

"I can't think of anything tastier." Axel rested his fingers lightly on her waist and guided her to the kitchen.

The table was already set and dinner made, so he helped fill the water and wine glasses and took the salad to the table. Piper turned off the lights and lit candles for their meal, which progressed just the way he wanted it to: romantic, sexy, yet chaste. A woman like Piper fell into the category of women he liked to take his time with. She probably expected him to try to seduce her tonight, but he didn't. She seemed surprised yet touched when, at the end of the evening, he told her that he was looking forward to many more times together and kissed her goodbye.

As he drove home, he reviewed the evening in his mind, feeling pleased. Things actually seemed to be looking up. He had found a big screen TV from a guy who had just lost his job and was desperate for money. Paid practically nothing for it. That divorcée he had screwed a while back had given him a beautiful cashmere sport coat. It was too warm for most of the weather in Incident, but when he made his big score and opened his restaurant in San Francisco, it would come in handy. In addition, that old lady he had scoped out at the assisted living facility was starting to warm to him. She didn't have any children, so he wondered whom she might be leaving her money to. Those assisted living facilities weren't cheap; she had to have some. There might be nieces and/or nephews, but he was fairly confident he could push them out of the way, given enough time.

And Piper. Innocent, sweet, trusting Piper. She was almost too good to be true. It was about time he caught a few breaks. About time.

CHAPTER 13

iper opened the door to her herbal practice and welcomed her client with a warm hug. Helen, a rancher in her mid-sixties who was still participating in cattle drives, had been coming to see her for various minor health issues for several years now, ever since Piper established her practice. Soon after she moved in, she had converted her landlord Frank's woodshop into an office and dispensary, with his permission. She loved the way it was tucked into a corner of the garden, framed by two magnificent, venerable redbuds that Frank and Mary had planted when they first built the house back in 1965.

Piper invited Helen to sit down in the comfy armchair that she provided for her clients and asked if she would like a cup of tea. Helen said she would love one.

"But first, before I select your tea, I should have an idea of your complaint," Piper said.

Helen nodded, then sighed. "Oh, I just can't seem to stop getting these darned bladder infections. I've tried taking antibiotics, but they always seem to come back, and I'm taking the whole dose like they tell me to. My doctor says that it's probably because I'm post-menopausal, that my hormones are different now and not as protective as they once were. Riding horses probably doesn't help. He suggested even more antibiotics, but I just don't want to take any more. I've been reading a lot about our microbiome and how important it is to our health."

Piper patted Helen's shoulder. "Helen, you are a wise woman," she said. "And a well-read one."

Helen smiled at her. "My doctor doesn't seem to think that's a good quality, my reading on the Internet."

Piper returned her smile and nodded. "Well, it's true that it's a mixed bag. There's a lot of bad information out there but there's also a lot of good information. He should know what a discerning individual you are, don't you think?"

Helen shook her head. "He's new, for one thing. My old doctor retired. I think this new doctor thinks all old people are stupid—and hopeless when it comes to things like the Internet. Besides, he only has time to spend about ten minutes with me. At that rate, I'll be dead before he realizes what a discerning individual I am."

Piper laughed and said she would be right back with her tea. She put the kettle on to boil in her kitchenette, then opened her cabinet, fragrant with earthy scents, and perused her stock of herbal teas. She selected some dried marshmallow root, mixed it with some peppermint, and placed the mixture in the strainer for the teapot. Then she went out to her office and took Helen's blood pressure. No problems there. She returned to the kitchenette to find that the water had come to a boil, so she filled the pot, then put it and a cup on a tray and brought it out to Helen.

Helen brightened visibly when she saw Piper coming into the room bearing the tea tray. Piper set the tray down and took a seat herself, quizzing Helen about her habits and symptoms while waiting for the tea to steep. When it was ready, she poured a cup and handed it to Helen, who accepted it with a contented sigh. Piper was convinced that a large part of what she offered to patients was simple caring and attention. Those two things were potent healers. She and Helen chatted for a half-hour, during which time Piper sought to get a feeling for how Helen's life was going in general.

Halfway into the conversation, she learned that Helen's brother, who lived in Chico, had fallen ill with a rare, aggressive cancer. She broke down while telling Piper about him. Piper handed her a clean, soft handkerchief, then held her hand quietly until she was able to stop crying. When she finally did, Piper observed that this could easily cause enough stress that there could be health repercussions; she asked about Helen's support network. Fortunately, her husband was in good health and they had a loving relationship, it sounded like, and she was close to their two children, one of whom lived in Incident, the other not far away in Portland.

Other than that, there didn't appear to be any underlying or related issues other than the ones Helen's physician had discussed. At the end of their session, Piper wrote down some recommendations.

"You might want to take D-Mannose supplements," she said, as she handed the paper to Helen. "D-Mannose is a sugar, and it's what makes cranberry juice so helpful for UTIs. It binds to the receptor sites on the *E. coli* bacteria so that they can't stick to the bladder walls. You can take it prophylactically as well as when you have a flare-up. When your symptoms are acute, take some *Uva ursi* and oregano according to the dosages I've written down here. Take the *Uva ursi* for five days only, because it's potent and has some toxicity associated with longer use. It should be safe for you because your blood pressure is normal and you're generally healthy. If it upsets your stomach, though, which it can, or you notice anything else untoward, stop taking it. You can take the oregano for one to two weeks."

"Thank you, honey."

"And I would wash only with pure olive oil soap, which you

can find on the Internet. Since I know what a big fan you are of the Internet."

Helen chuckled and reached for her purse. "Can I get all of those other things from you?"

"I can sell you the oregano, if you'd like, but you'll have to get the other two supplements at the Incident food co-op. You can get your oregano there, too, if you'd prefer."

"Oh, no, I'd much rather have yours," she said. "Your herbs and teas have a special quality to them, somehow."

"That's awfully nice," Piper replied, pleased to hear this. "And be sure to get plenty of probiotics in your diet – yogurt, kefir, naturally fermented sauerkraut …"

"This all sounds quite doable. And microbiome-friendly. What do I owe you for the visit and the oregano?"

Piper handed her a receipt, then went to her dispensary and picked out a bottle of oregano capsules for Helen. She gave her another hug before she left and told her, "Be sure to take good care of yourself while you're so worried about your brother. Be especially kind and good to yourself, okay? I'll be thinking about you both and sending healing energy to you."

"I'll do that, honey. Thanks so much for all your help."

Piper watched to make sure that Helen made it to her car safely—a light drizzle had begun—then closed the door, both warmed by her interaction with Helen and full of sadness. Piper didn't have a very good feeling about her brother's prognosis and he and Helen were clearly close. I hope everything goes as well as possible, she thought. And I wish for Helen to find comfort and solace no matter what happens.

The rest of her day went quickly, and before she knew it, it was time to drive over to Marion and Danny's house, where she was having dinner. She picked out some tea to bring as a hostess present, placing it in a decorative tin and dashing out into the rain to cut a few fresh flowers. Then she hopped into her Beetle—the color of a Japanese beetle, she often thought, a luscious metallic green—and headed over to Marion's.

The rain was coming down hard, now, which made driving more difficult, but it was the first rain of the season and so welcome after the long, parched summer. As she drove, she spotted a man on the opposite side of the road in shabby clothes trudging along the shoulder, hauling a big backpack. Probably homeless. Marion had talked her out of taking people like this into her home— "Honey, we are looking at a seriously sketchy scenario with these individuals!" —but their plight tugged on her heart strings. One afternoon as she was coming home from teaching, she had spotted someone sprinting from the back of her house into the forest. When she inspected the back yard, she found the end of the hose off the hose reel and the wind-fallen fruit she had noticed earlier that day was gone. It made her heart ache to think that someone was so desperate that they were taking water from strangers' hose bibs and eating fruit that she had left for animals. She couldn't know for sure, but maybe it was this same guy. *I wish for you to be warm and dry,* she thought as she passed him; *I wish for you to be safe and comfortable.*

Marion and Danny's house was lit up and inviting-looking in the falling dusk as she pulled into their drive. Marion had a flair for landscaping as well as interior design, and their front yard looked like a Zen garden, with beautiful quartz and granite boulders, dwarf conifers, and hidden lighting artfully arranged. Their house was modern, sleek and rectangular. It couldn't have been more different from Piper's house, but she loved it.

She rang the doorbell and Danny answered, giving her a peck on the cheek and ushering her inside. Danny worked as a district attorney and seemed most comfortable in nice clothes; tonight he was wearing an exquisite pair of slacks and a smartly pressed Oxford shirt. He and Marion had moved to Incident from San Jose, so they had an urban energy that Piper enjoyed and found familiar from her childhood. Plus, the three of them could rhapsodize for hours about the lack of traffic in Incident compared to the Bay Area, not to mention the difference in housing they could afford. He thanked her for the tea and flowers and beckoned her into the kitchen where Marion was putting the finishing touches on dinner. On their breakfast bar sat three champagne glasses and a bottle of champagne in an ice bucket.

Marion brightened when she saw Piper and threw her arms around her. "Hey, girlfriend!" she exclaimed.

"Hey yourself!" Piper replied, squeezing Marion tight. "So champagne, huh?" she said, once she had extricated herself. "What's the special occasion? I know it's not your anniversary or either one of your birthdays."

"No," said Marion, shaking her head and smiling broadly. She took a deep breath and grabbed both Piper's and Danny's hands. "We're pregnant!"

"Oh my God, you're kidding!"

"Nope!"

Piper found herself squealing, then started laughing. "Well … I—I'm just so tickled that no words can express how I feel!" she finally managed to gasp. "Only squeals, evidently." She grabbed Marion in a fierce hug once again, then turned and hugged Danny. "What a beautiful baby you will have! When are you due?"

"In April."

"So … an Aries or a Taurus."

Marion rolled her eyes. "Whatever, Omar."

Piper laughed. She knew that Marion hated astrology.

Danny stepped over to the counter and poured two full glasses and one half-glass of champagne. He handed the half-glass to Marion and a full one to Piper, then raised his for a toast.

"Here's to our baby!"

"Hear hear!" Piper cheered. "May she—or he—be blessed with great good fortune!"

They all took a sip. Then Danny faced Piper. "And here's to

our baby's godmother."

Piper's eyes filled unexpectedly with tears. "Oh, gosh, you two." She wiped her eyes. "I'm—wow—I'm so honored." She took a shaky sip. "Thank you," she said. "I will take this responsibility to heart, you know I will." Danny and Marion both beamed at her.

They all settled down at the breakfast bar then, snacking on the appetizers that Danny had prepared and catching up with each other's news. As they chatted, Piper couldn't help but feel a twinge of yearning for a baby of her own one day. She was still plenty young enough, but she didn't want to wait too long. Maybe if things worked out with Axel?

As if reading her mind, Marion said, "So tell us more about your new hunk of a boyfriend, Piper."

"Yes, do tell," Danny said, filling her glass.

"Well …" Piper smiled and took a swallow of champagne. "He's incredibly romantic. And so sweet! He showed up to dinner the other night with a dozen pink roses. And he's so interested in everything about me! You would totally approve, Marion. One thing Axel is not is a narcissist."

Marion laughed. "I'm so glad to hear that," she said. "And you wouldn't believe how handsome this guy is, Danny. Almost as good-looking as you." She winked at him.

"Where did you meet him?" he asked.

"He's the restaurant manager at Buffington's," Piper told him.

"Is he from here?"

"No, he's … well, that's funny! I don't even know where he moved from, but I do know he didn't grow up here."

"Clearly you need me to weasel more information out of him," Marion said. "How about you bring Axel over to dinner here soon?"

"Or I could have you guys over."

Marion shrugged. "Either way. We always love coming to your house."

Soon, dinner was ready, and they all grouped around the kitchen table. Piper adored their kitchen, with its glass countertops, black cabinets, and nickel hardware that glowed softly in even the dimmest light. The glass countertops were outrageously expensive, Marion confided to Piper one time, and everyone thought she was crazy for even wanting them. But she had installed lighting underneath them so that when she wanted to, she could illuminate them. They looked utterly amazing when she did that, but it was often so amazing it could be a little distracting. Tonight they were off, but they still possessed a lustrous gleam in the reflected light like the nickel pulls and knobs.

Marion had fixed crabmeat crepes with an Asiago béchamel sauce and a salad with ruby grapefruit, jicama, avocado, and dried cranberries. It was as beautiful as it was delicious. Marion loved to cook, something Danny enjoyed as well. He was king of the grill.

On her drive home, Piper felt warm and cozy, loved and buoyant. She was going to have so much fun with the new baby! She loved babies. And she was feeling so smitten with Axel. Fortune seemed to be smiling on her, finally, in her love life. She thought back to the cute musician who had approached her at the food co-op the other day, declaring, like Axel, that she had had some profound affect on him, and wondering if she would like to go out sometime. If she hadn't already had her first date with Axel, she just might have taken him up on it, but as it was … At any rate, maybe Marion was right, she was a lot of men's type. This thought cheered her as she parked in her garage, let herself in, and got ready for bed. As she undressed, she wondered what Axel was like in bed. She had a feeling he might be fantastic.

CHAPTER 14

Carson strummed gloomily on his guitar, not bothering to pay attention to the visuals the notes produced. He thought he had prepared himself for Sky Blue—Piper, that is—to not be available. Hell, he thought he had braced himself for never seeing her again. But. When he had a chance to interact with her at the food co-op, he fell even more head over heels. She was even more enchanting than he had imagined. He had never met someone that ingenuous, that kind, and that impish. And her voice. My God. Whenever she said anything, anything at all, he felt as if someone were gently, sensuously combing his body with maiden hair fern fronds. Or something. Something feathery soft, but more substantial than a feather … like how he imagined a sea comb's tendrils would feel if they didn't have stinging cells along their length. And whatnot. He shook his head. Impossible to describe. Just absolutely, addictively delicious.

He could tell she liked him. But she was seeing someone. Of course she was seeing someone! How could she not be? He had thought he could accept that. He would have to accept it. But he couldn't. God, this was painful. He had no idea how painful something like this could be. If he truly cared about her, though, he had to be happy for her if she was in a good relationship, he told himself. That was what was most important, right? If it wasn't about his ego?

At least things were going relatively well in his work. The demo he had sent to the producer had been enthusiastically received. They had sent him his first check, so he was able to buy the software he needed without having to take advantage of his mom's offer. He was working on the full score, finding that he was having no trouble writing music for the somber, haunting scenes. But for the beautiful, uplifting ones? He'd just have to get himself out of this funk. He'd love to do more of this kind of composing, quite frankly. The record business was fraught with proverbial land mines, disappointment, and frustration. And he thought that, with his synesthesia, he might be particularly well-suited for this kind of work.

He had a gig in Chico tonight, at The Rusty Nail, which he was only half-looking forward to. Bizarrely, he was feeling like he didn't want to get too far away from where Piper lived. How weird was that? They weren't even going out. He put his guitar down. He was getting too weird. He needed to get a grip. He thought about calling Heather and apologizing, asking if she would take him back. But that didn't feel right. He would feel like a dick. He would be a dick. He sighed and mentally ran down the list of girls he had been attracted to in high school who hadn't moved away from Incident and/or settled down with someone. He came up blank.

Then he remembered Olivia. She seemed nice. And smart. Jessie liked her. That counted for a lot in his book.

She had left her contact information with them, and his mom had thumbtacked it onto the corkboard she had for messages in the kitchen. He knew his mom wouldn't have any problems with his calling Olivia; she had been trying to set him up with her when she came over to install the video camera. Fortunately, Merilee was with some of her women friends, taking a ceramics class, so he could have some privacy. He didn't want to come on too strong, so he decided to ask Olivia if she'd like a walking tour of downtown Incident, and he could tell her about all the good places. He braced himself—he had never gotten to a place where he felt relaxed about asking a woman out—and punched her number into his cell phone. She answered, and when he told her who it was, she asked him if everything was okay with the equipment and with Jessie.

"Oh, yeah, everything's great. You'll have some good footage, I think. And I've been keeping track whenever I'm home."

"Wonderful! Thanks."

Carson decided to plunge in. No point in dragging this out. "Well, hey, I was wondering if you'd like a tour of downtown. Being new here and all. A walking tour."

"That would be fantastic, I would love that!" she exclaimed. "When?"

Carson glanced up at the kitchen clock. "We could go now, if you're free. I realize it's last minute. And if today doesn't work, we'll find another time."

"Now works great! In fact, your timing is perfect."

"Cool. How about we meet at the corner of Sugarloaf and Sassafras? In … say, forty minutes or so?"

She said that sounded perfect, too, and when he hung up, Carson was feeling glad that he had called. The fact that she sounded so happy to hear from him raised his spirits considerably.

He thought he would bring Jessie along, since they were walking, and she was so well-behaved. She was under excellent voice command, so she didn't need a leash, and she would sit and wait patiently outside any venue without hassling anyone. The shoppers and shopkeepers in downtown who were dog people loved her so she got lots of attention, which she enjoyed.

He brushed his teeth and ran his hands through his hair, then called Jessie, who seemed to know they were going out the minute he called her. She pranced out to the Corolla with him and leapt gracefully into the passenger's seat when he opened the door for her. As he put the car in reverse and turned the car around, he observed once again what a handsome dog Jessie was. He'd rarely seen such a pretty dog, actually, with her beautiful Husky markings and all the softness of a lab. Taking her home from the shelter was one of the best things he'd ever done.

He got to their meeting place before Olivia did, so he took a seat on a nearby bench and waited; Jessie sat down at his feet. A number of people petted her when they walked by. Carson often thought that if she ran for mayor, she'd win. He spotted Olivia before she saw him, and he watched her making her way down the street. She had a determined stride, but a feminine one. He liked the way she dressed, too. Today she was wearing a black tunic over black leggings and some ankle-high russet-colored boots almost the same shade as her hair.

He stood and waved when she got close and Jessie trotted over to greet her, tail wagging.

"Ohh, hey there, Jessie," Olivia crooned, giving her a pat. She straightened up and smiled at Carson. "Thanks so much for offering me a tour."

He shrugged. "It's the least I can do. You've really jazzed up my mom's life with your experiment. Gives her a sense of purpose."

"That's nice to hear."

Carson tucked a lock of his hair behind his ear. "Well, first things first. The best coffee in town is across the street at The Divine Bean." Olivia looked across the street to where he was pointing.

"That's good to know," she said. "I've already had some great coffee here."

"Well, this is the best," he said firmly. "I know some people who think Java Queen's better, but … no way, as far as I'm concerned."

"Noted," she laughed.

"Might as well head this direction," he said, as he began sauntering down the street, Olivia and Jessie in tow. "So, this is a really excellent brew pub right here, Badger's Breath. They make their own craft beer. And this store is pretty cool. They sell model trains but all kinds of train paraphernalia, if you're a train geek or have a friend who is. This place, The Hemp Store, has great clothes and bags, oils and snacks. Oh, and this is a terrific plant store. They also sell cut flowers. Then there's this place. We'll have to make a stop here, if you don't mind."

"Not at all."

Jessie already had her nose at the door of The Epicurean Pooch. Not only did she love this place, but the owner of the shop also adored Jessie. Half the time they went in there, she refused to take any money for the bison jerky or white-chocolate-covered dog biscuit that Jessie scarfed down in two nanoseconds. He didn't quite understand how Jessie could know that she loved something so much that she gobbled down so quickly, but clearly, she did.

"Jessie, hello!" she crowed as they entered. "And hello to you, too, Carson," she said. She gave Olivia a friendly nod.

"Hey, Lauren. Could you please give me one of those … wait, are those dog donuts?"

Lauren nodded proudly. "They are indeed."

"What flavor are they?"

"Well, I have bacon, peanut butter, and cheddar."

"Oh, man, Jessie. That's a hard choice. What do you think?"

Jessie, who had politely sat down, thumped her tail.

"Hmm, she loves all of those."

"She's got great taste."

"OK, give me a peanut butter and we'll try one of the

others next time."

Lauren handed him the donut and then rang up the purchase. He fed it to Jessie in several bites and despite the fact that she was salivating like crazy by now, she took each bite gently from his hand and managed not to slime him at all. She did, however, gulp each bite down with impressive speed.

As they exited the store, Olivia remarked that Jessie was lucky to have such a generous, thoughtful owner. "Or, person, I should say. That's the term Rupert uses."

Carson nodded. "I like that."

"So I take it that you're not one of those people who think that dogs should eat only dog food."

Carson snorted. "No way! What a crock. What do those people think dogs lived on before dog food? Scraps! People food! And anyway, how cruel. Dogs have such a rich sense of smell—I can't imagine withholding all the things we eat that she loves."

"She certainly seems healthy," Olivia observed, reaching down to give Jessie a scratch behind the ears. "And happy."

They continued on their way, Carson pointing out the green grocer that carried local, organic produce, the bakery, his favorite gift store, Dante's, and the gelato store that made all their gelato on site. As they approached Buffington's bistro, Olivia exclaimed, "Hey, I've heard this place is great! Can I treat you to lunch?"

"Oh, uh, sure, I guess. But I should take you!"

"Why?"

"Because … well, because I'm the one who invited you to go on a tour."

"So, let me do something to reciprocate. C'mon. I saved money on my moving allowance." Then her eyes fell on Jessie. "Oh, but I forgot about Jessie."

"She'll wait outside. It'll be fine. It'll give her a chance to mingle with her fan club."

As they went in, Carson quickly scanned the place to see if

Piper might be here. Chances were not high, necessarily, even though this was the first place he spotted her. But Incident was small enough that it could happen, especially if she ate here regularly. He was relieved not to see her. He didn't want to be distracted. Olivia seemed really nice and it would feel tacky to be lusting after another woman while he was with her. Not that he was necessarily thinking of Olivia romantically, but he had taken this first step. And he wasn't ruling it out.

A waitress showed them to a table and as they looked over the menu, Olivia exclaimed over the tempting fare. "One of the best things about moving to California is the food," she enthused. "I love California cuisine."

She chose Pad Thai with duck confit and Carson ordered a salmon burger with red cabbage and jicama slaw and killer sauce. Halfway through their meal, the oleaginous manager came by the table to ask if everything was served to their satisfaction. After briefly making eye contact with Carson, he spent all the rest of his time chatting up Olivia. Carson couldn't believe it. Was he really going to flirt with a woman who was with somebody? Of course, this guy hadn't bothered to come by his table the other day when he was eating alone. He guessed women probably found him attractive—he not only had conventional good looks, he also had that smug kind of self-confidence—but he was so slimy. God!

After the guy left, Carson couldn't help it. He knew he was going to sound like a loser, but he asked, "So, tell me. Do you find that guy attractive?"

She looked surprised. "Well, sure. Why?"

"Oh, I'm just trying to gain a woman's perspective, I guess."

Olivia shot him an amused glance. "He is very smooth."

"Slick."

She laughed.

Ugh, thought Carson. He would never understand women. That guy's voice alone was creepy. Not only did it sound phony, the colors it produced were ugly—brownish, greenish yellows. Ugly as shit. And bland patterns that reminded him of corporate logos for some reason.

Olivia's voice, on the other hand, was quite pleasant. It didn't do to him what Piper's did, but it created some terrific visuals—deep orange and violet polygons that occupied different planes, some of them edged in a vibrant green. He happily listened to her talk about her research, most of which he didn't understand, and about New England, which she loved. She seemed interested in his work as a musician and asked some insightful questions. He didn't like talking about his music all that much—what he had to say was in his music—but he ended up telling her about his synesthesia, which she found fascinating.

Carson saved a couple of bites of his salmon burger for Jessie, as a reward for being such a good dog to wait for so long. She was right behind the door where he had left her as they exited, and she got up when Carson called to her, a big smile on her face. She loved salmon. When they went on walks on the river trail, he had to keep her from rolling in the dead salmon that washed up along the riverbanks. He found it interesting that odors like rotting salmon smelled good to dogs, when their senses of smell were so much keener than humans'.

Olivia said that it was time for her to go and thanked Carson for the tour. He asked if she wanted to hear him play in Chico later, but she told him she had too much work getting up to speed in her new job. She said she'd take a rain check. Carson said he would call her. And he would, too. She wasn't Sky Blue, but she was nice. And nice was good enough for now.

CHAPTER 15

Olivia sat in her new office at the university, trying to curb her rising anxiety. She had just come from a conversation with Rupert about funding. The good news was, she was starting to get an idea for a way that she could test to see if a person could consciously affect gene regulation. She was homing in on a target gene, one that was well-known and whose product—a protein—could be easily measured from a blood sample. She was combing the literature for experiments that proved the efficacy of meditation, biofeedback, or guided imagery for physiological effects such as lowered blood pressure for her methods, and working her way through a list of endorphins produced by the body for her target, thinking that this could well be the mode of action: The meditation or guided imagery encouraged production of endorphins. Even if her hypothesis concerning the mode of action was incorrect, it wouldn't necessarily matter in the long run if she could get her subjects to intentionally alter the production of an endorphin under experimental conditions. This just helped her to have a place to start. She had a lot of details to work out, but she was feeling good about the direction her brainstorming was taking her.

However. She would need a fair amount of money to be able to conduct experiments like this, $150,000 or more. But after speaking with Rupert, she learned that most grant awards in the area of consciousness research were $60,000 or less, often far less, in the neighborhood of $2000 to $5000. She could try to get multiple grants, but compared to the kind of science she had been doing, they were fewer and farther between, and they were even more competitive. She couldn't go back to doing her old research, though, because the labs here weren't equipped to do that kind of work.

It wouldn't be so bad if she didn't feel the clock ticking. The Biology Department at Incident U might be more patient than some, but she couldn't put off getting results for very long if she wanted to keep her job. They could easily hire someone who was already performing consciousness research and who wouldn't have to get up to speed like she did. Though in fact, they easily could have, she told herself; she tried to take comfort in the fact that they hadn't, they had hired her. But then there were the journals in which she could hope to get published. She would probably have to give up her dreams of someday getting published in *Science* or *Nature.*

She sighed. Complicating everything were her nightmares. It was bad enough to have them, but they were coming true! There had been a terrible pile-up in a dust storm on I-5 a few days ago, somewhere down south. And a gunman had burst into a café in a small town on the California coast and killed eight people. And how could this be? She was willing to entertain the notion that consciousness could have an effect on systems in the present, but to think that anyone could access information from the future went against everything she believed.

And now she was dreaming about a commercial plane crash. The frustrating thing was, it wasn't like this information helped her to prevent anything. She didn't know where any of these things were going to happen, or when. And even if she did, what could she do? Who would believe her? Who would she tell in the first place?

She told herself that these kinds of tragedies happened all the time. Given enough people on the planet doing enough things, ferries were bound to sink, and cars were going to crash. But the timing was spooking her.

At least she had had a respite from all these worries on Saturday, when she had lunch with Carson. She and he were very different, but she liked him. She could imagine spending more time with him. She wasn't necessarily looking for a boyfriend, but she did need some friends. And who knew where it might go, over time?

Her stomach grumbled and she realized that she had forgotten about lunch. She had made herself a tuna sandwich at home and put it in the fridge in the faculty lounge, so she headed there now. As she was taking it out, Edwyn Ferguson, another faculty member, came in to get a cup of coffee. Olivia was just getting to know all the rest of the faculty and their specialties. Edwyn's area of expertise was Near Death Experiences and … wait a minute, his other specialty was dreams!

He nodded at Olivia as he grabbed the coffee pot and filled his mug, asked her how it was going. She knew he was just making small talk but she screwed up her nerve and asked if she could speak to him in private.

He obviously wasn't expecting that, but he invited her to his office. As she followed him in, she noticed that on one wall, he had hung a framed poster of "Flea Market of the Gods" by Barry Kite, a surreal landscape where shoppers browsed amongst table displays of planets. She knew this artist because her high school boyfriend had been a huge fan. On another wall he had a print by German illustrator Sulamith Wülfing, an ethereal artist of whom her mother had been fond. She kept a box of her notecards on hand at all times. In fact, her parents were both art buffs, so she had received an ample dose of art history and education while she was growing up.

Edwyn offered her the seat he had available for students while he settled into his desk chair and took a sip of his coffee. His coloring intrigued her as his skin was a beautiful ebony while his sparse, close-cropped hair had turned white on both his head and face. It gave her the impression that he was dusted with fine, sugary snow.

"So what's up?" he asked. "Are you getting along all right? Thinking about going into Near Death research?"

"I'm—doing fine," she said. "And no, not right now." Although, she mused, she wasn't ruling anything out at this point. "I—well, the reason I asked to talk to you is … I've been having these nightmares. All the time."

He nodded, but remained silent.

"And I never had them before! I never even remembered my dreams before. And—and the thing is … and this is going to sound crazy, but they're coming true."

"What do you mean, they're coming true?"

Olivia told him about the ferry, pile-up, and gunman. "They seemed to start after I was in this accident on my way out here," she said. "I hit my head somehow, and even though everything checked out medically, I started having these dreams that seem to be … well, prescient. And maybe there's no connection between hitting my head and the nightmares, but I just wish I knew why I was having them. And …" tears welled up unexpectedly, "how to stop."

Edwyn rubbed his beard as he pondered. "Well," he said, "I can tell you that there are, in fact, cases where a head trauma unleashes previously unrealized abilities, like musical or artistic talent, or mathematical prowess. It's called 'Acquired Savant Syndrome.' One guy, a high school dropout who got brutally mugged, came back to consciousness able to draw fractals. He's the only known human who can do that." He tugged at his ear as he continued to think. "And actually, now that I think about it, there was a case a few years ago of a man who suffered a blow to his head and went into a coma for two weeks. When he woke up, he started getting psychic impressions that were often borne out. They don't understand the mechanism, but because most of the brain injuries are to the left hemisphere, they think it's possible that these abilities were being somehow suppressed or throttled by the left side of the brain. They existed all along, they just weren't being expressed."

"So, you're suggesting that I've always had psychic abilities, I just didn't know it?"

He shrugged. "Maybe we all do. It's not like these are magical abilities. Those of us in this department believe that they're biological, with selective advantages. We might not understand how they work yet, but that doesn't negate the fact that they exist. The data are pretty overwhelming that they do."

"But … I don't get how precognition is possible. The future isn't set, right?"

"Not to my understanding. I would guess that if you are, in fact, getting information from the future, you're receiving future probabilities. They may or may not happen, depending on a number of factors."

Olivia felt the corners of her mouth droop. "But so far, all of mine have come true. And they're all bad. Why don't I have some precognitive dreams about something good?"

Edwyn leaned back in his chair and propped one leg on the other; the movement drew Olivia's attention to a small print that she hadn't noticed when she came in: Henry Fuseli's famous painting, "The Nightmare," in which a sinister incubus crouches on the belly of an exaggeratedly supine, sleeping woman. "A lot of people think that people receive information that we classify as psi as a warning," he said. "You might want to talk to Rupert about that sometime. He has some theories about this. It developed as a way of communicating over time and distance before we had telecommunications. 'Bad' information is more readily transmitted because it might carry a selective advantage. It might help in someone's survival."

"But these dreams aren't helping in anyone's survival. I'm not able to tell anyone not to do something or go somewhere on such-and-such a time—the information I'm getting isn't that exact."

Edwyn nodded. "I'm afraid I just don't know, Olivia. I can see why this would be distressing. Maybe there's some advantage or benefit that you're just not aware of yet. My advice would be to not take it personally. Look at these dreams as objectively as you can, as a phenomenon, not a curse, and not something you're meant to do something about. And try writing your nightmares down. See if maybe that releases you from some of the recurring ones. As a matter of fact, you might start writing down all of your dreams. There might be some clues there."

Olivia bit her lip. She wasn't sure what she had been hoping for, but evidently she had been hoping for more clarity. She felt disappointed. She stood up and held out her hand. "Thanks for your time, Edwyn. I really appreciate it," she said.

He rose and took her hand, gave it a brief shake. "Any time, Olivia. Feel free to come back and talk to me if you want to. I don't know if I'll be of any help, but I'll give it my best shot."

She thanked him once again and left, even hungrier now. She returned to the faculty lounge and ate her sandwich slowly, pondering everything that Edwyn had to tell her. For some reason, it comforted her to think of psi as biological abilities, not some kind of otherworldly, occult phenomena. That made it easier to take; she didn't feel quite so possessed by something that wasn't her. Still … she didn't like it. She supposed she could start writing her dreams down. It couldn't hurt. And maybe she would talk to Rupert sometime. He was awfully busy, but he had told her she could come to him with any problems. Not that this was necessarily what he had in mind.

She finished her lunch, regretting that she hadn't slipped in one of those chocolate chip cookies she had picked up at the bakery Carson had pointed out to her. Maybe she would talk to Piper about some herbs that she could take for nightmares. There might not be anything—she had very little knowledge about herbal remedies—but she didn't want to take sleeping pills.

And certainly, if she wanted to look at the dreams symbolically, it wasn't hard to equate her professional turmoil to all this disaster imagery. She sighed, crumpled her lunch bag into a ball and tossed it into the recycling bin. She just needed to focus on her work and not worry about the funding at this stage. Maybe there were some deep pockets out there for the kind of thing she was working on that she didn't know about. And if there were, she wanted to be ready with some good science and well-designed experiments.

CHAPTER 14

xel tightened his hands on the steering wheel. Some fucking asshole had blocked him behind a semi going up a hill, some dipshit in a Buick Enclave. Who the fuck would drive a Buick Enclave? This dipshit, apparently. Axel fumed until he got a chance to whip his car out from behind the truck, then stomped on the gas until he was passing said dipshit on the right. Then he cut in front of him, close enough that the guy had to slam on his brakes and nearly lost control. Would have served him right if he had. He glanced in the rear view mirror. Some old geezer. Who probably shouldn't have been driving in the first place. Axel floored it and got out of there in a hurry, just in case the geezer was a nut job with a gun.

He was put out that he had to make this trip in the first place, but if he didn't make arrangements to see Amanda, she'd no doubt come sniffing around Incident to find him, and she'd find out that he was going by a different name. That never looked good, even though there were plenty of perfectly valid reasons for someone to change their name. Like, if you were getting stalked or something. Or creditors were after you for some bogus bullshit. Or you just got tired of your old name. Still. He knew how important appearances were. And Amanda could potentially be useful in some capacity. It was annoying, though. He had lots of other irons in the fire, far more lucrative.

He arrived at her house fifteen minutes late—always good to keep girls like Amanda waiting, so they weren't sure if you were going to show up or not—and apologized profusely for his tardiness when she opened the door.

She looked thrilled to see him and once again threw her arms around him like he had just rescued her from a mugging, then invited him inside. She lived in a funky cabin that smelled like old wood smoke, bacon, and dogs, even though she didn't appear to have a dog. Her idea of home décor was to hang a couple of quilts on the wall—Jesus God—and some supremely amateurish landscapes painted in oil, several of the famous mountain that loomed over the small city.

"Wow," he said, stopping in front of one of them. "Did you paint this?"

Amanda said yes, while shaking her head with self-deprecaion. "I'm just learning," she told him. "I'm taking a class from an artist in town who is amazing! You should see some of his work."

"I'd love to," he said, as he continued his inventory. Sad, really. "I can see you've been working hard."

"Well, trying to, anyway," she said. "Thanks. Can I get you something to drink? Beer, wine? I can make mojitos, if you'd like."

"I'd love a mojito, if it's not too much trouble." He could only imagine what her taste in wine ran toward—or what she could afford. Beer was for plebes.

"No trouble at all! Would you like to join me in the kitchen?"

He followed her into the small kitchen, where he saw that she had a number of plaques on the walls, proclaiming such homespun wisdom as, "Wake up every morning with the thought that something wonderful is going to happen," penned in flowery calligraphy, and "Friends: A true friend is someone like you."

"So how are you liking Incident?" she asked, as she opened the freezer to load the shaker with ice.

"It's great. How about you? Are you liking Mt. Shasta?"

"I'm loving it!" she said. "This mountain is so spiritual. And there are so many things to do here! I'm taking a great yoga class, and this painting class. There's a bird-watching group that I'm thinking about joining, as nerdy as that sounds," she giggled. "And the people are so nice and so mellow."

"That's great," said Axel. "I'm really happy for you."

"Thank you!" She smiled at him, set the shaker down on the counter and added rum and sugar, then squeezed in some limes. She reached for the pile of fresh mint leaves she had lying on the counter and began tearing them into small pieces and dropping them into the mix.

"You don't miss Sacramento?"

She shrugged. "Not that much. I miss some of my friends, but after Kristy died … I don't know, it felt like a good thing to get out of the city. It just feels a lot safer up here, you know?"

"I do." He hesitated, then asked, his face mournful, "Do they have any leads on her killer?"

She shook her head. "Not yet. Not that I know of, anyway. The police are saying that they don't want to share anything while they're conducting their investigation."

He nodded. "That's probably a good idea."

"Yeah." She sighed, hastily wiping a tear away. She handed him the beverage shaker. "You want to do the honors?" she asked. "I'm guessing you're pretty good at something like this, being in the restaurant business."

"I'd be happy to," he said, taking the container and giving it several smart, practiced shakes. Then he held the strainer over the top and poured them each a glass, using the martini glasses that Amanda had on the counter. "Here's to Kristy," he said solemnly, holding Amanda's gaze. He was aware that he had said the same thing during their coffee date, but figured it couldn't hurt to say it again.

She took a sip, the corners of her mouth trembling. But the liquor seemed to revive her, and she drank the rest of it quickly, pouring herself another and topping off Axel's glass. She had fixed a quinoa salad and broiled salmon for dinner, so after they had a few drinks, they ate in her dining area. He was trying to decide whether to come on to her or not, weighing the pros and cons, when she got up from her chair and climbed in his lap. There, she began kissing him passionately, so he figured what the hell and ended up in bed with her. Afterward, as he was leaving, giving her a tender farewell and declaring how much he wished he could stay but had to work brunch in the morning, he wondered if that was such a good idea. He didn't want her glomming onto him. But maybe this would keep her satisfied for a while, especially if he sent her the occasional romantic text.

Besides, he didn't plan on staying in Incident all that long. His ideas for his restaurant in San Francisco were starting to take shape. That's where he needed to be. None of these piece-of-shit cow towns—some place classy, that's where he belonged. And not just any restaurant—he was going to have the hippest, most sophisticated restaurant in the city, one where people called to make reservations a month in advance, where all the most influential and important people came, where everyone wanted to be seen. And where everyone wanted to curry favor with him to get a decent table.

He slept well that night. The next morning he headed over to the Golden Oaks Assisted Living Facility to visit his special friend, Ethel. He had made arrangements to see her in advance, so one of the staff had her waiting for him in the lobby, her hair coiffed, her makeup applied.

"How's my favorite girl?" he called out as he breezed in, winking at the receptionist as he approached Ethel.

She giggled girlishly while he took both her hands and gave one of them a courtly kiss. He had considered bringing some flowers, but thought that might be piling it on a little thick and he hadn't found anything decent blooming anywhere that he could filch, anyway. He noticed that a couple of the other old women sitting in the lobby were casting envious glances at Ethel. Well, they might get their chance if Ethel croaked any time soon.

"So what have you been up to since I was here last?" he asked. "You haven't been on any hot dates, have you?"

Ethel twinkled and laughed and told him impishly that it was none of his business.

"Why, Ethel, you saucy minx!" he exclaimed, borrowing a line from Hugh Grant movie. "Well, listen, it's a beautiful day outside." In truth, it was rather chilly, but at least the sun was out. "I wonder if you'd like a little spin outside?"

She said that she'd love it. Axel asked the receptionist—a different girl than the regular girl, but just as impressed with his looks and charm—if it would be all right to take Ethel around the block. She gushed that this sounded like a wonderful idea.

Axel took his cashmere jacket off and wrapped it around Ethel's shoulders, then took his scarf and wound it around her head like a turban.

"There. Now you look like a star."

"But—won't you be cold?" she asked anxiously.

"Not at all. I'll be fine."

Axel wheeled her outside and across the parking lot to the sidewalk. Golden Oaks resided in a nice neighborhood close to the river trail that ran along the Sacramento River, so there were sidewalks aplenty. As they walked, he made light chit chat for a bit. Then he homed in on what most interested him.

"So tell me, Ethel, how much family do you have left in town?" He had learned by now that her only child, a son, had died in the Vietnam War; her husband had passed three years ago. She had asked about his family at one point, and he had given her the story about his parents dying in a terrible car accident when he was fourteen; fortunately, he told her, his maternal grandmother took him in.

"Well, I have a niece and a nephew."

"Any other nieces or nephews?"

She shook her head.

"So, I imagine that you must see a lot of them."

She shook her head once more, the turban wobbling. She looked rather ridiculous, actually. "No, they—they're very busy. You know how it is these days. Everybody's working so hard."

"Oh, don't I know!"

She craned around in her chair to catch his eye. "You're so kind to make the time to see me. I imagine you're busy as well."

"Not too busy to pay some special attention to a special person," he said.

She brightened, turned back around.

"So tell me more about your husband. You said that he was in real estate?"

"Oh, yes! And he was very good at it, too. Had wonderful instincts and a great personality. People loved him."

"I imagine that when the real estate bubble burst, he must have been hard hit, though, huh?"

"Actually, no. Like I say, he had excellent instincts. He was in a very good position to buy."

Axel's mouth began watering. Literally.

"Of course, I sold everything after he died and put the money in investments."

"That's prudent." He paused. "What a shame that you don't have a child to leave your and your husband's legacy to. But your niece and nephew will no doubt appreciate it."

She didn't reply, but he noticed that she had begun to twist her wedding ring on her finger. "No doubt," she said finally.

Axel felt that he had accomplished enough for one day, so he turned around and took Ethel back to the facility. He stooped to give her a peck on the check, then retrieved his scarf and jacket. "Till next time, my dear," he told her. He wasn't sure, but he thought he detected the glimmer of a tear in her eye.

As he walked jauntily to his car, his cell phone buzzed, alerting him to a text. It was from his dad. Since Axel wasn't picking up any of his calls, he had obviously decided to try another tack. Impatiently, he navigated to the text, then stiffened when he read it:

"Word on the street—police looking for one Eric Johnson as a person of interest in the death of Kristy Holloway."

He proceeded quickly to his car then called his dad. "What the fuck is this?" he said, when his father answered.

"What do you think?"

"I don't think you're looking out for me, that's what I think."

"My boy, my boy! So cynical." His father gave his phlegmatic, tubercular laugh. "Of course I'm looking out for you. We look out for each other, right?" When Axel didn't respond, he repeated, "Right?"

Axel ground his teeth. His old man better watch his step. "So what is it that you want?" he asked, his voice tight.

"Well, now, let's talk about that. You know I'm not greedy …"

Fucking hell you're not, thought Axel, chewing savagely on his thumbnail. And as he listened to his father's demands, he sunk lower and lower in his seat until he could barely see over the dashboard. He closed his eyes, fighting a wave of nausea. Money just got a lot tighter.

CHAPTER 17

hen Axel opened the door to his apartment, Piper couldn't believe how handsome he looked. He was wearing a beautiful cream-colored linen shirt that set off his dark good looks, and the twill slacks that he was wearing fit him perfectly. Before she could do or say a thing, he put his finger to his lips and held up a blindfold.

"Turn around," he said.

She did so, the most tantalizing feeling stealing over her. She trembled as he fastened the blindfold around her eyes and then gently took her by the hand.

"Come," he said.

She followed him obediently to wherever it was that he was leading her, and when he stopped and took the blindfold off, she gasped in delight. He had filled his small dining room with flowers—on the table, on pedestals, on the sideboard, in the windowsills. No devas; Piper had rarely seen a deva accompanying cut flowers. They tended to stay at the site where the original plant was growing, the one exception being the time she had caught sight of a pretty little deva hanging out in a vase of cut lilacs at Marion and Danny's home. The table was set with a white linen tablecloth and napkins, beautiful china patterned with strawberries, and elegant crystal. Lustrous silverware gleamed in the candlelight and low mood lighting; haunting New Age music played softly.

Piper whirled and caught Axel up in a fierce hug. "This is so beautiful!" she exclaimed. "It's enchanting!"

"Only the best for you, sweet girl," he said, as he gave her a smoldering kiss. They hadn't made love yet, and Piper wondered if tonight was the night. She hoped so. She had never wanted anyone so much in her life. She was a little worried that he didn't find her sexy, like Jared. That certainly didn't seem to be the case from the way he looked at her and kissed her. But it was a fear that nagged at her.

"Wait here," he said. He strode over to the sideboard where she noticed for the first time that he had champagne chilling in a bucket, two flutes standing beside it. Her heart beat faster.

Axel expertly popped the cork and filled both flutes, then handed one to Piper with a courtly bow. "To the most beautiful woman in the world," he said, devouring her with his eyes.

Piper blushed and took a sip, then held her glass aloft and declared with a smile, "And to the handsomest man!"

Axel took a large swallow, set his flute down, and pulled Piper's chair out for her. "Sit!" he urged.

She sat down and tried to time her movements with his, but failed miserably and completely thwarted his efforts to scoot her smoothly up to the table. "Sorry!" she exclaimed, laughing.

Axel shook his head in amusement. "No, it's charming. You're charming." He hesitated before he added, "I love the way you are."

Tears prickled her eyes; Piper felt at a loss for words. But Axel saved the day by announcing that he would serve the first course. He disappeared into the kitchen and reappeared with two shallow bowls filled with the most brilliant green she had ever seen.

"Dandelion greens soup, à la Alice Waters," he said as he set Piper's in front of her.

"Oh my gosh, it's gorgeous!" she exclaimed. "And I love Alice Waters!" She had several of her cookbooks at home.

Axel nodded thoughtfully as he took his seat and whipped his napkin from the table with great flair before settling it into his lap. "She's my hero—or would that be heroine?" he said, with a smile. "In fact, my dream is to open a restaurant like Chez Panisse."

"Really? Here in Incident?"

"Absolutely! I could work with local farmers and ranchers, brewmeisters and vintners … offer seasonal, organic fare … I know a lot of places already do that, but …"

"Oh, Axel, you would make a huge success out of something like that, I know you would!"

He shrugged modestly. "Well, I would certainly give it my all. I've been saving every scrap and I'm looking for some venture capitalists. I'm in conversation with a couple of them, actually. We'll see how it goes."

Piper held her champagne flute up once more and said, "Here's to your new restaurant! And much success!"

"Hear, hear," Axel said with a wry grin. "Thank you."

"And if there's anything I can do to help— anything at all! —just let me know. I could provide you with fresh herbs—for free until you're making a profit. Or … anything else! Just ask, okay?"

Axel shook his head, his eyes full of affection and gratitude. "What did I ever do to deserve you, Piper?" He gazed at her steadily, then got up and walked over, tipped her head back and gave her a passionate kiss. Piper thought she honestly might swoon. What had she ever done to deserve Axel? she asked herself as he re-seated himself and they tucked into the soup. Which was positively scrumptious. She felt as if she were eating a bowl of Spring.

After the soup course, he served a fish course, poached

halibut with capers, Sungold tomatoes, and fresh garlic, then a salad made with butternut squash and pomegranate seeds. For dessert, he served apple blossoms with crème fraiche, some ice wine as an accompaniment. Piper could only imagine how much money he had spent on this dinner, and given the fact that he clearly didn't have a whole lot—his apartment was sparsely furnished—she felt deeply touched.

After dinner, they retreated to the living room and shared the couch. It wasn't long before they were kissing, and soon the kissing turned into more. Axel stood up and offered his hand to Piper, then led her into his bedroom. There, he had scattered rose petals on the bed, and two fat, fragrant candles burned on the bedside table. He put his arms around her and tightened his embrace so gradually that it felt like a delectable eternity, until he was gripping her more ardently than she had ever been held. When he let go of her, he held her gaze for a moment. Then slowly, reverently, he removed her clothes, piece by piece, kissing her on her cheeks, her lips, her shoulders and her breasts. When she was completely naked, he whispered into her ear, "I love you." By then, she was in a daze. He lay her on the bed and gave her the most decadent yet romantic ravishing she had ever received. She was right; he was dynamite in bed.

She stayed the night, during which time she found out just how much stamina Axel had, which was pretty amazing in its own right. When she awoke in the morning to find him lying next to her, she marveled at her incredible luck and thanked the gods for the beautiful man in her life. He kissed her as soon as he opened his eyes, then told her that he needed to get up and get ready for work.

"But feel free to stay here as long as you like," he said. "No need to rush."

She replied that she should get going, too, and left the bed when he did, winding her arms around him and holding him close. Her heart was beating so hard that he remarked on it, and she giggled. "You make my heart race," she said.

And in fact, as she drove home, her heart continued to beat excitedly as she thought about the evening. She had never, in her life, been treated so well and so tenderly. She couldn't believe how lucky she was, and that Axel wasn't already in a relationship with someone. He alluded to having gotten his heart broken not long ago, so maybe that was the reason. She began to think that maybe having children wasn't so far off in the future after all.

When she got home, she showered, ate a bite of breakfast, and changed into a pair of soft, worn jeans and a heather-colored pullover. She added a light, lavender jacket and headed off into the woods with her basket, on the hunt for some wild rose hips. She grew roses in her garden, but she generally liked to keep them flowering for as long as possible, so they rarely formed fruit. The forest behind her house had a robust population of wild roses and some roses that perhaps had originated in someone's garden—maybe even her own. She hadn't heard any knocking since the night that Axel was over for dinner, so she hoped that the children whose game this was had grown tired of it. And anyway, what harm came from making knocking sounds?

She soon came upon a rose bush laden with rose hips, so she gathered up a number of them, thanking the beautiful deva who hovered about as she worked, then moved on. She wanted to leave plenty for the animals who liked them, too. As she wandered deeper and deeper into the forest, she began to notice that the sounds she was accustomed to hearing had gotten quieter and quieter until she didn't hear a single bird or insect. That seemed strange. And as she stopped and strained to hear a cheep from a finch or a cackle from a quail or the lazy buzz of a bee, she became aware of a feeling of being watched. Her hair on the nape of her neck literally stood up, just like in books she had read, and a prickle scrambled all over her body. She turned around in place, trying to discern where this feeling might be coming from when all of a sudden a blur of fur burst out of a clump of bushes. Startled, she cried out, then realized it was a dog. A beautiful dog, actually, with the markings of a Husky but the shape of a lab. He—or she—came trotting up to her, tail wagging. Piper leaned over to let the dog sniff her hand.

"Jessie!" someone called. "Jessie, come!"

Jessie turned to respond to whomever was calling her and before long, he came into the clearing. It was the musician she had spoken to the other day at the food co-op.

"Well, hey!" he said, as soon as he caught sight of her. "I hope Jessie didn't scare you. She's very friendly."

"Oh, no worries," said Piper. Jessie came back for a pat, which Piper obligingly gave her. "She's a beautiful dog."

"She is," he agreed. He fell silent then, perhaps remembering their last interaction and feeling shy.

"So … do you two hike these woods very often?" Piper asked.

He nodded. He turned and pointed behind him. "My mom's house is just a couple of miles back that way. Jessie loves these woods. As you might imagine."

"I do, too."

Carson peered in her basket. "Collecting rose hips?"

"Yes, I'm an herbalist."

"Oh yeah? That's cool."

Piper debated whether to ask her next question, then figured she might as well. "Listen, this might sound like an odd question, but do you ever hear knocking in the woods?"

"Knocking? Like, woodpeckers?"

She shook her head. "No, deeper and slower than that. Maybe kids. I'm not sure."

"Hmm." He thought for a moment. "Can't say that I have, but I'll keep an ear out. Do you live near here?"

"Yes." Piper gestured behind her. "I rent a house about a half-mile from here.'"

Carson brightened. "Frank and Mary's old place?"

"That's right! Do you know them?"

"Sure! I grew up around here. Frank used to take me fishing when I was little. But I sucked at it."

Piper laughed.

"But hey, I don't want to hang you up. You're obviously a woman on a mission." He smiled. He had a very nice smile.

"I should probably get back home," she said, "and get ready for my class."

"You're a teacher, too?"

"Yes, I teach a couple of classes at the university."

"Do you ever give tutorials?"

She shrugged. "Sometimes."

"Because I'll bet my mom would love to learn about herbs. Her birthday's coming up and I was trying to come up with something besides the same old, same old."

Piper grinned. "Well, you can look me up at the university or on the Internet. Piper Fairchild. I'd give you a card, but I don't have any on me."

"That's fine. I'll find you." Carson seemed to want to take her hand but to think better of it; he gave her a little salute instead. "Come on, Jess, we should be on our way ourselves."

Jessie, who had settled down on the soft forest duff, jumped to her feet. And as they disappeared into the forest—quite a cute pair, she reflected—Piper headed back the way she had come. Now the birds were singing and chittering, and a hummingbird came zooming noisily by. She didn't know what to attribute that lull she experienced earlier, but figured it must have been the presence of some animal like a bear or even a bobcat or a raccoon. Maybe even Jessie!

Whatever it was, she shouldn't let her imagination run away with her, she told herself. And anyway, she had plenty to keep her mind occupied. As she savored her night with Axel, she felt a foolish, dreamy smile steal over her face and was glad that she didn't feel anyone watching her now. She would hate to be that vulnerable to anyone. Except Axel, she supposed. Her soul mate, she felt sure.

CHAPTER 18

he front door to The Contrarian opened, then closed, splashing a brief rectangle of light across the stage where Carson was setting up the equipment for the band's gig. Matt, the sound guy, was in the back of the room, coordinating. Carson had played The Contrarian a number of times and worked with Matt even more often; they had a good relationship, which Carson appreciated. He straightened up, hoping to see Evan, but it was Buster, the drummer.

"Hey, Buster," Matt called out. Buster nodded. He was a man of few words. He was dependable, though, and knew a lot about sound. He had worked as a sound engineer before, but preferred playing.

Evan had promised to be here a half-hour ago, to go over some notes Carson had put together for a new song, but he hadn't even texted to let Carson know what had delayed him. Carson suspected nothing had; he was just in a pissy mood. Carson hadn't shared his news about the soundtrack he was working on with either Evan or Buster because he was afraid that Evan might find some way to belittle it.

"Heard anything from Evan?" Carson asked Buster. Buster

shook his head and began fiddling with the drum mic.

Carson sighed, went back to what he was doing. The smell of stale beer was making him want one, but he never drank before a gig. Fifteen minutes later, Evan came sauntering in.

"You're late," said Carson.

Evan shrugged. "Sorry."

"Sorry doesn't really cut it, man. What's going on with you?"

Evan met his eyes with a flat, unfriendly gaze. "With me?"

"Yeah, you."

"I'm just not into it, man. This isn't my kind of music. In fact, this is my last gig with Tachyon."

So there it was. Carson had been waiting for this. He tried to pretend he didn't care, but he did. In high school, he and Evan had been inseparable. They had started a band their freshman year with two other classmates, and they had done awfully well for a high school band. Without ever even discussing it, they had assumed that they would all attend Incident U together and keep their band together. But then Carson decided to attend Santa Cruz instead.

The problem was, things just didn't seem to work here after his dad died. All the color seemed to go out of his world. And his mom was no help. She had retreated inside. She did her best; he couldn't really blame her. But he needed something and he wasn't getting it here. He would have thought that Evan could have had a little compassion for what he was going through then. But Carson was starting to think that he had always been self-centered.

"Okay, so … fine." Carson wanted to say something snarky, but he was afraid that Evan might just walk out. And they needed him tonight. He glanced over at Buster, but Buster lived in his own little world. From his affect, it appeared as if he hadn't heard a word that Evan said. "Can you help me with these wedge monitors, at least?" Fuck the notes on the new song.

Evan grudgingly ambled over and they worked together silently. Evan always smelled like Lawry's Seasoned Salts, and Carson had never been able to figure out why. He had never seen a container of it in Evan's cupboards. As they ran through their sound check with Matt, various colors and patterns shimmered in front of Carson's eyes. He often used his visuals to fine-tune the sound for his music. When everyone was satisfied, Evan took off, saying he'd be back in time for the gig, while Matt, Buster, and Carson decided to hang out and watch the football game between Stanford and Berkeley. Carson wasn't a big sports fan, but he didn't mind watching a game here and there, especially if it was part of a social scene. Evan lived close to The Contrarian, but for Carson to go home would mean a half-hour's drive each way. The gig would be starting in a couple of hours, so there wasn't really any point.

Olivia had told him that she planned to come hear the band play tonight; he hoped she would. A few regulars started drifting in, getting settled at tables here and there. Tachyon Fundicle had a good following in Incident, and there wasn't a whole lot else going on in the music scene tonight, so he expected a good turnout. Buster's girlfriend showed up and joined them, and then, a half-hour before the music started, she and a couple of her friends staked out a table close to the stage. He asked them to save a seat for Olivia, should she show up.

Evan straggled in three minutes before they were due to play their first set and laconically took up his bass while Carson and Buster got into position as well. They had a fairly wide repertoire, from dreamy ballads to some kick-ass hard rock; they started out with a rousing version of one of Carson's favorite songs to get the energy going in the room. As they were playing, he spotted Olivia coming in the door. He managed to catch her eye and nodded at the band widows' table. She grinned and made her way up to the front, giving him a shy half-wave. She looked good tonight in a burnt sienna—his synesthesia had fine-tuned his vocabulary for the very specific colors his mind produced—and dark orange dress that grazed the tops of her ankle boots and buttoned up the front; it clung to her nicely and looked stylish and hip. Carson had decided that Olivia was a hot shit. There weren't really any sparks there yet, but Carson figured it could happen. He still hadn't been able to get Piper out of his mind, as much as he wanted to. But he had decided to give it all time.

So when break time came and he scanned the audience as he prepared to go join Olivia, his heart nearly stopped when he saw Piper in the back of the room at one of the more private tables tucked into a corner. She was with someone, probably her boyfriend. Carson squinted to make out his features in the dim light, curious about his competition, forgetting about the fact that he was thinking of making a go of things with Olivia. When he realized who it was, he froze. She was with that smarmy, phony shit who managed Buffington's Bistro.

How could you?? he wanted to scream. Of all people! When he had run into her in the forest the other day, he had honestly thought that maybe there was a special connection there. But this made him doubt it. Jesus, he wanted to think better of her. Maybe she wouldn't be a good match for him if that was the kind of guy who rang her chimes. He was torn between disliking her for being with this creep and utter despair— for her, for his romantic chances as a man just in general, for the state of the entire world.

He told himself to get a grip and grabbed a ginger beer from the bar before sitting down next to Olivia and thanking her for coming.

"I wouldn't miss it!" she exclaimed. "You guys are terrific!"

Carson glowed at her compliment, making the mental observation that she clearly had a discerning ear. He noticed that her glass of red wine was running low and asked if he could get her a refill. She said that would be nice, so he caught the waitress's eye, another acquaintance from the music club circuit. She came by the table and remarked that she thought Tachyon was sounding fantastic, pleasing Carson even more, and took Olivia's drink order.

Carson noticed that Olivia's color was particularly high this evening, her eyes bright. He speculated that, as a scientist, she might not have spent a lot of time in the music scene and probably had never dated a musician. This could be really fun for her. He hoped it would stay that way. Most girls who dated musicians quickly got tired of the fact that when the rest of their friends were going out and partying, their boyfriend was working. Of course, they weren't technically dating yet. Although—he snuck another peek at the corner where Piper was cozied in with that asshole—he might want to speed things up. He noticed the way the guy never took his eyes off Piper. He supposed that she might find that flattering and romantic, but seriously? It reminded him more of a snake trying to mesmerize its prey.

He wrenched his attention away from Piper and focused on Olivia. Even without the music playing, there was enough ambient noise that it wasn't easy to hear her, but he made a supreme effort. Still, it wasn't a good environment for anything but chitchat—the cluttered jumble of visual patterns from all the noise didn't help—and soon he needed to get back on the stage. Evan detached himself from a group of jazzy-looking guys huddled around a table near the front—goatees all around—who seemed to smirk at Carson as he picked up his guitar. God, who needed it. He would be glad to make this break with Evan, despite the fact that he would need to find another bass player. As much as he hated to admit it, Evan was the best in town. He thought of his film score job and felt glad that he had a fallback position. But as he played, he realized how much he loved the energy from a live audience, and when they launched into one of their early songs, one that

Carson and Evan had co-wrote, he found himself blinking back tears.

They had written it for their high school band, right after Carson's dad had died. His dad's death was one of the stupidest, freakiest ways to die that he had ever heard, and that fact compounded the horribleness of it all. He worked for Cal Trans and he was on a road crew the day that it happened. A driver was texting when a squirrel ran out in front of him, and in his efforts to avoid the squirrel, he yanked his wheel, lost control of his car, and plowed right into Carson's dad. He was pronounced dead on the scene. He was such a mess that they didn't bother to have Carson or his mom identify the body. Carson was glad that he never saw it. It would have haunted him forever. As it was, his imagination produced enough grisly images to last a lifetime.

When Evan heard, he showed up at Carson's house with a bottle of Jack Daniels. They drank half the bottle and jammed all night, producing this song, which seemed to channel all of Carson's rage, frustration, and grief. Despite that, it was a very beautiful song. "You colored the world with magic," he sang, "You gave me the gift of song. When you died, the world fell silent and every hue seemed wrong …" He glanced at Olivia and saw that her eyes glistened with tears, which made him like her even more. When he looked back to the table where Piper was sitting, he saw that she and her boyfriend had left. So she didn't even hear it.

Not meant to be, he thought morosely. Yeah, maybe he was giving up without making much effort, but what would the point be? He had never found busting his ass for some lost cause to have a big pay-off. And one thing his father's death had most certainly taught him was that there were no guarantees of anything, except that life would bring everyone a whopping share of disappointment. Best not to get too emotionally involved with anyone or anything. But when the gig was done, and Evan packed up his bass and left with his friends, Carson felt almost as bereft as he did the day his father died. Buster, evidently picking up on his mood, told him not to worry, that he knew about a bass player who'd recently moved to town and was looking for a band. He'd call him tomorrow, he said.

Carson was so involved with his gloomy thoughts that he didn't even realize that Olivia had stayed while he packed up until she approached the stage and asked him if he'd like to have a nightcap at her place. The thought of going home by himself filled him with a deep and terrible ache that filled his vision with a gauzy black haze, so he accepted with enthusiasm. As he snatched up his guitar case, he asked himself if he was hooking up with Olivia for the wrong reasons, but he shoved that question aside. Doing something for the right reasons was no guarantee of anything, either. And anyway, he got the feeling that right now, she felt just as lonely as he did. He saw nothing wrong with trying to feel a little less lonely in a world that didn't make any more sense than this one.

CHAPTER 19

livia ran a brush through her hair, then grabbed her purse on her way out the door. When her cell phone rang, she almost didn't pick up, but she recognized her sister's ring tone. She figured she was probably calling to chat, which she didn't have time for right now. Rummaging through her purse for her phone, she answered with, "Hey, Emily, I'm running late for an appointment. Can I call you back?"

"Uh, sure," she said. "But let me just tell you why I'm calling."

Her tone put Olivia on guard. She closed the door and sat down on her sofa. "Okay. What's up?"

"Well, Dad's not doing so great."

Olivia wasn't prepared for the surge of icy electricity that shot through her limbs at hearing this. "He's not? What's wrong?"

"He's having more and more trouble walking. And he tore his calf muscle the other day just from stubbing his toe on a rug."

Olivia swallowed, trying to ease the lump in her throat. "Do they have any idea yet what might be causing his symptoms?"

"Nothing has turned up so far. He's had dozens of tests at this point."

God, not a mystery disease. As horrible as some of the possibilities were—ALS, Guillain-Barré Syndrome, a series of small strokes—at least they would know what they were dealing with. "Do you think I should come home?"

Her sister sighed. "Probably not. Not yet. I just wanted to let you know."

Not yet? That sounded ominous. It would be a terrible time to fly back home, but if she needed to, she damn well would. "I can get on a plane anytime you think I should."

"That's good to know. But I don't think it's to that point. Call me back later when you have more time, okay?"

"I will. I'll give you a call back this evening, Sis."

Olivia was so rattled that she forgot to lock her apartment and then had to run back and do so. When she got to her car, she sat for a full five minutes staring at her key, trying to get focused enough to start the car. She arrived at Piper's out of breath and off-balance, something that didn't escape Piper's notice. She told her to come in and relax, and asked her if she'd like a cup of chamomile tea.

"I would love one," she gulped, blinking back tears. Something about Piper's kind solicitousness caused her self-possession to melt, and soon, tears were trickling down her cheeks. Piper yanked a couple of tissues out of a nearby dispenser and handed them to her, giving her a squeeze on the shoulder before disappearing into another room to make her tea. When she reappeared, the steam rising from the mug in her hand, Olivia had managed to get her emotions under control. She accepted the tea gratefully and took a trembling sip. Piper sat in her chair and waited for Olivia to speak.

"I'm sorry," Olivia said, setting the cup down on the end table next to her chair. "I—just received some worrying news about my dad."

Piper's sweet features creased into sympathy and concern.

"Oh dear, I'm so sorry to hear that," she said. "Do you want to talk about it?"

Olivia shrugged. "Well, there's not much to talk about. He's starting to have trouble walking, and he's in increasing pain, from his muscles, it seems—which are also becoming more fragile. But none of the tests have turned up anything."

"Hmm." Piper's gaze became unfocused as she pondered for a moment. "This might sound a little off-the-wall, but is there any possibility that he might be exposed to some toxins? You came from back East—do your parents live in an old house?"

"They do."

"Is it possible that some of the old paint might be leaching into the air?"

"Oh, right—lead poisoning. Well, it's certainly something to look into. Thanks for the suggestion."

Piper smiled. "You're welcome. But that's not what you've come to see me about."

"No." Olivia shook her head. "I'm—well, I started having nightmares on my way out here. I was in an accident where I bumped my head. It didn't seem all that bad at the time. The paramedics didn't even think I had a concussion. But after that, I started having nightmares."

"About the accident?"

"Yes and no. I dreamed about the accident for three nights until the other people in the accident died."

Piper looked puzzled. Olivia proceeded to tell her about her other dreams, prescient dreams, all of which had now come true. She told her about talking to Edwyn, and his advice, which she had been following. She was writing her dreams down and trying to see how they might be giving her some information that could prove helpful in one way or another, but it only seemed to increase her sense of helplessness. She wasn't able to warn anyone about anything. She felt like a psychic voyeur, peeping in on other people's misfortunes to no good purpose. And these nightmares definitely seemed to be crowding out any other dreams she might normally have.

When she finished, she sat staring at the floor for a few moments while she drank her tea. Piper joined her in silence for a while, then said, "And what is it you hope I can help you with?"

Olivia set her mug down with a sigh. "I was hoping you might be able to give me something to stop the nightmares."

"Well, I can give you an herbal mix that might help. But I've always felt that nightmares were trying to get our attention about something, something important that we're unable to face when we're awake."

"I might think that if my dreams were about me or people I know," Olivia said. "But they're not. It feels like this bump on my head jammed something on and it's just picking up white noise, not anything meaningful."

"Are there concerns in your waking life besides your dad's health?" Piper asked.

"Well, sure. Aren't there always?" Olivia gave a evasive smile.

"Specifically in your life." Piper smiled back.

"Oh, I'm trying to find funding for my research, but there's not a lot out there that I can find so far. And my professional viability depends on getting some good research under my belt after my doctorate."

Piper nodded. "Well, I certainly hope that you get the funding that you need."

"Thanks, Piper."

"How's your love life?"

Olivia blinked. "Umm, I broke up with my boyfriend before I moved out here. And other than that … well, there might be something happening, something nice."

"That sounds promising." Piper beamed at her so happily that Olivia felt her heart unfolding, like a poppy in the sun. No wonder she was a healer. Olivia often thought that, despite the great strides that modern medicine had made, many human complaints responded to an ineffable something that resided in a true healer.

Piper lapsed into silence again for a few moments, then said, "Well, I can give you some herbs. They may or may not help, but they're worth a try, I think. Keep writing your dreams down, if you still have them."

Olivia waited while Piper disappeared once again into her back room. She glanced around the room and noticed what a lovely, soothing environment she had created, with hanging pots of obscenely healthy fuchsia, standing Dracaena, and flowering cyclamen on plant stands. Their floral and earthy scents mixed with the fresh air that breathed through the windows from the outside. Most soothing. And the framed botanicals on the walls modestly conveyed the ancient, venerable history of herbal medicine, which filled her with pride for human curiosity and resourcefulness. It was what had drawn her into the sciences, that's for sure. Even the fabric on the armchairs were of a botanical nature, stylized patterns that reminded her of William Morris. More and more, it seemed, she had been coming into contact with the intersection of science and art. Carson had told her about his synesthesia the other night, which she found fascinating and wanted to learn more about, neurologically. She even felt a little jealous, it sounded so interesting.

Piper came back with a cellophane bag containing an intriguing mixture of dried plant parts that gave off a musty aroma. She hugged Olivia before she left and asked her to let her know how she was doing. Olivia promised she would, feeling better already. There was something just so very comforting about Piper.

After she left, she decided to stop by Carson and Merilee's place to pick up the video footage on Jessie. When she had spoken to Merilee yesterday, she had said she'd be home in the afternoons today and tomorrow. She smiled as she thought about her night with Carson. They had ended up going to bed together that night after his performance at The Contrarian. She hadn't really planned on it, but Carson was so cute, and she was feeling lonely. He was a nice guy, Carson, and thoughtful in bed. He didn't make fireworks go off, but to be honest, neither did Lance, even during their best days. Maybe she just wasn't a very passionate person. Or, perhaps her passions lay elsewhere.

On her way, she called her sister back and told her about checking into lead levels at their parents' house. The fact that their mother wasn't also suffering symptoms did undermine this hypothesis, but Olivia knew that different people had different genetic propensities for clearing toxins out of the body. Emily thought this sounded like a great idea and said that she would follow up on it immediately. "Because to tell you the truth, it's getting a little scary," she said, her voice breaking. "It feels like every day matters somehow."

Olivia told her to keep her posted and that she would keep thinking and researching to see if anything else came up. "And remember that I can come home whenever you need me," she said. "Love you, Sis."

"I love you," she said, her voice wobbling. "I miss you. I wish you weren't so far away."

Olivia promised to come home during the Christmas break if not sooner, and hung up feeling wretched. She hadn't realized what it would feel like to be so far away from her family. She also hadn't realized how much her younger sister's vulnerability would affect her. Emily was always so committed to Grant, whom Olivia found self-centered and demanding, wanting everyone to cater to him the way she did. She could imagine that right now, Emily's concern over their father wouldn't please him as he would no longer be the center of her attention. Her children were so young that they wouldn't be able to understand their mother's needs, and their own mother was probably so worried about her husband that she wouldn't be able to provide much support, either.

Which left her, Olivia. Who now lived three thousand miles away. And what on Earth was going on with her dad? He had always been so healthy and vigorous, going on regular hikes in the nearby woods and mountains, biking all around town. She was starting to realize that certain genetic time bombs could reside unexpressed for decades inside a person, only to reveal themselves once a person passed the age of fifty. Her grandparents had lived to a ripe old age on both sides of the family, which meant that she had never worried about her own parents. But different generations faced different stressors.

She phoned Merilee to let her know that she was on her way over, Merilee's obvious pleasure in that fact warming her heart. She hoped things would go well with Carson over time. Because she liked his whole family, Jessie included. And she needed all the moral support she could get right now.

CHAPTER 20

xel scanned the online *Sacramento Bee* as he sipped his first cup of coffee, looking for news items about Kristy's death. Over a week had passed since his dad called, claiming that he was a person of interest in the investigation, but he had so far found nothing to corroborate the claim that he indeed enjoyed that status. He was starting to think his old man was blowing smoke up his ass.

Then an article leapt out at him. It was a little buried—Kristy's death was old news, after all, and other murders had taken place since the discovery of her body—but there it was: "Person of Interest Sought in the Murder of Kristy Holloway." And there he was: "Sacramento police are searching for Eric Johnson, former boyfriend of murder victim Kristy Holloway, according to a news release from the Sacramento Police Department. Monday morning, police announced that they were looking for Johnson, stressing that they did not consider him a suspect but did want to talk to him in hopes that he might help shed some light on the case. Johnson is believed to have moved from the area, and police are asking anyone who might have any information on his whereabouts to contact the Sacramento police. Eric Johnson is thirty years old, stands at six feet and weighs 190 lbs, according to his DMV records. He has dark hair, brown eyes, and drives a 2004 Ford Mustang …"

Fuck! Thank God he swapped cars in Woodland before he moved up here. Anxiously, he scanned the rest of the short article, then the comments. None posted so far. God, had Amanda seen this? Quite possibly. He chewed his lip, trying to come up with the best strategy. Should he wait for her to call him and then tell her he had already contacted the Sacramento police? The problem with that plan was, she might call them before he talked to her. But if he called her, would that seem suspicious? He could call later today on the pretext of setting up their next date, and see if she said anything. But even that gave him cause for worry in terms of timing. He glanced at the clock on his computer screen. 9:15 am. She was probably either at work or on her way to work.

Finally, he decided to text her, working out his text on a piece of paper before punching it into his phone. "OMG! Sacto police looking for me. Am calling them now – let's get together soon! Miss u." He worried over it for a couple of minutes before hitting "send." Then he waited for her reply. When it didn't come right away, he set his phone on vibrate and shoved it in his pocket. He had work to do.

He had gotten Ethel to agree to make him a co-signer on her checking and savings account, telling her that he was studying accounting at Incident U as part of his business education. He told her that he had noticed she was a little forgetful here and there, that he didn't want her to have to worry about her day-to-day finances, and that he didn't want anyone unscrupulous taking advantage of her. The amount that wasn't being withdrawn automatically to pay for her assisted living each month didn't leave a lot, however. He was still working on figuring out her other assets. But even if he managed to replace her relatives on her will, unless she croaked soon, it wasn't going to help him out with his dad's fucking blackmail.

Axel had put him off for a while, telling him he needed to raise the money, but he wouldn't be able to delay him forever. He briefly considered snuffing out the bastard, but the truth was, he was afraid of him. He was extremely shrewd and crafty, generally had all angles figured out, and probably anticipated something like that. Plus, the guy had contacts. How had he found out, for instance, that Axel was a person of interest a week before it broke in the news?

He had hit up his cougars for an investment in his new restaurant, but they all said they wanted to see it further along before they put their money into it. He had thought about maybe lifting a few pieces of expensive jewelry when he was at their homes, but he would be the prime suspect when they went missing. He didn't need that kind of complication. And the owners at the bistro had gotten suspicious lately, telling him to pay close attention to the cash register and inventory; he should probably lie low there for a while.

So he was on his way to the Senior Citizen Center to play some bingo. As he was parking, he felt his phone buzz. Amanda had texted back. "I saw that! OMG for sure! How about this Sunday? I can come down if u want."

He relaxed. She must not think he was a murderer if she wanted to see him. The only problem was, he was already booked for Sunday. He'd have to cancel those plans. "I love coming up to Mt Shasta," he replied. "See u Sunday."

She answered, "Sounds great! xox"

Axel shoved his phone back in his pocket and checked his appearance in the visor mirror, as he always did. He sauntered into the hall where a number of the more senior of the senior citizens sat at long tables, some of them in wheelchairs They probably weren't even awake after 6:30 pm when the other games were scheduled. The place reminded him of a small plane hangar. It smelled like cheap coffee and disinfectant. He scoped out which senior looked the best dressed and coifed and most likely to find his con appealing, then took a seat next to her and gave her a wink.

"Hi," he said, offering his hand. "I'm Axel."

"Rose," she replied, giving him an appraising look. "What's a young hottie like you doing in a place like this?" She cracked herself up with this observation and gave a loud cackle.

Axel gave her a shy smile and dropped his gaze to his hands, cradled loosely in his lap. "I was supposed to meet my great aunt here this morning." He craned his neck, pretending to search the room. "She asked me to help her play since her eyesight isn't what it used to be. But I don't see her. Mind if I play along with you until she does?"

"Knock yourself out," she said. "She's got another five or ten minutes before they start." She leaned back in her folding chair and squinted at him. "So what do you do, Axel?"

"Well, my current job is restaurant manager, but I'm working on my dream business, and once I get enough donations, I'll be starting it up."

"And what might that be?"

"I'm putting together a nonprofit organization to take care of pets that survive their owner's death," he said. "I've often thought it would give such peace of mind to know that your pet would be well-placed and taken care of in a good home. It might even help more seniors make the decision to get a pet, you know? … if they didn't have to worry about their pet outliving them."

Rose's eyes misted up. "It sure might."

Axel gave her a sympathetic glance. "Do you have a pet, Rose?"

She shook her head. "I did. I had the cutest little Boston Terrier. He died last spring and I thought about getting a puppy—or even an older dog from the pound—but my children said that I was too old. It would be irresponsible, they said." She blinked back the tears that rimmed her eyes.

"So there you go. My idea is that my organization would

board the dog—or cat—until the right home was found. So there would never be a time when the pet wasn't being well cared for."

She gazed at him steadily for a few moments, then reached for her handbag. "Well, let me be one of the first to support your dream, young man." She fumbled inside it, then withdrew her checkbook. Her action drew some disapproving glances from her neighbors on the other side, which didn't escape her notice. "Axel here has the most wonderful idea," she said. "Listen to what he's planning."

Axel gave his spiel to the other seniors at the table. Two of them wrote him a check as well, while one wasn't a pet person, she said. But they all told him what a great idea he had. He kept a careful eye out for the people who drew and called the numbers, shutting down his fundraising efforts when they took their places. He excused himself, saying that he needed to call his aunt and see what had happened, then got in his car and drove away. Three hundred bucks. Not great, but not bad for a first outing. And it told him that he had struck a chord. Actually, it was a good idea. Somebody should do it.

He contemplated the fact that if he wanted to continue this charade, he would need to come up with a faux great-aunt to accompany him. Ethel was an obvious possibility. He made a note to see if he could get permission to take her off the premises. She'd probably want to contribute to his nonprofit company, actually—and her enthusiastic presence would enhance his sales pitch.

But his best prospects lay with Piper. He was going to have to cancel his date with her Sunday night in order to see Amanda, unfortunately, so as soon as he got home, he gave her a call. She answered on the fourth ring, sounding delighted to hear from him.

"Axel!" she exclaimed. "I was just thinking about you."

"Were you?" he said playfully.

"I sure was," she replied. "What's up?"

"Oh, I'm afraid I'm going to have to reschedule our date for Sunday night."

"That's too bad," she said, clearly disappointed. "I invited Marion and Danny over to join us."

Christ. He just dodged a bullet. "I'm so sorry," he said. He paused. "Though, to tell you the truth, sweetheart, I wish you would check with me first before doing something like that."

"Oh, I know, it's bad manners," she said. "I'm sorry. I just thought, you know, with us as close as we are now that you'd want to get to know my best friends."

"Of course I do!" he protested. He was going to have to figure out some way to derail that friendship. Marion struck him as a nosy bitch. And Piper had told him her husband was a DA. Not exactly a profession he wanted to cozy up to. "I just—it's just that—well, right now, I'm having a hard time sharing you," he said. "I know it's silly …"

Piper laughed her musical laugh. "No, it's not! It's romantic."

"God, I love your laugh," he said, softening his voice. "How about if I come over right now?"

"I wish you could! But I have to leave to teach my class in just a few minutes."

"How about if I come over after work tonight? It'll be late."

"I don't care how late it is! Please come! I would love that."

"All right then," he said. "Keep a candle burning for me."

"Oh, I'll do more than that." She tried to sound sexy, but it fell rather flat. Sexy was not her forte, that's for sure. Fortunately, she had a great body, in addition to being pretty. And there was something about despoiling innocence that got him off big time.

"Mmm," he said. "Looking forward to it." Then he hung up. He wasn't working lunch today, so he had a few hours to kill. Once he made his big con, he'd have to leave here right away. He should be ready. And if the police somehow tracked him to this alias in this town, he'd have to scoot, too.

As expensive as cities were, he was starting to think that it was easier to get lost in them than a small city the size of Incident. Before moving here, he hadn't realized how easy it was to run into people. The other night when he took Piper to this music show she wanted to go to so bad, it turned out the lead singer was this loser that showed up at the bistro from time to time. That was the other thing. His job put him in contact with a lot of people here. He was dreading the day that two of his cougars showed up to lunch or dine at the same time. Another reason to see if he couldn't speed things up, pay off his fucker of a parental unit, get the hell out of Dodge, and disappear off everyone's radar this time. He might even want to leave the country.

So he logged onto his laptop and started his search. God, he was annoyed that he'd have to waste an entire evening with Amanda. Why the fuck did she have to move up here, anyway? Time spent with Piper after work was helpful, but he needed more time to lay the groundwork for his plans. He'd spent a goddamned fortune on all those flowers, fancy food and drink, and rented place-settings for Seduction Night. He needed to be able to coast on that and the further away that night got, the more pressure there would be to follow up. He knew how voracious women were, how needy, even the sweet-seeming ones like Piper. In fact, they were often the neediest of them all.

He started off with his wildest fantasies before having to get more pragmatic: Rio? Honolulu? London? Just thinking about being a big shot in one of those places helped him to relax. He'd get it all worked out, he felt sure. He'd rarely met as easy a touch as Piper. And then he'd blow this fucking puke hole.

CHAPTER 21

Piper was on the hunt for some stinging nettles today, and therefore had brought her garden gloves with her to protect her hands and forearms. She had once accidentally brushed up against one of these plants and the sting was something she would never forget—a burning, searing pain that lasted until she found a curly dock plant nearby and applied it as an antidote. Thankfully, they often grew near one another. They both liked wet conditions, so they grew along the creek that ran through the woods. The nettles had a whole host of applications, from allergies, to arthritis, to issues related to an enlarged prostate, so they were well worth the trouble they took to harvest. Unsurprisingly, the devas associated with stinging nettles were a sassy bunch, but they were fun; Piper enjoyed interacting with them. Today was no exception. At one location, they had fashioned some sort of trampoline out of a large fig leaf and they were taking turns bouncing each other into the air. Sadly, fig season was over. But Piper had stashed away several jars of homemade fig jam in September.

As she walked along, she thought about Axel, and how romantic he was. He came by after work the other night and they had an amazing time in bed, once again. She blushed thinking about it. And … he intimated that he thought the time was approaching that they might want to live together. He had asked about her home, and how much her landlords wanted for it, how much she thought she would need for a down payment and how much she had saved toward that end. He told her that he might want to help her with that, once he got his restaurant up and running. Piper dreamily fantasized their life together, with children—he had told her he was eager to start a family, once he felt financially stable—and maybe even a dog. He loved dogs, he said. Piper remembered Jessie, Carson's dog, and what a lovely spirit she had.

And as if she had summoned them both, here they came along the trail, Jessie out front with Carson not far behind. "Hey, you two!" she called out happily, delighted to have run into them once again.

Carson looked up, apparently lost in deep thought, and gave her an appraising stare. Not exactly what she was expecting. Jessie, however, was as friendly as before, frolicking around her and licking the hand that Piper offered her.

"How—how are you?" she faltered.

"Good."

"Glad to hear it." She hesitated. "I loved hearing you play the other night at The Contrarian," she said.

His brow furrowed. "Yeah, I saw you in the audience. Guess your boyfriend wasn't as enamored with the music as you were."

Piper laughed. "Oh, he's just … well, we, uh, wanted to be alone." As she said that, she remembered what he had said about not wanting to share her. At the time, she had thought it sweet and sexy, but now, watching Carson's expression, doubt nagged at her. Maybe he was possessive. She hadn't thought so, but she supposed it was possible. Still, compared to all the wonderful things about him, this seemed like a small wrinkle.

Carson's face became even stonier. "You know, I have to

admit—he's not the kind of guy I would have imagined you with."

Piper shook her head. "I know. To be honest, I wouldn't have, either! I know he seems awfully …"

"Slick?"

"Well, the word I was looking for was 'urbane,' which isn't exactly my style—"

"No."

"But inside, he's a prince, really. If you got to know him, you'd like him."

Carson shifted impatiently. "I seriously doubt it. And honestly? I think you should be careful with a guy like that. He strikes me as a player."

Piper didn't know how to reply. "Jealousy doesn't suit you," she said finally. "I think I know him better than you do." She bent down and gave Jessie a scratch behind the ears, then turned to go. "See you around," she said.

"Wait!" Carson burst out.

She turned back. Carson looked genuinely distressed. "I'm sorry. I was out of line."

"Yes, you were."

"I'm sorry," he repeated, then stuck out his hand. "Friends?"

Piper relaxed and removed her glove to accept his peace offering. "Absolutely."

Carson held her hand just a fraction too long, then let go and shoved both his hands in his pockets. "I wish you both the best," he mumbled.

"Thanks, Carson."

"So … looks like we both hike these woods a fair amount. Nice to run into you—hope it happens again sometime."

"I hope so, too," she said warmly. Jessie nudged her hand for an extra pat, which she was glad to give. "You two take care."

Piper decided to go a different direction then, and found a

place to ford the creek as she headed deeper into the woods. Last year, she had found a patch of chanterelle mushrooms and if she were lucky, she might find some again.

As she hiked, the sun dipped lower in the sky; soon it would be behind the ridge, creating an early sunset. She shouldn't dawdle, she told herself. Even though she knew these woods well, if it got too dark, she could have trouble finding her way back. She was debating whether she should turn back when she spotted a beautiful cluster of apricot-colored chanterelles tucked underneath a stand of poison oak. She put her gloves on and carefully gathered some choice specimens, thanking the shy devas dressed in ruffled smocks and mushroom caps. She thought she might call it a day when she spotted yet another cluster a little farther into the woods. As she set her basket on the ground and bent down to gather up a few, she noticed the hush that often fell this time of day. She loved it. But suddenly, the hair raised up on the nape of her neck.

She whirled around, knowing that cougars preferred to pounce from behind; but she didn't see anything out of the ordinary. Despite this, she felt an overwhelming sense of panic and dread. All cognitive thought deserted her, and she snatched up her basket and began racing back to her house. Once, she tripped over a blackberry vine and went sprawling. She lost half the contents of her basket but didn't bother to gather up what she had lost. She didn't stop running until she was inside her house, the doors locked, the shades drawn for every window. She stripped her clothes off and dashed into the shower, staying there until the hot water began to run out, then toweled herself dry. She picked out her fuzziest pajamas and coziest robe and padded into the kitchen to make herself a cup of chamomile tea. She even rummaged around in her odds and ends drawer for a roach that a friend had left behind a few weeks ago.

As she sat at her kitchen table, attempting to get her emotions under control, she tried to understand what, exactly, she found so frightening and upsetting. She felt a desperate need to talk to someone about it, but what would she say? She freaked out in the forest? She sighed as she took her last swallow of tea. She should make dinner. She should deal with the remaining contents of her basket. But all she could do was sit at her table and ponder the blinding sense of terror she had encountered in her familiar and beloved forest.

CHAPTER 22

Carson poked along the trail, halfheartedly throwing the giant stick that Jessie had picked up for her fetching obsession. He felt depressed. He could see that Piper was totally snowed by that cheeseball restaurant manager, and after seeing just how clueless she was, he couldn't dislike her. He could only feel sorry for her. Why were women like her so easy to fool? But even Olivia didn't think that guy was all that bad, not that she'd had all that much interaction with him. Nor had he. Piper was right, she certainly had spent more time with him —but did she know him better? Maybe he was prejudiced by the ugly colors and bland shapes that the guy's voice produced, but Carson had found his synesthesia to be a fairly reliable judge of character. Although, he had to admit, he hadn't suspected that the business manager for his old record label was a crook.

So was he jealous? He didn't think so. He'd never felt all that jealous about anyone before. In fact, the opposite problem seemed to be the charge most often leveled at him, that he just didn't care enough, didn't put enough of himself into a relationship. Well, whatever the case, she was off-limits, and he was determined to make a go of things with Olivia. She deserved it. He should probably try to forget all about Piper. She had made her choice and it didn't involve him.

While he trudged down the trail, lost in his gloomy thoughts, Jessie came prancing back to him. He reached down absentmindedly to grab her small tree limb and throw it for her, when he realized she didn't have it. But she was poised as if she did. He stopped and tried to figure out what was going on. That was when she spit out a tiny little twig, then immediately sprang back into her stick-chasing stance. It took a moment to register, but then Carson burst out laughing. That Jessie! She had stopped getting a reaction from the logs she had been fetching, so now she was offering him the tiniest stick in the world. The workings of her mind sometimes just blew him away. He pondered the thought processes that she would have to go through to play this little joke of hers and he was once again awed by her intelligence and insight into human behavior and humor.

He knelt down and ruffled the thick fur around her shoulders. "Jessie, you crazy dog!" he exclaimed. She gave him a few licks on the cheek and he reached over and scratched her on the butt. Well, if she wanted to cheer him up, he wasn't going to disappoint her. "Thanks, girl," he said. "You're a good dog."

He picked up the twig and held it up between his thumb and forefinger. "You realize there's no way I can throw this, don't you?" He flicked it into the air. It flew six inches before falling to the ground where she pounced on it. "Come on," he said. "We need to get dinner started." The royal "we," he guessed.

His mom was working at the food co-op until six, so he usually cooked those nights. He liked cooking, actually. His dad had been the parent more interested in food, so he had done most of it whenever he was off work. He excelled in Asian cuisine, which neither Carson nor his mom had learned how to fix since he was so good at it and enjoyed making it so much. He loved super spicy foods, often piling tons of extra hot sauce and peppers onto an already spicy dish, sweat popping out on his forehead that he swore was the key to his health. Not that it ended up doing him any good. After he died, neither Carson nor his mom could bear to take up his specialty, so bottles of fish sauce, jars of chili bean paste, and tubs of miso went unused. But they couldn't bear to throw them out. They should be discarded at this point—if anyone tried to use them, they'd get food poisoning, probably. But they sat in the pantry, as if expecting to be used any minute.

Merilee had always liked cooking what Carson called "hippie food," but he had to give her credit—it was generally pretty good. Carson loved Mexican food, so he had become expert at making enchiladas, tacos, chili verde, and mole. Tonight he was making chile rellenos, one of Merilee's favorites.

When he and Jessie got home, he got busy making the batter for the chiles, and once they were all stuffed and coated, he stuck them in the oven while he made the sauce. His mom came home shortly before they were ready, delighted that dinner was pretty much waiting for her, and that Carson had been so thoughtful as to fix a favorite dish.

"You're a sweet boy," she sighed, as she sat down and propped her feet up on an adjacent chair. She leaned over and massaged her ankles and lower legs. "Damn, standing for hours at a time is getting old," she said. "Well, I guess I'm getting old."

Carson nodded absentmindedly.

Merilee balled up a paper napkin from the dispenser on the table and threw it at him. "You're not supposed to agree with me!" she exclaimed, exasperated.

He grinned. "Well, you are getting old, Mom," he said wickedly. "What am I supposed to say?"

"I take back what I said about your being a sweet boy," she grumbled.

Carson took a peek at the chiles in the oven, then sat across from his mom at the table. He reached over and took her hand. "I'm sorry you have to do work that requires you to stand for so long every day," he said. He was, too. He had worked at a music store one year during high school; his feet ached at the end of those days. And he was a teenager. "And you're not that old! Come on."

She laughed. "That's better."

Carson let go of her hand and picked at a thumbnail, against his better judgment. In point of fact, he really wished that he could earn enough from his music that she could retire, or take a different job, or devote full time to her crafts. It just totally sucked that most of the fun ways to make money made practically no money at all. He couldn't see himself becoming an accountant or going into real estate. He knew himself well enough to know that he would suck at sales. The idea of working in the medical field made him feel slightly panicky—he was squeamish, big time—and he didn't want to work for Cal Trans like his dad. Not that he'd be able to get a job with Cal Trans. He would die if he had to work for a bureaucracy or do office work all day, and he wasn't cut out for construction.

He might have liked to be a teacher at some other time in history, but when he talked to his friends who were teachers, it sounded like that sucked these days, too, with all that standardized testing and crazy parents and administration breathing down your neck. Besides, if he had to enforce any kind of discipline, forget it. The one thing he could see himself doing was working in a commercial kitchen, but it didn't pay all that well, either; he'd never become a head chef. He didn't want to risk injuring his hands, anyway.

"Well, hey," he said. "I think dinner's ready." His mom got up and set the table while he took the chiles out of the oven and served them on plates. The sizzling that they made created a spritz of pale, foam-green bubbles in his vision.

"How are things going with Olivia?" his mom asked, once they were seated.

Carson groaned. He didn't know why, really, but he hated talking about his romantic life with his mom. "Fine."

She waited for more, then nodded. "Great!" She paused. "I sure enjoyed seeing her last week when she came to pick up the video footage."

"She is very cool." Carson could at least say that with conviction.

"She thinks Jessie is maybe a little special. More than most dogs. Which is saying a lot."

Jessie, who was lying next to Merilee's chair, pricked her ears up at the mention of her name.

Carson laughed. "Well, of course Jessie is special!" He told her about the twig-throwing incident on the trail. Merilee laughed and laughed, reaching down to smooth her ears, which Carson knew she loved. Her happy whine corkscrewed in vivid teal through his field of vision.

"So what's so special in Olivia's opinion?" he asked.

"Well, her faithfulness, for one thing. When she's here and I'm headed home, she invariably goes and waits by the door. Most dogs do it some of the time, or even most of the time, but not all of the time. But … and here it goes into a little bit of woo-woo territory … Olivia swore that Jessie was mugging for the camera. That she knew what the camera was doing and that there was a person on the other end, somehow."

Carson thought that any number of dogs might do either or both of these things, but he didn't say so. He thought Jessie was pretty special from his own personal experience, and why pop his mom's balloon? He remembered his idea about giving her some one-on-one classes with Piper and thought it might be one of his better ideas, like bringing Jessie home. He'd get online and check out Piper's contact information, set something up.

After dinner, Merilee insisted on doing the dishes and told

him to scoot, go make some music or something. She was excited for him that he had this scoring opportunity; and when he had told her about Evan, he could tell from her expression that she knew just how hard their split was on him. He thought that sounded like a fine idea, so he ambled out to his music studio, looking forward to doing some composing. He was still struggling a little with the lighter moods, so he was focusing on the darker ones. The beauty of that was, it lightened his mood. Playing and composing music was one of the most therapeutic, restorative things he did. Both the music and the visuals were transporting—not always, of course. Not when he was having trouble with a piece. That was work. But when he was in the flow, and things were going well, he felt like a different person almost, a lighter, brighter, more fluid person. It was what kept him from getting completely swallowed in a black pit when his dad died.

Carson sat down at his keyboard and began noodling as his mind drifted. He remembered the time when he was five that he had decided an umbrella could serve as a parachute. So, when he was supposed to be taking his nap, he had climbed onto the roof through the dormer window in his room, the umbrella in his back pocket. He steadied himself, plucked the umbrella from his pocket and opened it, then bounded purposefully off the roof. His elation turned to dismay as the umbrella turned inside-out immediately and he found himself plummeting toward the ground. But at the last second, his dad appeared out of nowhere, like a super-hero, and caught him safely in his arms. At the time, he didn't question it. Of course his dad would have showed up to rescue him. Of course! He *was* a super-hero!

It wasn't until he was ten years older that he thought about it, and wondered how his dad had known. He had been too shocked and stunned to cry out. He asked him about it, and his dad shook his head saying, "I can't explain it myself, son. I was turning the compost pile on the other side of the house when I heard you call out."

"And there you were." He said this wonderingly, not sure what it meant.

His dad had reached over and given his shoulder an affectionate shake. "I'll always be there, bud."

But he hadn't. He died six months later.

Carson sighed, forced himself back into the present. What did he want to work on tonight? Despite Jessie's antics, he was falling back into melancholy. He ran through the video that the producer had sent, looking for a scene that would catch his fancy, take shape musically. Nothing was doing much for him, and some of it he had already composed music for. And then he saw it: a picture of the earth from space, an impossibly beautiful, sparkling gem in a vast, black, velvety emptiness. He wasn't sure why it moved him so deeply, but it did. *The music of the spheres,* he thought, filled with the same wonder that he had been the day he learned his dad had heard his unspoken cry. And he had never heard anything so glorious in his life.

CHAPTER 23

livia stirred in her bed, savoring the dreamless sleep she had just awakened from. Piper's concoction had really helped—she hadn't remembered a dream since she had started drinking the tea a few nights ago. Although, a wisp of a dream memory darted through her mind … something about … hmm, she couldn't grasp it, though she had a fleeting visual memory of that handsome restaurant manager at Buffington's Bistro. She laughed to herself as she threw the covers back and rolled out of bed: probably an erotic dream. That guy had some powerful pheromones.

She headed to her small kitchen to put the coffee on before tending to other needs, and opened the blinds a tad to see what kind of a day greeted her. A little overcast and chilly, it looked like, from the way passersby were dressed, but compared to what she could expect back East this time of year, she couldn't wait to get outside. She had always loved Massachusetts, enjoying walks with her dad in the forests of western Mass., or the Back Bay in Boston, the occasional summer bike ride through pastoral countryside and quaint villages. But she had always been so focused on her studies and her work that she was realizing that she had really never immersed herself in her larger environment. She was determined to change that in her new location. Why not? She was starting over in so many ways; why not that one as well?

Once dressed, she ran downstairs and picked up a mini-baguette from the bakery a few doors down, then came back and settled at her kitchen table with a generous pat of butter and a pot of apricot jam. Sipping on her coffee and munching on her bread, she pondered her day. She should do some work this afternoon, but she was giving herself the morning off. The recurrent theme of art in her life right now seemed so insistent that she decided she should put some time into making her own furnishings more aesthetic. Piper's office had been so sumptuous in that way. Piper's style wasn't hers, of course—Olivia gravitated toward Steampunk—but that didn't mean she couldn't put more effort into her place.

She also thought she could put a little more energy into cooking. Lance had been a good cook, so she hadn't bothered much, especially now that she was living alone. But right now she wanted to provide more stimulus to all senses and not dwell so obsessively in her brain with all its abstract molecular models. Carson's synesthesia was a prompt in this direction. His sensual experience was so rich. She didn't have his gift, unfortunately, but she could certainly enhance what she did have.

After breakfast, she called her sister to see how their parents were doing. Emily had come up with the brilliant idea of treating them to a week at a new eco-friendly resort in the Berkshires while their house was being tested for lead.

She answered after the second ring, sounding more relaxed than she had in some time. "Olivia, hi!" she said.

"Hey," she replied, reflecting as she did so that she was already picking up a more Western way of speaking. "How's Dad?" Emily had managed to get them in right away, so they had been at the resort for three days.

"He's doing a lot better!"

"Well, thank God," Olivia said. "Any information about lead levels yet?"

"No, the inspectors came on Thursday—they said they'd have the results for me on Monday."

"Okay, well, keep me posted."

"I will for sure. How are you doing?"

Olivia reflected. "Pretty good, all things considered. I didn't realize how hard it would be to live so far away from all of you, though."

"Yeah," Emily sighed.

"Maybe we can all chat soon."

"That would be great! Mom and Dad would love it."

"And what about you? How's Grant? How are Madeleine and Zoe?

"They're all fine. Thank goodness. Madeleine just won a blue ribbon at the children's art show at the Museum of Fine Art, so she's thrilled. Zoe is starting to tell stories, mostly about tadpoles. That pop out of children's closets. Somehow."

Olivia laughed. "That's pretty cute." They chatted for a bit more, then signed off. Emily was going to take a trip out to the resort tomorrow with her family, so she would have more news then, she said.

Olivia sat at the table for a few more minutes, thinking about how she'd like to spend her morning, and settled on the Saturday Market. Incident was famous for its market, which featured not only local produce, dairy, and meat products, but arts and crafts as well. She might pick up something decorative for her apartment, and she had heard that the mushroom foraging in this area was outstanding. A couple of vendors sold wild mushrooms at the market that they had harvested from the surrounding mountains.

She grabbed her pea coat, slouch beanie, and purse—more of a daypack, actually—and clattered down the stairs and out the door. Her street was busy on a Saturday, and she reveled in the colorful clothes that most of the residents here liked to wear: purple, fuchsia, yellow, and turquoise. It was a beautiful, brisk November day, too. The air here smelled so different from the air back East, though she didn't know exactly what to attribute it to. She suspected it was the higher percentage of conifers as opposed to hardwoods, and quite possibly a ubiquitous tall, sinuous bush with satiny red bark and frosty green oval leaves called manzanita that she had never seen anywhere else. Back home smelled fecund and moist, whereas the air here smelled sharp and fresh.

She caught a glimpse of Mt. Shasta to the north as she made her way to the market, its flanks thick with snow from autumn storms. It was so intriguing to live near such a tall mountain—actually, a volcano, something she had a hard time truly wrapping her mind around for some reason. Mt. Shasta stood over 14,000 ft. and it rose from a plateau of only 3,000 ft.; so 11,000 ft. of it stood in relief. It created its own weather and bizarre lenticular clouds, often shrouded when the rest of the surrounding landscape lay under clear skies and sun. It could be rather treacherous, as well. A lot of people hiked to the top, though part of the climb required crampons and ice axes, so it required some mountaineering skills; people skied and snowboarded on it, too. But it claimed lives upon occasion, the locals told her.

As she approached the market, she could hear the band that was playing this morning, one that featured steel drums, and she could smell the scents wafting off the food court, too—Cajun shrimp and grits, Thai stir fry, and spicy Middle Eastern fare. She decided to visit the craft booths first, then finish up with the produce vendors, though she wasn't seeing a lot of Steampunk. As she perused the colorful T shirts and hats, sensuous wood crafts, and fanciful jewelry, she heard someone call her name. She turned to find Rupert and his wife bearing down on her, Rupert beaming, which seemed to be his usual expression, unless he was deep in thought. And even then, the burning curiosity that he carried inside him lit him up.

"Olivia! How lovely to see you! I don't believe you've met my wife, Jill."

Jill was a striking middle-aged British woman with thick, long hair. Olivia knew, from researching the department here before applying for the position, that she was an expert in the use of sound for healing, an author, biophysicist, and therapist. She took Olivia's hand in an admirably strong grip and told her how lovely it was to meet her. "Rupert's told me a great deal about your research," she said. "And he so appreciates your help on his studies."

Olivia grinned. "Well, Rupert's a treat to work with," she said. "He's taught me an unbelievable amount in a very short time."

Rupert turned to his wife. "I predict big things for our young scientist here."

Olivia sighed. "Yeah, if I ever find any funding." Olivia had honed her research proposal to the point that she felt she could start seeking funding. But so far, she had not located any good funding sources, not for the amount she would need. She had approached one dot.com philanthropist based on an article she had read online, but that hadn't gone anywhere.

Jill took on a thoughtful air as she studied Olivia, then burst out, "Have you considered crowdfunding?"

"Crowdfunding?" Actually, no, she hadn't. She always thought that was for making movies.

Rupert laughed delightedly. "Brilliant idea, dear!" He grasped Olivia's shoulder with excitement. "That's exactly what you should do!"

"For science experiments?"

"Absolutely!" exclaimed Jill. "You might start with Experiment.com."

Olivia was so dumbstruck by the idea that she couldn't reply for a moment. The idea shocked her, she had to admit.

What kind of credibility would crowdfunded research carry? Although, given that she was already out on a limb in terms of scientific credibility, would it hurt to creep out a little farther? Especially if this were the only way she could follow through on her work.

When she found her voice, she thanked Jill for her suggestion and said that she would look it up first thing. They parted ways then and Olivia had just about decided that she would have to go elsewhere to find something for her apartment when she came upon a Steampunk booth. The vendor had Steampunk-inspired light switches, lamps, clocks, and flash drives. So many items intrigued her that she ended up buying one of everything, making arrangements to come back and pick them up later. She strolled over to the produce section of the market then and purchased some chanterelles and hedgehog mushrooms, some apples, persimmons, and patty pan squash. She saw a couple of her students there, stopping to chat briefly. The students at Incident were pleasant, she had decided, easy-going but interested in their education.

After getting everything back to her apartment, she stashed her groceries in the fridge, and put her new household items in place, admiring them and feeling proud of herself for making some frivolous purchases. Then she slipped her new flash drive in her pocket and headed over to her office at the university.

There, she logged onto her computer and started perusing Experiment.com, her spirits rising the longer she browsed. She was surprised, now, that she had never heard of crowdfunded scientific research, but then again, she had been so firmly entrenched in mainstream science that it wasn't talked about in her circles. Everyone was lusting after an NSF, NIH, or Big Pharma grant. Most of the scientists on Experiment.com were asking for far less than she hoped to have for her research, but she saw that a few asked for even more than she would need. She felt that her research would be something to benefit everyone, a true boon to humanity.

It was interesting to ponder the fact that most mainstream funders would probably find what she wanted to do a threat. If people could use their own directed thoughts to affect their gene regulation, it could make a lot of pharmaceutical approaches obsolete. She remembered reading once that the combined profits for the ten drug companies in the Fortune 500 were more than the profits for all the other 490 businesses put together. She supposed the numbers could have changed since she received that information, but she knew that their global economic presence was enormous. If her work were successful, it could topple a massive economic engine.

That thought gave her pause for a moment and she wondered if pursuing this research was even the right thing to do in the big picture. But nothing was going to happen overnight. And she thought about all the people who couldn't afford the pharmaceutical option, and those for whom such an option didn't even exist. She also knew that 100,000 Americans died each year from taking prescription drugs as prescribed. Most people didn't realize that a number of genes did different things in different tissues; introducing a regulatory product into a complex biological system in a non-targeted fashion whether by mouth or injection or patch ensured that there would be side-effects. It was physiologically unavoidable. Some people just tolerated various medications better than others, given their unique genetic makeup.

Anyway, what she was looking for was undoubtedly the mechanism by which the placebo effect worked, so it wasn't as if she would be inventing something new; she would simply be demonstrating that a known phenomenon had a reproducible, biological basis … as well as, hopefully, improving the ability of patients to target the proper regulatory systems successfully and predictably. How could that be a bad thing in the big picture?

It couldn't. It just couldn't. So she hummed a tune (one

of Carson's, she noted with a smile) as she began creating an account for herself on Experiment.com … and allowed her most idealistic fantasies to run wild as she crafted her proposal.

CHAPTER 24

xel decided that it would be a good strategy to take Amanda out to dinner, so he selected one that wouldn't be too expensive, but didn't seem cheap, either. He settled on The Green Man, which featured vegetarian food but also offered some beef dishes, the meat from a nearby ranch that raised cattle for pharmaceutical purposes, he had learned, and sold the meat as a by-product. It was beyond organic, evidently. Temple Fucking Grandin had designed the slaughterhouse, for God's sake. He was finding all this New Agey, PC crap wearing. He'd be glad to get the hell out of Insipid, his new nickname for his current location. All this cheesy goodness and earnestness. Ugh.

He picked up Amanda right on time tonight, to keep her off-balance, bearing a bouquet of flowers that he had put together from discarded table-settings at the restaurant. She apparently didn't notice or decided to overlook the slightly wilted blooms and fussed over them as if he had brought her a bracelet from Tiffany's. She put them in some water before they left, giving him an extra kiss for his thoughtfulness. He was glad he hadn't sprung for a more expensive restaurant, the way she was dressed. The longer she lived in Mt. Shasta

City, the hippy-dippier her wardrobe was becoming, and it wasn't an improvement. She was wearing harem pants tonight with a long tunic, lots of jangly bracelets and several beaded necklaces. Put her in a craft fair and she wouldn't even need a booth.

Once they were seated, their glasses of wine in front of them, Amanda fixed her wide-eyed gaze on him and said, "So what did the police want to know?"

"Oh, they just wanted to know the last time I'd seen her. And they asked me if I knew anyone who might have held a grudge against her, or who might want to hurt her—you know, might be stalking her or something."

Amanda nodded, playing with the stem of her wineglass. "They asked me the same things. I talked to them twice, actually—once when she disappeared, and again when they found her—" tears welled up in her eyes and she took a hasty swallow of her drink. "—body," she finished, blinking hard.

Axel's eyes filled with tears as well and he reached across the table to take Amanda's hand. "I couldn't think of a soul, could you?" he said.

She shook her head violently. "No! I mean, you know what a sweetheart she was. I suppose she could have had a stalker, but she never said anything about someone like that."

Axel sighed, allowing his eyes to go out of focus while he pretended to ponder. "There was this one guy at the restaurant where we worked," he mused.

"There was?" Amanda sat up straight. "Who?"

Axel hesitated, then exhaled heavily. "Nah, I shouldn't speculate. And anyway, it sounds like she was just in the wrong place at the wrong time."

"Axel, if you think you have anything, anything at all, you should mention it to the police. You could be saving someone else from harm!"

He gazed at her steadily, so that she would think he was giving her admonition careful consideration. "You're right," he said finally. "I'll call them tomorrow."

She relaxed. "Good," she said. Then gave his hand a squeeze before letting go.

They dropped the subject for the rest of the evening. Afterward, they went to her house where they had sex and she had the atrocious judgment to tell him she loved him afterward. God. That was of absolutely no use to him. But he whispered that he loved her, too, and when he left—saying he had to get up early in the morning to take care of a friend who was undergoing chemo—he figured he would disappear from her life. She clearly didn't suspect him of Kristy's murder, and if, on some off chance she came looking for him, she didn't know the name he was going under these days. And no one in Incident knew him as Eric Johnson.

His dad called while he was driving home. He ignored him until he got home, then phoned back, anxious about what he wanted, calling so late. If pure hatred could kill, his dad would have been dead a long time ago.

"Sonny boy!" his dad exclaimed when he picked up. This nickname was new.

"What."

"Hey, listen, I appreciate the paltry sums that you're sending my way, but I hope we're clear that this isn't anywhere near the ballpark I had in mind."

"I need time, you old fuck."

"Whoa! Dial it down a notch, junior. I don't think you really want to piss me off." He paused. "More than I am already." He said this last with a dangerous softness that Axel knew only too well.

"Jesus Christ, Dad, this isn't exactly Palm Springs! I didn't relocate here thinking I'd need to keep you in style!"

"Maybe you should have planned ahead better."

Axel didn't respond.

"So here's the deal. You've got a month, got it? Max. If I get antsy before then, or I don't think you're making an honest effort" —these two words produced a wheezy chuckle— "I may call in my chips before then. So if I was you, I'd get busy. Son."

Axel punched the screen on his phone to end the conversation so savagely he bruised his finger. He wanted to rage around his apartment and bust things up, but he couldn't really afford to. So he controlled himself with steely resolve, sitting on his sofa and taking deep breaths until his impulse cleared. Then he stripped down to his boxer shorts and went to bed, falling into an agitated sleep. When he awoke in the morning—early—he decided he needed to get moving. He glanced at the clock on his bedside table and saw that it was a little before seven. He dialed Piper's number, certain that, even if he woke her up, she'd be thrilled to hear from him.

"Axel?" she answered, her voice buoyant.

"One and the same," he replied.

"What a lovely surprise to hear from you so early!" she said.

"I couldn't wait."

"What's up?"

"Do you have a couple of hours before you need to get to work?" he asked.

She paused, presumably checking her calendar before responding, "I do!"

"Okay, I'll be right over. I've got something to share with you, a little outing I want to take."

She sounded intrigued and excited as she hung up. Axel took the briefest of showers, decided his five o'clock shadow looked sexy, and dressed casually in a pair of gabardine slacks and a well-worn Oxford shirt. As he drove over to Piper's house, he ran through the list of places he'd checked out the week before as possible locations for his faux restaurant in Incident. The restaurant business had high turnover, so he had found a handful of promising venues for sale. He decided on the one in the best location, so that she would know the height of his aspirations.

She came to the door looking radiant in a dark blue cotton knit dress that brushed her knees and brought out the color of her eyes. Whereas Amanda looked like a wannabe fortuneteller, Piper always looked tasteful, even when she was in her hippiest garb.

She stood on her tiptoes and took both of his hands while she kissed him on the lips. "Hi," she said, tipping her head back to smile at him.

"Morning, ma'am," he said softly before giving her another kiss. "So, are you ready?"

She nodded. "Just let me grab my purse." She snatched it off the hall table and locked her arm in his as they descended the stoop. "Where are we going?"

He shook his head. "Nope, I'm not telling. It will just have to be a surprise." Women loved surprises.

She chattered as they drove, a little more nervously than usual, and he wondered what was up. He tried probing a little, but didn't seem to get anywhere, and decided it was just her mood. A lot of insecure women got chatty like that. And he was a bit more quiet than usual, plotting his moves, which, to tell the truth, often worked in his favor. Women usually decided that if he was quiet, it was because of something they had done.

When they pulled up in front of the vacant storefront, tucked between a well-patronized gallery and a high-end women's clothing boutique, Piper's eyes widened and she exclaimed, "Don't tell me!"

He laughed. "Okay, I won't."

She squealed and grabbed his nearest hand, giving it a hard squeeze. "Oh, Axel, this is the perfect location!"

He grinned at her. "Isn't it?"

"Ohhh." She returned his grin. "So have you come up with a name yet?"

"Not yet. Maybe you can help me with that."

She nodded. "So how far along are you? Do you have the

capital you need?"

He shrugged. "Well, to be honest, one backer that I was counting on fell through. But I still have others. Unfortunately, someone else is interested in this property, so I need to get my act together as soon as possible."

She fell silent, thinking. "Well, look, I have some money in savings."

"Oh, no. No. I wouldn't even consider it," he said firmly.

"No, listen! It could be a short term loan. I know that you'll be good for it."

He wagged his head violently back and forth. "Piper," he said solemnly. "That's the money you're saving for your house!"

"I know it is. But you can pay me back as soon as you get another investor on board."

He pretended to consider, leaning back in his seat and massaging his stubble. "I don't know, Piper."

"Axel, don't be proud! Let me do this for you," she pleaded.

He gazed at her with his best imitation of adoration, then pulled her to him and kissed her lingeringly on the lips. "I don't deserve you," he murmured.

"I'm the one who doesn't deserve you," she replied, snuggling into his arms.

Axel sighed in relief, and tightened his hold. He might just get out of his current predicament. Ethel hadn't come through all that well, except as a stopgap measure, unless she kicked the bucket tomorrow. But Piper was another story. Another story altogether.

CHAPTER 25

Piper slipped into the crowded room, looking for someone she knew. The dean of the college that housed the Biology, Psychology, and Parapsychology Departments threw a faculty party once a semester at his home, a grand house built at the turn of the 19th century from some impressive timbers that existed in the forests at that time. Logging had felled most of the old giants, but many of the forests were making a comeback, despite the wildfires that raged every summer and early fall. The living room was carpeted with Oriental rugs, wainscoted with dark wood paneling, and a baby grand piano sat in one corner. Mellow afternoon light slanted through the tall windows. She spotted Halil, the cryptozoology professor, ladling himself a cup of punch at the table that served beverages and joined him, accepting the ladle from him after he finished with it.

"Hello there, Piper," he said, giving her a warm smile. He was short and a bit chubby, with soulful brown eyes and a shock of dark, glossy hair that liked to grow forward, covering half his face. "How is life treating you these days?"

Piper pondered his question as she served herself a cup of punch and wondered if Halil might be a good person with whom to share her strange fright in the woods. She took a sip as they stepped away from the table, deciding she might as well. "Actually … I had an odd experience in the woods behind my house the other day."

He gazed at her with interest. "Did you now?"

She nodded, took another sip. She found herself trembling, remembering how powerful the sensation had been, and for no discernable reason. "I was picking chanterelles and suddenly I … well, this sounds so stupid now. But I felt like something was watching me. And then out of the blue I was seized by this feeling of abject terror."

"Hmm," he mused, pushing the hair out of his face. It flopped back immediately. Carla Sanchez joined them at that point. Carla was Halil's partner, a professor in the Folklore and Mythology Department.

"Hi, Piper," she said, giving her arm a friendly squeeze.

"Hello, Carla. Lovely to see you."

"Likewise." Piper had always found something very appealing about Carla, though no one would call her a beauty. But her dusky coloring and deep brown eyes were beautiful, and she carried herself with grace and poise.

"Piper was telling me about getting seized by an inexplicable sense of terror in the woods the other day," Halil told her.

Now Carla was examining her closely. "Really? Anything you can attribute it to?"

Piper shook her head. "Well, I suppose it could have been a cougar."

"That could be," Carla agreed.

"But it was just so … extreme. It seemed a little … well, this sounds odd, but it seemed almost otherworldly. I've never experienced anything quite like this before."

Halil and Carla exchanged glances. "Anything more you can tell us?" Halil asked.

Piper shrugged. "Not really." Then she remembered

whatever had traumatized the devas to her snapdragons. But she felt a little silly bringing that up.

"Well, I'd say one possibility is Sasquatch."

"Bigfoot?" she said dubiously. "I thought that was just a myth." As she said this, she realized that most people would think the same thing about her devas. Then again, the community of Findhorn certainly believed in them.

Halil shook his head. "Nope. Check out reports on the Bigfoot Research Organization website. You'll be amazed. There are thousands of credible, vetted eyewitness testimonies, some recordings of Sasquatch vocalizations, and some photos and videos. Of course, the photos tend to be few and far between, blurry, and from a distance. A lot of the sightings are by hunters, who aren't carrying a camera, and most people aren't looking for them. They come across them by chance and by the time their mind has registered what they're looking at, they're gone. Same thing with video. Bizarrely, the Forest People seem to have some idea that a camera is a threat and they avoid them or destroy them."

Piper noted his use of the term, Forest People. "But no carcasses, no bodies."

He shook his head. "There's some speculation that they bury their dead, that they have a social structure, hominid-style psychology, and intelligence equivalent to a twelve-year-old human. I'm sure they feel that their survival depends on the cryptic nature of their existence. And even if they don't bury their dead, how many animal carcasses do you see lying around? Not many, even for far more common creatures. They get eaten by scavengers. And you'd have to know where to look for them in the first place. As you no doubt know, they prefer remote locations."

"Have you ever seen one?"

"Regrettably, no."

"But—are they otherworldly?"

Carla tilted her head to one side. "It's speculated that they possess the ability to produce infrasound. It's not otherworldly, but it can sure feel that way."

"What's infrasound?"

"It's sound whose frequencies are so low that we can't consciously hear it," Halil said. "A number of animals ... elephants, whales, and giraffes, for example ... produce infrasound. It can travel very long distances. Impending earthquakes may produce infrasound and this might be what alerts animals to head for safer ground. Experiments have shown that even though humans can't hear it, it can still create feelings of uneasiness, panic, fear, and even cause heart palpitations and fainting. It's possible that the Forest People use it for protection as well as communication."

Piper fell quiet for a moment, mulling over this information and thinking about the knocks she had been hearing in the forest. "Are they dangerous? Do I need to be worried?"

Halil sighed. "To be honest, there are reports of possible deaths and abductions."

"A few reports date back to 19th century folklore," Carla told her. "A trapper claimed he was abducted to be a mate for a young female Sasquatch. He spent a few days with her family group before he managed to escape."

"And some Indian tribes tell stories about Indian maidens being snatched for similar purposes." Halil added. "The deaths—well, it's speculated that these individuals could have either been threatening or not respecting territory. Teddy Roosevelt famously wrote about the death of a trapper in the Badlands that was attributed to a Sasquatch, in fact. And ... actually, to be honest, some researchers think some cases of children disappearing without a trace in wilderness areas might be related to Sasquatch."

Piper gaped at him. "To what purpose? To—to eat them?"

"Maybe," he admitted. "Or, you know, think about us. We're hominids. We adopt all kinds of animals for pets. Maybe Sasquatches think human children are cute. There have been a couple of reports of human children sighted in the company of a Sasquatch."

Tears sprang into Piper's eyes. She found this discussion extremely disturbing.

Reading her expression, Halil said, "But Piper, bear in mind, these stories are only a handful out of literally thousands and thousands of reports. There are only a few reports of aggressive behavior on the part of Sasquatches, usually if they're being attacked or harassed in some way. Dogs that come after them don't fare well. But most of the time, they just run away. They will throw big rocks to scare people from their territory, but they have excellent aim. They almost never hit the person, though they'll plunk a small boulder right next to them." He hesitated. "There is something that you should probably know about them, though, if they are in your area. One is that they hate guns. Hate them."

"I don't even own a gun."

"You don't seem like you would, but I just wanted to let you know. Shooting at them is a very dangerous thing to do. You would need an elephant gun to take one down, and shooting them with a conventional weapon just enrages them. Oddly, a flashlight seems to be better protection than a gun. They'll run away from light, but charge someone with a gun."

Piper stood silently for a moment, digesting all this information. "Wow," she said finally.

"Truth be told, though, it seems that they're mainly just a pain in the ass the way most hominid species are, including us," Halil said. "They're territorial. They often prey on people's pets and livestock. And sometimes they'll destroy stuff that pisses them off, like logging and mining equipment that's left in the woods."

Carla cleared her throat. "There is another possibility as to what caused your fright."

"What's that?"

"The Gentry."

"The ... Gentry?"

Carla gave a self-deprecating laugh. "Well, it's a catch-all term that I've adopted for these entities. I've borrowed it from the Irish. It's their name for a number of different magical humanoid-type beings—fairies, leprechauns and the like. As you probably know, humans have been spinning tales about these creatures from time immemorial. These stories span every culture, every continent, and every century. Today, we think of fairies as being gentle, harmless creatures."

Piper nodded, thinking about her devas.

"But that certainly hasn't been the historical perception of them. They were known as mischief-makers, and the term 'mischief' was far harsher in ancient times. Some of the 'mischief' included abductions and luring people to their deaths. They include missing time and injury."

"But nowadays, people don't believe in those kinds of beings, right?" Piper said. "I mean, this is from folklore, correct?"

Carla shook her head. "As it happens, there are reports of strange humanoids in recent history and up to this day. In 1977, three teenagers in Dover, Massachusetts all separately spotted a strange-looking being with a watermelon-shaped head, glowing orange eyes, and tendril-like fingers. In 2009, a man was relieving himself behind a shed in rural Pennsylvania when he was suddenly seized with a massive feeling of dread that punched him in the gut like a physical blow. He ran to his truck to peel out and his lights swept across a strange humanoid-type being crawling out of a nearby ditch that he felt certain was stalking him."

"I know that feeling," Piper gulped.

"And just recently, several witnesses in a remote park in Costa Rica spotted a group of what they at first thought were children walking along a trail. But their faces weren't childlike, and they all reported experiencing an unaccountable sense of fear when they saw them."

Piper swallowed, her eyes continuing to water. "I wonder why?" she said. "Why the feeling of fear?"

Halil gave a low chuckle. "Self-preservation, perhaps?"

Piper shivered, chafing her arms. "I'm sorry I asked now," she said uneasily.

Carla patted her on the back. "Don't worry, Piper. Chances are, if there was anything tangible behind that feeling you experienced, it was a cougar."

"Right," she sighed. She hated thinking that there was anything at all in her forest that she needed to fear. She comforted herself with the thought that cougar attacks were extremely rare. She had heard quite enough by now, so she thanked Carla and Halil for their information and sought out other faculty she knew, chatting with Rupert and some others before leaving, steering the conversations to gardening and heroics performed by dogs.

She needed to pick up some groceries before returning home, so she headed to the food co-op. Tonight, she was having Axel, Marion, and Danny over for dinner, and she wanted to fix something special. She planned to have a Polish hunter's stew, which called for sausage, pork shoulder, and ham, and the food co-op had organic, locally-sourced meat from small farms, as well as ham cured without nitrites or nitrates. She was also serving a beet-and-gorgonzola salad and poached pears for dessert.

After she got home and put her groceries away, she picked flowers from her garden, with the blessing of her devas: marigolds, some late roses, and snapdragons, arranging them in vases and placing them on the dinner table and around the living room. She was so excited about this evening and feeling so relieved to have shared her encounter with Halil and Carla that she bounced around the house, like Tigger, she laughed to herself, one of her favorite characters of all time. Then she put the stew on to simmer, chopping onions, mushrooms, and cabbage, and adding an entire jar of sauerkraut that a neighbor of hers sold at the farmer's market. The scent of caraway seeds and allspice filled the house, swelling her heart with contentment.

Marion and Danny arrived first, bearing a bottle of wine and some ginger cookies that Marion had made to go with the pears. She got them settled, poured glasses of wine, and asked after Marion's pregnancy, which was going beautifully.

"Except for barfing several times a day," she said, with exaggerated gloominess.

"But we understand that this is a good sign," Danny added, putting his arm around Marion and giving her a squeeze.

Piper started to say something when the phone rang. She saw that it was Axel calling, so she took the phone into the hall. "Hey, sweetheart. What's up? Are you delayed?"

He groaned. "Worse. I won't be able to come."

Her heart sank. "Oh, no, Axel. What happened?"

"My mom had a stroke. A pretty bad one, according to my dad."

"Oh my God, that's terrible! I'm so sorry!"

"So I'm driving down to Santa Rosa to see her. She's been asking for me."

"Well, by all means!" she exclaimed. "Is there anything I can do?"

"Just keep being adorable, lovable you. Listen, I have to go, but I'll give you a call the first chance I get, okay?"

"Okay. Be careful."

"I will."

Piper hung up, worried about Axel and his mother, and disappointed that he wouldn't be coming to dinner.

"Who was that?" asked Danny.

"Axel," Piper sighed. "His mom had a stroke so he won't be able to join us."

"That's such a shame, sweetie," Marion said, getting up to give her a sideways hug. "At least you know he's a dutiful son."

Piper nodded. "That's true." She tried to cheer herself up with that thought. "Anyway. Next time. How is work going, Danny?"

He wiped his lips with his cocktail napkin before answering. "Actually, we've got a bit of excitement going."

"Really? What?"

He gave a rueful laugh. "Well, you know Incident. Not much happens here. But we've got an APB out on a possible murder suspect."

"In Incident?" Piper didn't remember hearing about any murders recently.

"Well, the murder took place in Sacramento. They don't know that he's here, but they think he headed north. So we got the alert along with every other town up here. A young woman was found dead in the American River not long ago. She'd been missing for a few weeks before that. Anyway, at first they thought that she might have been a random victim—running alone on the river trail along there, where some dicey people are known to frequent. The back of her head was bashed in."

Piper's hand flew to her mouth. "How awful!"

"But it turns out to be more complicated than that. This is not to be repeated beyond these walls, but they found bruising around her throat and nowhere else. It looks like she was strangled first, which opens the possibility that she knew her attacker, trusted him enough to get close. Then he smashed her skull to make it look like a stranger did it."

"Lotta scumbags in the world," Marion observed, shaking her head.

Piper shivered. "Well, let's hope he's not here. This doesn't seem like a great place to hide out."

"No."

Piper changed the subject, finding this one to be disquieting, although, frankly, Incident seemed like the last place someone like that would come to. And if he had, he had no doubt moved on by now. So she told them about her new student, the mother of a musician in town whose band they had probably heard of. Her son had bought her a series of one-on-one tutorials for a birthday gift, she told them, and she was not only an enthusiastic student, she had a real feeling for plants, she could tell.

Marion and Danny were delighted for her, as they always were, and they scarfed up the appetizers that Piper made: blanched zucchini that she had sliced into rounds and then hollowed out in order to hold one of three toppings: a whipped salmon and cream cheese spread, a sundried tomato and caper paste, and a finely minced salsa of watercress, garlic, and avocado, tossed with lemon juice. Her *bigos* was a big hit—Danny loved sausage—and the cookies that Marion made were heavenly, crispy crunchy on the outside, chewy and succulent on the inside. They stayed late, splitting a bottle of chilled Moscato before leaving, Piper's heart glowing as she bid them goodnight. She was so lucky to have such lovely friends.

This in turn reminded her of Axel and how disappointed she felt that he once again missed meeting them. They were all going to enjoy each other so much. Her heart ached, too, thinking about how distraught Axel must be about his mother, and she waited up a while before going to bed, hoping he might text or call. The fact that he didn't worried her all the more. The only reason she could come up with was that it was worse than he had even known, or that another stroke had occurred after he got there. She had some herbs that she could have given him to help his mom, but of course, there was no time.

Finally, she went to bed, but she had a hard time getting back to sleep. Something was nagging at her, but she had no idea what it might be. She decided that it was simply concern about Axel and his mother. But when she fell asleep, she had frightening dreams about being chased by some shadowy, malevolent force. She awoke more than once with her heart pounding, wishing Danny hadn't shared that disturbing information about the escaped murderer. I wish Axel were here, she thought miserably. And she sent a prayer that his mother would be okay.

CHAPTER 26

arson rummaged through his T shirt collection, feeling more rattled than he had in some time. It was Thanksgiving and he had invited Olivia. His mother had invited Piper.

"The poor thing is estranged from her family," Merilee told him yesterday. "I could tell when I asked about her plans that the thought of spending Thanksgiving with her parents and brother made her awfully sad. Not to mention that horrendous Thanksgiving traffic."

Carson had to suppress the groan that this information elicited. How would his mom know that he had any feelings for Piper? She wouldn't. He was going out with Olivia. And he had only himself to blame by setting up those classes. He knew that they would hit it off. But he hadn't expected her to do something like this. Of course, who would have predicted that Piper would be estranged from her family? She didn't seem like the type. Then again, he knew very little about her. Little enough that the intense feelings he had for her made no sense whatsoever. It pissed him off, quite frankly.

He selected two T shirts from his drawer and laid them out on the bed. Why did he care so much what T shirt he wore, he asked himself, annoyed. Usually he just grabbed the handiest one in the drawer. He finally settled on a wheat-colored one that had an enso symbol painted on it in black. He pulled it over his head, then checked to see how his hair looked in the mirror. It was fine, he decided. He was never one to fuss over his appearance, but today … he wasn't sure whom he wanted to impress more: Olivia or Piper.

Sighing, he headed into the kitchen where his mom was making a salad. The turkey was in the oven, fragrant and golden, the pies made yesterday. All that remained to be done was set the table and cook the potatoes and green beans. And make the gravy, of course, once the bird came out.

"You look nice," his mom told him with a smile. He couldn't tell if she was being ironic or not. He did know that she didn't share his opinion that a T shirt and pair of jeans was suitable for pretty much every occasion but she had given up trying to talk him into wearing anything else.

"Thanks," he said.

Jessie was lying in the middle of the kitchen, on the lookout for any stray tidbits that might fall to the floor. It didn't matter how many times either he or his mom asked her to move, or how many times they tripped over her, she always ended up right there. Carson reached down to pet her ears, which prompted her to start thumping the floor with one of her back legs, like a rabbit. Carson loved that. And the clouds of dark blue paddle shapes that the sound produced.

He grabbed the potatoes from under the counter and washed them in the sink. Gold and silver sparkler patterns filled his vision from the sound of the spray. He put the water on to boil, then fetched the green beans from the fridge and piled them into a colander.

"Piper was telling me that stinging nettles, cooked, are quite tasty," said Merilee.

"Huh," said Carson.

"And apparently, in the spring, the fiddleheads on ferns are edible. They sell them in the grocery store in Japan."

"We'll have to try them sometime." Not. He tossed the potatoes into the now boiling water, turned the heat down, and began slicing the ends off the green beans.

The doorbell rang then and Merilee asked Carson to answer it. Her hands were slimy from cutting up avocado, she said. Much to his relief, he opened the door to find Olivia standing there, holding a casserole dish covered with aluminum foil.

"Hi," she said, giving him a kiss. "Thanks so much for inviting me to Thanksgiving dinner!"

Jessie nosed in between them, tail wagging, delicately sniffing Olivia's leg while angling for a pat.

"Hey there, Jessie," Olivia said, handing the casserole to Carson and obliging her with a thorough rumpling of her ruff.

"Smells delicious!" he said. "What's in here?"

"Creamed pearl onions. A family favorite."

Carson noticed a pang in her voice and put his arm around her as they headed toward the kitchen. She had confided in him that her dad wasn't doing well and that no one had figured out what the problem was yet. They had suspected lead poisoning, but the tests had shown no appreciable levels of lead in her parents' house. He had done well at a resort her sister treated them to, but once he returned home, the symptoms came back.

Merilee greeted her effusively, throwing her arms around her and welcoming her. Olivia glowed, Carson noticed, which made her even prettier than usual.

Merilee took the foil off the top of the casserole and peered inside, giving Olivia a delighted squeeze. "Thanks so much for bringing these, dear. I love pearl onions but I never have the time to peel them."

"It's a once-a-year kind of dish, that's for sure," Olivia laughed.

"Pour Olivia a glass of wine, won't you, sweetie?" Merilee

nodded at the glasses she had sitting out on the counter. "We've got a bottle of white chilled and a bottle of red breathing," she said to Olivia.

As he was pouring Olivia a glass of red, the doorbell rang again.

"Carson, be a dear and let Piper in," she said.

Olivia turned to her happily. "Piper Fairchild? She's joining us?"

"Yes! You know her?"

"She was one of the first people I met here! She spotted me in the student center the day of my interview here and ..."

Carson steeled himself as he headed to the door. This time, Jessie scampered ahead of him. He noticed that her entire behind was wagging and that she was whimpering excitedly in way that she reserved for very special people.

He let Jessie bound forward as he opened the door. She caught Piper by surprise, but her face flushed with pleasure as she hitched her basket over her shoulder and bent down to stroke her soft ears. She was looking gorgeous in a heather blue dress that draped her figure beautifully, Carson noted glumly.

She straightened up, seemed not to know whether to hug him or shake his hand. She ended up taking both of his hands in hers. "Hi, Carson," she said. "Happy Thanksgiving."

The electric jolt he experienced from the combination of her voice and her touch threw him completely off-balance. God, this was going to be the longest Thanksgiving of his life. "Thanks," he mumbled. "Come on in."

Both Olivia and Merilee fussed over Piper as she entered the kitchen, and the grateful look on her face tugged at his heart. He was also feeling outnumbered in terms of gender and for a moment, he missed his dad so powerfully that he had to blink back tears. He covered by pouring himself a glass of wine and returning to the vegetables.

"Good God, you didn't!" His mother was exclaiming. He

turned to see her lifting the cloth from Piper's basket.

Piper giggled. "My grandmother's recipe."

"Homemade dinner rolls!" Merilee said, rolling her eyes heavenward in ecstasy.

"Wow, cool," said Carson, trying to be friendly, though his insides were in complete turmoil. Piper rewarded him with a dazzling smile. Which made things even worse.

He turned his attention to getting the turkey out and putting it on a cutting board to rest. Then he started on the gravy while Merilee took care of steaming the green beans. Piper and Olivia filled glasses with water and set out the side dishes, everyone chattering away, having a grand old time except for Carson. He slugged down his glass of wine and hastily poured himself another before they got seated. Merilee sat at one end of the table while Carson took a seat at the other, Piper and Olivia between them. Jessie lay down between Piper and his mom. Merilee held her hands out for everyone to join in a blessing, some goddess shit that she always liked to do. He focused mainly on the sound of her voice, which always reminded him of warm, buttered toast. Carson ended up holding hands with both Piper and Olivia, and he thought his brain might shoot out his ears before it was time to let go.

Carson tried to act as normally as he could, but halfway through the meal, he noticed Olivia observing him carefully, then turning her thoughtful gaze to Piper. His hands started sweating; he wiped them covertly on his napkin under the table.

"So, Olivia, how is your crowdfunding going?" he asked.

She grinned and laid down her fork. "It's going great!" she said. "I'm already halfway to my goal."

"That's fantastic!" Piper exclaimed. "What are you funding?"

"My research. It's rather fringe and it doesn't stand much of a chance of getting any kind of regular funding."

"Can you give us a laymen's synopsis of what your research

involves?" Merilee asked. "I assume it's different from the work you've been doing with pets."

Olivia rested her cheek on her hand briefly while she pondered. "Basically, I want to figure out how we can turn on the placebo effect consciously, and in a targeted fashion. All of our cells have the same genes, but different ones are turned on and expressed in different tissues and at different times. The way this works, in a nutshell, is that molecules interact with each other like a lock and key. When genes, which are made up of molecules, are covered up with certain other molecules, they aren't read. But other molecules can come along, fit their locking mechanism into the key of the covering molecule, and reveal the gene to the gene-transcribing machinery, which is also molecular."

"Wonderful description," said Piper.

"So how does the placebo work?" asked Merilee. "Is it more molecules?"

"Well, at some point. At some point there is some kind of molecular interaction that shuts down misbehaving genes or stimulates ones that need to be read that aren't. But the shape of molecules, and therefore their reactivity—their "keyness"—can be determined not only by their interaction with another molecule, but energy as well. Heat, light, UV radiation … all of these energy sources are known to affect the configuration of certain molecules. But our minds and nervous systems also produce electric fields. It's possible that the position of the molecule in one of these fields could affect its shape and therefore its activity."

"So our thoughts, being electrical in nature, could affect the way our genes are read," said Carson. She'd walked him through her theory earlier, so he had some grasp of what she was doing.

"Theoretically. It's what I'm out to prove."

Piper gazed at her admiringly. "That would be … absolutely groundbreaking!"

Olivia shrugged. "Possibly."

Merilee raised her glass in a toast. "Here's to Olivia getting all the funding she needs!"

"Hear hear!" Piper enthused.

Carson reached over and squeezed Olivia's hand while he took a sip from his glass. The smile she gave him seemed enigmatic.

The rest of the meal passed more or less in a blur. He drank more than he normally did, so things became a little fuzzy. He managed to comport himself in a reasonable manner, though, all things considered, he thought. After everyone had finished their pie and coffee, and sleepiness began to catch up with them, Piper, then Olivia took their leave. Carson let Merilee and Jessie escort Piper to the door, and he took the opportunity to give Olivia a heartfelt hug and fervent kiss. But she felt different somehow. Not unfriendly, but not the same.

He told her he'd call her tomorrow and she said that would be great. Then she headed for the foyer to say goodbye to Merilee and thank her for the evening. Carson accompanied her, and he and Merilee stood at the door while Olivia walked to her car and Piper pulled out of the driveway. Merilee waved and waved.

"Aren't they delightful young women?" she sighed, leaning against the doorjamb as Olivia drove away. Moths batted around the porch light, the soft fluttering creating a billow of putty-colored lozenges in his field of vision. Carson was touched by how happy she seemed. It had been a long time since she had exuded this much happiness. He felt bad for resenting the fact that she had invited Piper. And yet … God. What was he going to do? Well, there was nothing to do, he thought miserably.

He just hoped he hadn't blown it with Olivia.

CHAPTER 27

livia paced her apartment nervously, waiting for Carson. She had invited him over for a glass of wine because she felt that they needed to talk, but she wasn't exactly sure about what or how to get started. She had noticed the chemistry between Piper and Carson at Thanksgiving dinner yesterday and was trying to figure out what it meant. Piper seemed willfully oblivious to it while Carson seemed tortured by it, trying everything he could to give the opposite impression. She appreciated the valiant effort he made to focus his attention on her instead; however, it was definitely a case of protesting too much. Carson wasn't very good at hiding his feelings. But she knew that Piper was in love with someone else, and she assumed that Carson knew, too, given the way he had behaved.

He was a good guy, but she didn't think that the comfortable feeling that existed between them was strong enough to ward off something like intense chemistry. And what was the feeling she and Carson had for each other, anyway? She was starting to suspect it was friendship, not romance. Though she had liked the feeling of being someone's love interest, especially someone as cute as Carson.

She sighed wistfully and uncorked the wine so that it could have some time to breathe. Not that she could afford any kind of fancy vintage. She got out the cheese, too, some local artisan cheeses, one a hard, sharp cheese, the other a soft runny cheese with a tasty, mellow rind. Incident was an artisan town, like her hometown in western Massachusetts but even more so. If a person wanted to buy local, they certainly wouldn't have any problems living in Incident. Small mom-and-pops and cooperatives thrived in every sector here, from health care to farming, food and drink, to social services. Merilee told her once that a collapse in social services a few years ago had led to some visionary and effective local solutions. A neighborhood of tiny houses was built for the homeless, a recycling center set up nearby to bring in some income and give residents some job skills. It wasn't long before they were building furniture out of recycled pallets and materials from demolitions, and Incident had managed, in cooperation with the university, to come up with a an employment program that ensured everyone could obtain work that paid enough to cover their basic expenses.

Some people with disabilities needed subsidizing, so a fund was created from sales tax to help those people. The city found that these solutions reduced the need for law enforcement, and in fact, turned out to be cheaper. And the money given as subsidies ended up spent mainly in Incident, so the money didn't really go anywhere. On the more hedonistic end of the spectrum, Incident was famed for its beer, organic wine, cheeses, and chocolates.

The doorbell rang as she was slicing a baguette, causing her to jump. She smoothed her hair back, opening the door with a smile that she could feel was too wide and too bright. Carson regarded her warily.

"Hey," he said, giving her a kiss on the cheek as she stood back to welcome him in.

"Hey yourself," she said, giving him a brief hug. "Come on

in."

She thought that sitting at the kitchen/dining room table might feel the most casual, so she offered Carson a seat, poured them each a glass of wine and took the chair across from him.

"Cheers," she said, holding up her glass.

Carson dutifully clinked his glass into hers.

Olivia rushed to fill the awkward pause that followed. "I had such a great time at Thanksgiving dinner with you guys," she said.

"Well, we enjoyed having you. I haven't see my mom so happy in a long time."

Olivia nodded, swirling the wine in the glass as she tried to craft the best approach to her topic. "So, um, Carson ..."

"Yeah?" She could see him tense.

"Listen, I ... well, I couldn't help but notice how attracted you are to Piper. Believe me, I don't blame you! She's gorgeous and smart and kind—"

Carson interrupted. "Yeah, and she's hooked up with that jackass restaurant manager at Buffington's." He glared at the table. "The one you think is so hot."

Olivia blinked. She decided to ignore his last comment. "Oh, is that who she's going out with?" she said. "I didn't know who it was, I just knew that she was seeing somebody."

"Now you know." Carson continued to avoid eye contact while he took a large gulp of his drink. His shoulders were starting to slump, which made Olivia feel guilty.

"So ... well, this isn't anything against you at all, Carson. But I just wonder if it makes sense for me to invest my emotions in you if you're actually smitten with someone else."

His head jerked up and the intensity in his eyes took her aback. "It'll pass, for God's sake! She's not even my type! I don't even know why I have this attraction towards her, but I don't want it! If that's the kind of guy she wants, she couldn't possibly find someone like me interesting."

Olivia fought the urge to go put her arms around him. It somehow didn't seem like the right move, as much as she wanted to. "I don't think that's true," she said. "Like you say, who knows why we're attracted to someone on a gut level—maybe he represents something to her, maybe he treats her like a queen, who knows? But whatever happens with Piper, whether it involves you or not … I guess I just realized yesterday that in my romantic life, I want those kinds of sparks. Maybe I'll never find them, but I think you'll admit that you don't feel the same way about me that you do Piper."

Carson sighed, his eyes full of pain. He didn't answer, which was an answer. "But look!" he exclaimed suddenly. "I think you're a total hot shit, Olivia! I might not be 'in love' with you, but I adore your ass! You know? Maybe it's not love, but it's a whole lot of like. Neither one of us are seeing anyone else right now, what's wrong with us hanging out?"

Olivia drummed her fingers, thinking. He had a point. "Well …" She hesitated, unsure what to say next.

"Friends. We can be friends! We are friends, aren't we?"

"Of course we are." Olivia smiled warmly at him and took his hand. She actually needed a friend more than a lover right now.

His face relaxed but he held on tight to her hand. "You're a really great presence in my life right now."

She got up then and went over to give him a hug. He pulled her into his lap and put his arms around her.

"How about snuggle buddies?" he said. "How about we just indulge in the affection we feel for each other and see where it goes? I respect you. You respect me. We each have the other's best interests at heart, don't we? We don't want to hurt each other or use each other. We've already slept together so we don't have that tension hanging over our heads."

Olivia laughed, tickled by his picaresque pragmatism. It held a powerful appeal, she had to admit. "Okay, let's give it a whirl," she said finally, giving him a squeeze.

"Good," he sighed.

Olivia stood picked up the cheese board. "Want to watch a rerun of *Leverage*?" she asked.

Carson grabbed the wine and they settled on the couch for a couple of hours. Carson left soon after the second episode, giving her a wonderful hug that warmed her heart. She closed the door behind him, rubbing the back of her neck, thinking that there was a lot more to Carson than met the eye.

She returned to the couch and poured the last dregs of the wine into her glass as she turned her thoughts to her dad. She had spoken to her parents yesterday after she came home from Merilee and Carson's, trying to puzzle out why her dad had done so well away from home but had had a relapse when he got back if there was no lead threat. She suggested getting the house tested for radon, which her mother promised to do. But something was nagging at her, something in the back of her mind. Something that it seemed like she had considered before but since forgotten.

She bolted upright. It was his medication! She had never researched the side-effects the way she had promised to do. She had been in the middle of moving, and then she had had that accident, then those awful nightmares … not to mention taking on a new job and having to figure out her research. But surely they took his medication with him to the resort.

She glanced at her new Steampunk clock that she had added to her collection and hung on the wall. It was too late to call. But she couldn't wait. She dialed her parents' number, hoping that they would pick up. Her mother answered after the fourth ring, sounding sleepy and panicked.

"Olivia? Is everything okay, sweetheart?"

"I'm fine, Mom. Listen, did you take Dad's blood pressure medications with you to the resort?"

She paused. "No, we didn't. It all happened so quickly that we forgot, since they were on the kitchen counter. We figured going a week without would be okay. Why, do you think that was a problem?"

Olivia strode over to her laptop and flipped it open. She typed, "ARB side-effects" into her search engine. "No, actually, Mom, I think just the opposite. I mean, normally, it would be a very bad idea. But let me research this a little bit. Don't give him his morning dose, all right? Call his family practice doc and let her know; she'll probably want to put him on something else, something in a different class." A patient forum came up in her search results and she clicked on it. "Horrible headaches, muscle pain, tendon damage ..." read the first post. "Dizziness, blurred vision, severe muscle pain. I only hope no permanent damage was done," read the next.

"But—what if the new medication is a problem?"

"We'll keep working on the best solution. But I think the most important thing right now is to get him off of this particular medication. Have him drink a lot of water to flush it from his system, okay? And I'll call you first thing to see how things are going."

Olivia hung up and continued to scroll through the posts. She was taken aback by how many there were and how severe some of the side-effects were for patients. Not everyone, of course. Some people tolerated this class of drugs just fine. But the vast majority of posters in the forums had serious problems from taking it. "I tried to tell my doctor about the side-effects I was experiencing," wrote one poster, "but he told me these drugs 'didn't do that.'" This was echoed by several others. Olivia surmised that if the physician didn't take the person's experiences seriously, he or she didn't report them to the FDA. These side-effects were therefore underreported, which exacerbated the information gap.

She did a rough calculation of pros versus cons on the forum and found that ten percent of the posters had a positive experience whereas ninety percent had a bad one. These individuals were self-reporting, and those who had a negative reaction were far more likely to post online than those who had a good experience. But even so, the sheer number of people who suffered serious side-effects was concerning.

"High blood pressure alternative remedies," she typed into her search engine. And hunkered down for some in-depth research.

CHAPTER 28

xel pulled onto I-80 in his rental car, cursing the traffic. And the high prices of everything in the Bay Area. Rents were insane, even in Oakland these days, finding a parking garage an exercise in extortion, and the lease on a commercial hole-in-the-wall in a decent part of The City astronomical. Still. If Piper really did come through with everything that she promised, he might just be able to swing it. Assuming, that is, his old man didn't get any greedier.

He had spent the last few days in a cheap motel in Vallejo, checking out the places where he might want to open a bistro-style restaurant in San Francisco. Once he told Piper he had to rush to his mom's side, he couldn't let her see him in Incident. He always hated Thanksgiving anyway—no happy memories there—and he got a discounted rate for his motel because most people spent the holiday with family.

When he checked in with Piper after bailing on her dinner party, she had invited him to Thanksgiving at her parents' home in San Francisco, which made his skin crawl just thinking about it. So he had told her that his mom was a little better, but he just didn't feel that he could leave her side. Piper then offered to come down and spend the day with his family, volunteering to cook most of the meal. He yammered on how touched he was, how sweet she was, how he didn't deserve her, yadda yadda, but in the end told her in his most mournful voice that his mom was feeling self-conscious about the fact that half her face was drooping, and that she wanted to meet Piper when she was at her best.

Piper had given him pretty much everything in her savings, $10,000, the last time he saw her, before her dinner party. For earnest money on the place in Incident. But the rest was tied up and she was going to have to go to a little bit of trouble, she said, to make it liquid. He was dropping the 10K by his dad's place, hoping this would get him off his back. He hated going into Sacramento, especially now that he was hot, which was why he had rented a car in an abundance of caution. The police didn't have an inkling of his Mercedes that he knew of, but better safe than sorry. Another goddamned expense, of course. But he was going to try to appeal to his mother, see if she could get the old geezer to back off.

He'd given up thinking that his dad had a single paternal bone in his body; to him, every other entity on the planet, even if it had his genes, was simply a mark. But maybe his mom had some milk of human kindness for her son hidden away in there somewhere. His mental image of her was a wraith, a ghostly sidekick to his dad shrouded in the smoke from her cigarettes, her worn, hazy face an odd combination of blank and hard. Not exactly warm and fuzzy, but she didn't carry the same menace that his dad did. He might find a chink in her bland armor.

He parked down the block from his parents' depressingly shabby bungalow in a declining neighborhood. The lawn was basically a bunch of weeds that got mowed occasionally, and the rest of the landscaping consisted of a couple of scrawny rose bushes spotted with blight. The dingy yellow house with tatty white-ish shutters desperately needed a coat of new paint. Axel couldn't figure out what the hell his old man did with his money. Probably spent it on gambling, near as he could figure.

He rang the doorbell, even though this was the house he grew up in. You never knew what might be going on inside, what shady character might be in there. No point in getting his head accidentally blown off. His mother answered the door, her face registering nothing more than mild surprise. No pleasure, that's for sure. He set his jaw and walked in. The house smelled like mildewed carpet and cigarettes, as always.

"How're you doing, Mom?" he asked, in a solicitous tone.

She shrugged. "Same old," she said.

He cast about for something in particular to ask about, but as far as he knew, she had no interests besides her job as a blackjack dealer in an Indian casino on the outskirts of town. And drinking cheap vodka.

She led him into the kitchen where his dad sat counting out some bills and putting them in different piles.

"Sonny boy!" he crowed, not bothering to get up. He waved him into the seat opposite. A cigarette was burning in a glass ash tray sending up a plume of acrid smoke. Axel hated cigarette smoke.

Axel sat down and made a show of removing the bundle of bills from the inside of his coat pocket. Then he hesitated. He glanced over at his mom, who was fixing herself a cup of instant coffee on the peeling Formica counter.

"So I've got ten thousand in cash here for you, like I explained over the phone," he said, holding onto it. "But I need to know if this is going to take care of things. It's not easy for me to raise this kind of money. I don't have your expertise." He hoped that flattery might help him.

His dad snorted. "Save it for somebody who falls for that kind of crap."

"Well, it's true! I'm trying to get started in something legit. If I can do that, I'll be good for a lot more later."

His dad regarded him through narrowed eyes. He picked

up his cigarette and took a drag.

"And—and you know I didn't have anything to do with that girl's death."

"Do I now?"

"Come on, Dad! I'm not a murderer for Christ's sake." Axel turned to his mom, his eyes pleading. "You know that, don't you, Mom?"

Her eyes went even blanker. She took a sip from her cup without responding, directing her gaze at the corner of the room.

Axel sighed. So much for maternal love. He stood up and threw the money on the table. "Okay, whatever. Here's the money. It's all I can come up with. This is it. I'm done."

His dad leaned over and picked up the bills, took his time counting them. "You're done when I say you are," he said matter-of-factly, once he had finished and laid them back down, throwing Axel an amused glance.

Axel repressed the desire he felt to lunge across the table and wrap his hands around his dad's scrawny, wrinkly neck. He was a lot stronger than he looked. Well, his dad didn't know it, but his only son was about to pull a disappearing act and he had only himself to blame. Axel was already working on his new alias. He had nabbed a credit card offer from a rural mailbox outside of Incident and rented a temporary P O Box in Oakland. He sent the credit card company an application for Trevor Wilson before he left Vallejo, and got himself a library card and buyers' club membership under that name, too. With those, he got himself a state photo ID, and the next time he was in the Bay Area he would get himself a new driver's license. Before Trevor figured out what was going on, Axel would be established in his new identity, having chucked the P O Box once he got his apartment.

He stomped out to his car and sat there fuming for several minutes before starting the engine. He was so sick of people fucking up his plans. Why the hell did his dad have to be such a greedy prick? And his mom such a tool? Why the hell, as a matter of fact, did Kristy have to get so goddamned nosy and high-handed? Jesus Christ, everybody stole from the restaurant where they worked. Oh, except for her. Miss Priss. She even threatened to turn him in to the police! Was that necessary? Was it? He thought she loved him, that bitch! He had apologized, he had groveled, he had promised to pay back every cent. But it had hardly moved her. He suspected that she knew he was fucking another waitress who worked at a Japanese restaurant in the same neighborhood. So what did that mean? That she was spying on him? She had only herself to blame for what happened, the stupid twat. And here she was, still making trouble for him.

Grinding his teeth, he started up the rental and pulled out of his parking place, making sure that no one was coming. Last thing he needed was a fender bender. At least his dad was pacified for the moment. And by the time he made his next attempt to lean on him, he'd be long gone. He couldn't rest easy, though, until he was reestablished in his new location. Piper needed to hurry up.

He was so preoccupied, he didn't pay attention to where he was going, and ended up driving right by the section of trail where Kristy met her maker. This expression amused him with its double entendre, though he shuddered as he remembered their encounter. He didn't enjoy it. Didn't enjoy it at all. It was messy and hard work. And it turned out she weighed more than he thought, the cow. Dragging her body over to the river was no picnic. He wasn't lying when he told his parents he wasn't a murderer. It didn't come naturally or easy to him. He didn't get off on it, the way he imagined serial murderers did. But what the fuck was he supposed to do when faced with a situation like this?

He didn't like how angry all this was making him, so he turned his thoughts to other matters. Depending upon how much Piper coughed up, he might actually be able to afford a fairly decent apartment on Lake Merritt. And he had his eye on a small railroad-style storefront in a gentrifying area that was attracting a young, hip crowd. It would be the hottest new restaurant in town and people would wait in line for hours just to eat there. He would bestow tables on the most deserving customers and everyone would curry his favor just to be able to say they had eaten at his place. He caught his reflection in the rearview mirror and wondered if he might want to alter his appearance. He could end up being high-profile enough that it might not be a bad idea. He could bleach his hair and eyebrows for starters. He had always thought he'd look good as a blond.

This thought entertained him enough to make the rest of the drive through the godforsaken Central Valley pass by in a blur. He'd call Piper as soon as he got to town. And see what kind of progress she had made in his absence.

CHAPTER 29

Piper tucked an extra sprig of firethorn into her centerpiece, then stood back to admire it. She loved cooking and decorating according to the season; something about the procession of seasons made her feel more alive, more grounded yet more sublime. Along with the firethorn, she had gathered holly, snowberries, and a few beautifully gnarled branches of manzanita with its smooth, crimson bark and sage-colored, medallion-shaped leaves. She had set the rest of the table with care, too, in wintry shades of scarlet and ivory and soft charcoal gray, wanting to make this brunch special for Axel. He had had such an emotionally wrenching week. It was hard to believe he had been away only a week, she had missed him so much. For some reason, his absence had instilled an anxiousness in her that she couldn't identify.

The doorbell rang then and she ran to the door. Axel snatched her up in a crushing embrace and murmured in her ear that he had missed her like crazy. A sudden wave of desire seized her so strongly that she almost dragged him up to her bedroom, but she didn't want to burn the cheese strata she had baking in the oven. Instead, they made out feverishly in the foyer for several minutes until the timer went off in the kitchen.

"Hold that thought," she said, smiling, as she pulled him behind her, clinging tightly to his hand. He looked tired and stressed, she noted, and she resolved to do whatever she could to comfort him.

She seated him at the breakfast bar and poured him a glass of champagne into which she dropped an ice cube of frozen strawberry puree. She had picked and frozen the strawberries last spring—such a refreshing treat during the short, dark days of winter.

"How's your mother?" she asked.

"She's doing better," he said. He took off his coat and slung it over one of the bar stools. "She still hasn't regained the use of the muscles on her right side, but her doctor thinks that she'll be able to make at least a partial recovery over time."

"That's good. I'm sure it was such a comfort to have you there."

"Oh, yeah." Axel took a large swallow of his champagne, practically emptying his glass.

Poor thing. She could tell how upset he was. "So, were you able to celebrate Thanksgiving?"

He shrugged. "Sure. You know. We managed."

"That's good. I had a fun time with the family of one of my students." She smiled at him. "Though I missed you terribly."

"Great." Axel drained his glass. "So how are things going with the funds you're helping me out with?"

Piper blinked. That wasn't the response she had been expecting. "My financial advisor is working on it. Some investments are more liquid than others. Why? Is there a problem with your other investors?"

He grimaced as she reached over to refill his champagne flute. "Oh, not really. I mean … well, maybe."

"What's going on?"

Axel glared at her, startling her. "Can we please not talk about this right now?"

"Sure," she stammered. Wasn't he the one who brought it up? And if she was going to be loaning him this much money, shouldn't she be able to talk to him about it?

He must have noticed her expression because he wiped his face with a trembling hand and sighed. Then he reached over and squeezed her wrist. "I'm sorry, sweetheart. I'm just dealing with a lot right now."

Her heart melted. She came around the counter and put her arms around him. "Of course you are. I'm sorry."

He practically crushed her in return. "The only two things I have going for me right now are you and this restaurant," he muttered. "I just—I just want this to work out so much."

Piper reached up and stroked the back of his head. He had such gorgeous, thick hair. "It will, I just know it will, sweetheart," she murmured.

Axel relaxed his hold to furtively wipe a tear from his eye. "Too much emotional overload, I guess," he said ruefully.

"Well, it's not surprising. Here, let me refill your glass." She disentangled herself and grabbed the champagne bottle.

She made an effort to keep the conversation light for the rest of the morning. Axel seemed to enjoy the brunch she had made, but he appeared distracted in a way that didn't seem like him. She wondered if his mother was worse than he was letting on. Or if his concern about his restaurant was overshadowing everything. She needed to call her financial planner and see if he couldn't speed things up a bit.

She had hoped that they might make love after brunch, but he told her that he needed to leave, that he had to go check out some leads. Her obvious disappointment apparently put pressure on him that she didn't intend; after taking in her fallen face, he told her brusquely that while he got his restaurant up and going, she couldn't expect as much from him as before.

"I—I'm not expecting anything," she said, taken aback. "I just … have hopes. We all have hopes, right?"

His expression softened. "Of course. I'm sorry, Piper." He reached over and caressed her cheek. "This was wonderful and I appreciate it so much."

"You're welcome." Piper made a valiant effort not to let her hurt show.

He grabbed his coat and she walked with him to the foyer. "You'll let me know as soon as you know something about the money?" he asked.

"Absolutely," she said.

"Thanks. I owe you big time." He gave her a quick kiss before turning up his collar and heading out to his car. High, thin clouds covered the sky, making the wintry light even weaker. Was that what plunged her into such a funk when she closed the door? It had been overcast for several days, yet no rain had come. It had been rather gloomy.

As she stood pondering, she reasoned that it was not surprising that Axel was testy and on edge. She tried to put herself in his place and felt tremendous sympathy for him. She remembered how anxious she had felt when she set up her herbal practice, wondering if enough people would come that she could make a living. Trying to run a small business wasn't easy and there were all kinds of hidden costs. This was going to be his first restaurant, and they were notoriously difficult to make successful—of course he was not going to be at his best. Not to mention the added stress of his mother's health. This was the first time he'd been anything other than overwhelmingly attentive and sweet. She should give him a break.

She cleaned up the breakfast dishes and then decided to take a walk in the woods to center herself. Nothing soothed her more than nature, and at times like these, when she felt disheartened, she could always count on the devas to comfort her. She hesitated for a moment, thinking about the feeling of fear she had experienced while collecting chanterelles and her conversation with Carla and Halil. No doubt it was foolhardy to go into the woods alone. But she had been exploring and walking these woods for years now, and she had never experienced anything frightening or disturbing before. She had never heard of anything untoward happening in this forest, either. In all truth, she was probably safer in the woods than she was in downtown Incident.

So she put on her cloak, a scarlet one that a friend of hers had made, a woman in her woman's group, which she had been neglecting lately now that she was seeing Axel. She made a mental note to remedy that. In her backyard, the devas came out to greet her, wearing their winter garb as well, fuzzy seed pods forming the sleeves to their jackets, hollow gourds for hats, supple lichen for skirts and breeches. In the weak, chilly light, they seemed especially ethereal and the light they gave off all the brighter. Some flew over to kiss her on the cheek, giving her the most delectable shiver. She thanked them and told them what a joy they were. They glowed even more brightly.

In the woods, more devas appeared, clothed in pinecone bracts, acorn caps, and moss, vermillion berries serving as buttons and accents. She felt honored; the forest devas often hibernated during the winter months. In a couple of weeks, they no doubt would be. The way they crowded around her made her think that they sensed her to be upset, but there seemed to be an intensity to their energy that she didn't think quite merited the circumstances. Yes, she was feeling melancholy, but in general, things were fine. Wonderful, even. Which was why, to be honest, she didn't quite understand her melancholy.

As she walked, she took a different path than the one that had taken her to the chanterelles, and she saw nothing more than some bear scat and a blue jay that scolded her for simply being there, as near as she could determine. The air smelled crisp and musty, like fallen leaves and hoar frost. Apart from the harsh cries of the jay, the forest lay silent. She thought about the times that she had run into Carson and Jessie; she sure wouldn't mind running into them today. But she didn't.

After awhile, she turned around. Olivia had invited her over for a glass of wine this afternoon, wanting to discuss options for managing her father's blood pressure, offering to pay her for a consultation. But Piper wouldn't hear of it. If she couldn't actually meet with her dad, she didn't feel comfortable charging for a visit. But she was happy to help any way she could.

When she returned home, she put a little time into packaging up some teas and tinctures, then tended to her houseplants, sweet things that they were. As she drove over to Olivia's, the skies darkened even more. Some rain would be nice, but as cold as it was, snow wasn't out of the question. She found a parking place on the street and walked up the stairs to Olivia's apartment, noting that the stairwell smelled like citrus, probably from a citrus-based cleaning product. She appreciated the fact that most of Incident was on board with nontoxic cleaning supplies. Interestingly, Incident had been identified recently as a cancer oasis; cancer rates in the county were three times lower than the national average.

Olivia opened the door when she knocked, and another scent wafted out into the hallway: baked apples and cinnamon.

"Come in! Welcome!" she said, as she gave Piper an enthusiastic hug. Piper smiled, thinking how much different her hugging style had become after a couple of months in Incident. "Let me take your wrap. Wow, this is a beautiful cloak!"

"Thanks, a friend made it for me," Piper told her as she handed it to her, savoring, as she always did, the lovely, soft wool.

"Come on in to the kitchen—I made some apple blossoms and some mulled wine."

"Sounds heavenly," said Piper. And it did, too. She realized how desperately she needed some nurturing right now.

She took a seat at Olivia's kitchen table, which was painted sable brown, although she noticed that Olivia had added some decorations to the apron, some watch gears and small metal rosettes which gave it a distinctive, retro tech look. "What did you use to attach your decorations to your table?" she asked, as Olivia filled a cup for her with a dipper and set it before her. The fragrant steam that rose up from it warmed her all the way to her toes.

"Silicone caulking," she said. "This is a new direction for me—decorating."

"Well, keep it up!" Piper grinned at her and raised her cup in a salute."Thanks," Olivia laughed, serving herself a cup before setting down two small plates bearing apple pastries and joining Piper at the table.

They chit-chatted and snacked for a while before getting to the topic of Olivia's father. She seemed a little apprehensive about bringing it up, so Piper finally broached the subject.

"Tell me about your dad's health situation," she said. "How's he doing?"

Olivia sighed. "Well, he's doing better. He improved immediately after quitting his medication. I've learned that this medication interferes with the P450 cytochrome pathway, which, as you probably know, is one of the main mechanisms for producing ATP in the cell."

Piper nodded. She had studied cytochrome systems while obtaining her degrees in botany and herbology. They were part of what was known as an electron transport system. As electrons bounced down the molecules in the electron transport pathway, molecules of ATP, the energy currency of the cell, were generated and used by the cell for metabolic work. Nothing could happen without it.

"I'm guessing that some people must have alternate pathways to cover this loss, or perhaps they have more cytochrome P450 than others do, and therefore, they're able to tolerate this and not have too many side-effects. But for my dad, it was starving his muscles of the energy they need, and he's been experiencing muscle pain, weakness, and wasting."

Piper felt a little horrified by this list of side-effects, but kept her face neutral though sympathetic.

"He's feeling better, but he's still experiencing some of these effects, and the new medication his doctor prescribed doesn't seem to be as effective. I started some research on herbal alternatives, but there's a lot of information out there, and it's just not my area of expertise. I wondered if you could point us in some directions to try."

Olivia looked so distressed as she spoke that Piper couldn't resist reaching over and squeezing her wrist. She felt a twinge of sadness, wondering what it would be like to have such a close, caring relationship with her own dad as Olivia obviously had with hers. "You know what? I'll write some things down," she said, reaching for her purse and pulling out her note pad and pencil. "Tincture of reishi mushroom is good, as is tincture of dandelion. The dandelion serves as a mild diuretic and also contains a lot of vitamin K, which is important since a lot of herbal remedies for hypertension have blood-thinning properties. Hawthorn berries and flowers will help keep his diastolic down, and coenzyme Q would be good not only for his hypertension, but also to help repair some of the muscle damage."

Quite a few remedies existed, actually, and she wrote them down in order of what she considered to be most promising. Hibiscus tea, pomegranate juice, and beet root powder all had hypotensive properties, and there was a device that helped people to slow their breathing down, which often resulted in lower blood pressure. Fish oil, garlic supplements, and olive leaf had all been used with good results. And wheat germ oil and cod liver oil would help with his muscle problems.

As Olivia watched her write, she commented, "Considering how serious some of the side-effects of these drugs are, it's surprising that these remedies aren't tried first before resorting to something as powerful as a drug." Piper gave her a sardonic smile. "Well, yeah, I know. It's about money. Not health." She exhaled heavily.

"The day that the profit motive becomes secondary to other, more humane motives will be a beautiful day," Piper observed. "I don't know if it's at all possible, but I love to imagine that world."

"No kidding." Olivia paused while Piper finished up her list, then said, "I sure had fun at Carson and Merilee's house for Thanksgiving."

Piper grinned widely. "I did, too. It was so lovely of Merilee to invite me."

"Yeah. And Carson is such a lovable guy. He seems to be struggling with some issues right now. But I think his heart is in the right place. I can tell that Merilee adores him."

"I don't know him all that well, but he does seem like a sincere person. And good-hearted, like you say."

"He—he sure seems to like you."

Piper lifted her eyebrows. "You think so?" She felt her cheeks flush. The last thing she wanted to do was interfere with Olivia's relationship. "I'm not sure about that."

"Oh, I'm sure."

Piper gave a light laugh. "Well, I can tell he's crazy about you. As well he should be."

Olivia gave her a long look. "If the truth be known, it's more like a brother-sister relationship."

"Is it?" Piper searched Olivia's eyes for any signs of pain that this confession might have elicited, relieved that she didn't see any.

"Yes. But it's sweet. Nicer than I would have thought. You're seeing that guy who manages Buffington's, aren't you? I would imagine there are some pretty intense sparks flying there." Olivia's expression was friendly and kind, but for some reason, her words caused tears to well up in Piper's eyes.

Olivia's eyebrows immediately bunched together in regret and concern. "I—I'm sorry," she said. "Are you having problems?"

Piper grabbed her napkin and wiped her eyes. Olivia reached across the table and clasped her free hand. Piper shook her head in embarrassment and tried to laugh. "Oh, just a bump in the road," she said. "It had to happen sometime."

"I suppose." Olivia's voice was soft with concern. "I mean … I hate to stereotype people but sometimes I think that guys who are as handsome as he is might not be the most sensitive meter in the lab."

Piper smiled at her metaphor. "Oh, he just has a lot going on in his life right now. He's starting up his own restaurant and his mom just had a pretty bad stroke."

Olivia nodded. "Well, that could do it."

"Most of the time, he's the most loving, romantic, thoughtful guy in the world."

Olivia's expression cleared. "That's good to hear. You deserve someone who's good to you, Piper."

Olivia's kindness touched her deeply and cheered her a great deal. "Thank you, Olivia. I appreciate that."

"No problem." Olivia let go of her hand and asked if she'd like a little more mulled wine. Piper thought that sounded like a wonderful idea.

As they chatted about other things, she suddenly remembered that she knew an herbal practitioner who had set up a practice in Northampton, Massachusetts after graduating. They had stayed in sporadic touch over the years. She fetched her notebook once again and wrote herself a note. "I just remembered I have a friend and colleague who practices not too far away from where your parents live," she said. "When I get home, I'll email you her contact information."

"That would be wonderful! Thank you!"

"My pleasure entirely," she responded, letting her gaze rest fondly on Olivia. What a lovely person she was. Carson was an idiot not to be madly in love with her, in her opinion. But then, love was a funny thing. Why had she been so attracted to all the guys who had broken her heart? Marion's observation that she had terrible taste in men intruded into her thoughts then, creating unease. Had she done it once again with Axel?

She firmly pushed these thoughts away. One bad day didn't mean squat. If anything, he proved that he was human, that he trusted her enough to let her see him when he wasn't at his best. And for that, she told herself, she should feel grateful.

CHAPTER 30

arson clenched his teeth while his student fumbled his way through the piece Carson had given him to learn at his last lesson. Clearly, he hadn't practiced. At all. Which was fine, to be honest. It wasn't as if his life or even livelihood depended on it. He was a student. But the kid was wasting not only Carson's time but his time as well. All he was interested in was being famous someday and making a lot of money, which was so deluded and so sad. Carson could tell him how that would turn out, but Noah didn't want to hear it. He clearly thought that Carson was a loser but he was not.

Carson sighed, blocking out the jumbled, busy visuals that the poorly executed piece was generating. To be honest, he remembered thinking the same thing when he was just starting out. And now, trying to figure out what to say to Noah that wouldn't piss him off but wouldn't make Carson feel like some kind of pushover, he realized that in fact, he had not revised his life's goals since he was eighteen, the same age as Noah here.

The even sadder thing was, his previous student, a young woman from China, worked her ass off and was incredibly talented. And she didn't necessarily have any better chance of making a living as a musician than Noah did. People loved music, but they didn't want to pay for it. He wasn't sure how they thought musicians would be able to practice and perform enough to be good enough to listen to if they had to do other things to pay the bills. But that never seemed to factor into their thinking. Most, like Noah, thought there was a fortune to made as a rock star. For a handful, maybe. But not for the vast majority. Even big names could get totally screwed by their record label.

He finally couldn't stand it any more and held up his hand. He was annoyed, but was that the best way to teach Noah something? Anything? "OK, let's stop here and analyze what's hanging you up."

Noah let his hands fall to his lap, his expression sullen. "The piece sucks, man. That's what's hanging me up."

"Okay, well, tell me why it sucks."

Noah shrugged. "It just does. It's not my thing." Echoes of Evan, Carson thought, anger flaring reflexively. But he didn't want this kid to make him lose his cool.

"No, come on, analyze it," Carson said. "Is it too repetitive? Do you not like the melody? Do you think it's too busy, not enough variation in rhythm or chord structure? What?"

Noah remained quiet for so long that Carson figured he was not going to answer. But finally he said hesitantly, "It … it doesn't look right when I play it."

Carson froze. Did Noah have synesthesia? "Can you explain that a little more for me?"

Noah avoided Carson's eyes. "It starts out okay. But then it blows everything out. Everything falls apart and I can't follow it."

"You mean musically?"

"I guess."

Carson decided what the hell, he was going to probe, ask some leading questions. He remembered the first time he shared his synesthesia with his class in fourth grade. Everyone laughed at him, told him he was crazy. That was the first time he realized that not everyone saw sound the same way he did. Only his teacher took him seriously. But when he told his parents what happened, his dad was thrilled, bursting with pride, which totally made it okay. Made it special, even. He wondered what kind of experience Noah had had. "So … what do you see when you play this piece?" he asked.

Noah's head shot up. He searched Carson's eyes, and when he was evidently satisfied with what he saw, he said, "At first I see these dark blue shapes floating around that remind me of a spinnaker or something like that. They're really great. But then I get into this part here—" he pointed at the chart "—and they just collapse, like all the air goes out of them. It's really … um, just …" he gazed helplessly at Carson.

"It looks wrong," he said softly.

"Yes! It looks wrong. It feels bad."

Carson nodded. "Okay, well, look, how much do you know about synesthesia?"

"Jack shit, man. What the hell is synes-whatever?"

Carson took a deep breath and explained the phenomenon to him. Clearly, Noah had met with nothing but ridicule from everyone he had tried to share it with, including his parents. His dad sounded like a major dick, actually, which made Carson feel sorry for him. But which was worse, to have a dick for a dad, or to have a really great dad who died when you needed him most?

As he spoke, he could see Noah's defensiveness soften a little. He told him that it was a really special gift, one that he could use for his music. He said that in his experience, it was better to keep what he saw to himself in most cases, unless he knew the person well and trusted him or her.

"But listen, let me know what looks right to you and what doesn't," he said, wrapping up his discussion. "I can work with you on this. Tell me more about what you like."

Noah said he would think about it. He seemed to need

some time to digest everything Carson told him. Carson didn't necessarily expect miracles or for Noah to become a model student, but he did hope that maybe he could help him to not feel like a freak. He would leave the whole rock star thing alone for now. People didn't like having their fantasies challenged. He should know.

After his lesson with Noah, Carson drove home to pick up his keyboard and amp for the gig that he had in Yreka this evening. It was a solo gig at the College of the Siskiyous, a junior college. His mom was at work, Jessie hanging out in the front yard. She came to the car to greet him, tail wagging as he opened the door and patted her on the head.

"Hey, girl," he said, grateful for her loyalty and love. Dogs were, in his opinion, superior to most humans emotionally. Including himself, he thought somewhat guiltily, remembering his interaction with Olivia the day after Thanksgiving. Maybe it wasn't fair to push her to keep seeing him. But he just couldn't bear the thought of not having her in his life right now. Not after Evan. And why was he thinking so much about his dad these days, feeling his absence so acutely? He had thought he was over that loss, that he had moved on. It was his mom who couldn't let go. Lately, though, it seemed as if they had reversed their roles.

He gathered up everything he needed for his gig, Jessie following him around, which comforted him. He was beginning to suspect he might have picked Jessie up from the shelter for himself as much as for his mom. All of a sudden, in the middle of zipping up the bag to his keyboard, he found himself crying. He sank into a nearby chair, wondering what the hell was going on. Jessie sat down beside him, poking her nose into his hand, giving him a lick. He petted her absentmindedly.

Well, for starters, he reflected, he didn't have any idea where he was headed or where he even wanted to head. The producer was really liking the scoring he was doing, but he didn't see any other jobs like that on the horizon. And it could take this guy years to get his next project funded and to the stage of needing a soundtrack—assuming he wanted the same sound, which he might not. Carson was realizing that he just wasn't the kind of guy to hustle his ass off, the way he now knew most successful bands and musicians did. When he was younger, he assumed that talent and dedication would be enough. But teaching today, being reminded of his youthful dreams and just how short he had fallen, he felt depressed. He needed to replace those fantasies with something more attainable but even that thought depressed him.

Still, if he wanted to get anywhere at all, he needed to do something different than he had been. He had been drifting, mourning his losses, wanting to blame other people, like the business manager who killed his label, like Evan … like his dad. If only his business manager hadn't taken all the label's money, he might be making a living now as a musician; if only his dad hadn't died, his life would have been so much better and happier and so much more successful. If only the world weren't so fucked up, if only jerks weren't the only ones who seemed to get ahead … if only women like Piper didn't have their heads completely up their asses when it came to men.

He stood up angrily and finished zipping his keyboard case with a savage tug. Where the hell did that last come from? He tried to put these thoughts from his mind as he drove up I-5 to Yreka, but because he had only himself for company, they returned as he drove past Shasta Lake, its striped, russet banks exposed from years of drought, an ugly bathtub ring. What did he want? What did he want his life to look like ten years from now? Fifteen? Twenty? Did he want to be fifty years old, still living with his mom, never having found his soul mate, never having accomplished anything he felt truly proud of? His music was important, yes, but it wasn't the only thing that made life worth living. He wanted good friends, he wanted family … an unbidden image of holding an infant son came into his mind's eye, devastating him with the yearning it produced. His dad's death had made him think he never wanted to have a family, that he couldn't bear to take that chance emotionally. What if something happened to his son or daughter? Could he handle it? And could he be the kind of father his dad was to him? Did he have it in him?

Mt Shasta loomed into view then, a recent storm having coated the massive twin peaks with thick snow, smoothing out the rugged features and making them look as creamy and inviting as a Matterhorn pastry. But a snowboarder had died on the mountain only two days ago, bringing the yearly death total up to three so far. In the summer, a climber got stuck in a storm near the peak and altitude sickness caused his brain to swell so much that he died before he could get down; and a couple of months ago, a father of two in his fifties had fallen through the crust concealing a fissure and broken his neck. Temperatures were warming, so the ice pack wasn't as stable as it had been in times past.

In fact, a few years ago, he wouldn't have even booked this gig, as the chances of running into heavy snow would have made his chances of arrival iffy. Yreka lay to the north of Mt. Shasta, which served as a magnet for even the tiniest scrap of weather nearby. Mt Shasta and Mt Washington in New Hampshire were tied for having the most unpredictable and violent weather in the contiguous United States. His dad liked to tell him that. They had attempted to summit not long before he died, but a storm had moved in and prevented them from going above 11,000 ft. The fog was so dense they had to just sit in their tent and tell each other stories until it lifted enough to allow them safe passage down. They were both disappointed, but they vowed to try again. Which they never did, of course.

Once he reached the college, he parked in a visitor's spot, grabbed his equipment, and headed for the music department to meet with his contact. His liaison was a music teacher, the guy he had booked the gig with, a young adjunct professor named Scott.

When Scott saw Carson walking through the door to the music department office, his face lit up. He jumped up from his desk and hurried to grasp Carson's hand with both of his. Carson hastily set down his keyboard and amp so he could accommodate him. "Carson!" he exclaimed. "I can't tell you what an honor this is."

Carson batted his compliment away, then told him how much he appreciated his support.

"No, seriously, man," Scott said, his pale, freckled face earnest. "The solo work you're doing is nothing short of brilliant. Maybe the unwashed masses can't see it, but …"

Carson actually felt himself blushing. "Well, I sure appreciate your comments, man," he said. "It can feel a little lonely sometimes."

Scott nodded. "I hear you. Let me just say how much I—and everyone else in the department, whom I expect will all be coming to your performance—appreciate the fact that you keep making music. Here, let me take one of those," he said, as he picked up Carson's amp, "and I'll show you to the auditorium where you'll be performing."

He led Carson to the main theater stage, showing him where he could set up and what the lighting would consist of. "There's a theater student here who does amazing lighting," he said. "So she'll be taking care of you." He pulled his phone out of his pocket to check the time. "She should be showing up in twenty minutes or so. Let her know if you have any special requests."

"Will do."

"And I'm going to leave you to get situated. If you need anything, call me."

Carson thanked him and spent a few minutes just standing in the middle of the stage after Scott left. The theater smelled the way countless other small theatrical venues smelled, and he wasn't even sure what constituted it. It smelled a tad dusty, a tad like worn fabric, a tad like some kind of electrical discharge.

Truth be known, Scott's compliments had touched him deeply. He would make music no matter what—he had to, he couldn't stop himself—but he honestly did want to share his work and he wanted people to like it. Other people's taste didn't drive his musical choices, but he still always hoped to make a connection, to surprise listeners with something fresh and evocative, to elicit emotions they might not even know the names for or know that they felt.

So he welcomed this chance to perform, and as he set about preparing for the evening, he pondered the ways in which he could make enough money to live on his own without giving up a least a portion of his dreams. Maybe he hadn't been creative enough in his approach to life, he mused. Maybe he had been too passive, too content to adopt conventional dreams. He didn't know what steps he needed to take next, but he did know one thing: It was entirely up to him. And if he failed, he was the only one he could blame.

CHAPTER 31

Checking her email at work, Olivia saw a familiar name, a former colleague from U Mass who had taken a position at UC Berkeley. Ted and she were in the same lab and had worked together on a couple of papers, but once Olivia changed her research focus, their paths had diverged. She had always liked Ted. He was one of the few—the only, to be honest—of her colleagues who didn't trivialize her new direction. In fact, he had found it intriguing. He was emailing today to ask her about her opinion on his methods and materials for his latest 3D genome-mapping study; the rush of gratitude she felt for this mark of respect surprised her and left her feeling morose. If she hadn't switched gears, she might have been teaching at some place as prestigious as Berkeley. Some feelers had been extended during her last year of doctoral research.

Moreover, the initial momentum on her crowdfunding had slowed to a trickle and then stopped. No new contributions had been made in the last week, and her deadline was approaching. If she didn't meet her goal, she would lose all the contributions that had been pledged since this particular venue was an all-or-nothing funding source. She could try another crowdfunder, one that didn't have this policy, but she would lose valuable time and she liked the fact that Experiment.com was limited to funding the sciences. The gap was far too much for her or anyone she knew to cover. She had wracked her brains trying to figure out how to jumpstart her campaign, but this wasn't exactly her forte. She just wanted to do the research; was that so much to ask? For something that could conceivably alter the wellbeing of the entire species? It might even unlock previously unexpressed abilities, such as regenerative ones, like the ability to grow back a limb or organ.

She got back to Ted, who responded right away; he was online, obviously. He thanked her for her reply and asked her how her research was going. She decided not to tell him that she was scrambling for funding, but mentioned that, given her radical new direction, she was raising the money for her work via Experiment.com. She winced a little as she sent her reply, feeling woefully outclassed. Ted had not only received an NSF grant, but he was also getting funded by a well-known genetic engineering company. True to his kind nature, however, Ted wrote back enthusiastically and told her he'd look up her project and see if he couldn't contribute a little.

"Thanks," she wrote back. "How are you liking Berkeley?"

"Loving it!" he wrote. "You should come down for a visit sometime!"

She told him that sounded great and that she'd be back in touch. But when she logged off, she reflected that it might be too painful. She was starting to fear that she had made a terrible mistake. Several of them, actually.

It wasn't just her research. And her position at the least well-regarded campus in the UC system. And her precarious funding. She was feeling horribly, terribly homesick. Because she had never lived anywhere but New England, she couldn't have anticipated how much she was going to miss its familiarity. The scenery was grand out West, but she missed the softness of her home, the rounded mountains, the luscious deciduous forests, even the gentleness of the humidity. The mountains here, while spectacular, of course, were jagged and sharp. There was even a peak in the Cascades named "Broke-off Mountain," for Pete's sake. Most of the trees and shrubs had needles, or tough, prickly leaves, like the live oaks, not exactly inviting to the touch.

But worst of all, she missed her family and could hardly bear to be so far away when her parents were struggling so much. She was worried about her dad's health, but it was her mom who was suffering the most emotionally. Her parents had one of the happiest, most enduring marriages of anyone she had ever known. And even though she was not someone to yearn for children, she was wishing, now, that she could see her nieces more often. As for her sister Emily … well, they had gotten closer, bonding over their father's health issues, and now being so far away felt agonizing.

She was even starting to miss Grant, that insufferable egomaniac.

She glanced at the clock on her computer, thinking that she might call home, but she was meeting Merilee for lunch at a little Mexican place that Merilee loved on the outskirts of town. She would need to leave post haste to make it on time. The experiment with Merilee and Jessie was over now, all the data collected. Unexpectedly, this had dampened Olivia's spirits considerably until she decided that she didn't have to let this relationship go just because the data collection was over. She adored the whole family, Jessie included, and in fact, they felt a little bit like a surrogate family, her West Coast family. She was feeling very glad that Carson had wanted to remain friends.

She grabbed her pea coat and knit cap, slung her purse over her shoulder, and headed for the faculty parking lot. The day was cold and drizzly, which she liked, as it reminded her of Massachusetts. And she knew how much this part of the world needed the rain. As she drove, she pondered her professional status. It wasn't out of the question, she supposed, that she could pick up her old research. She could expect to get some decent funding if she did, even though, at this point, with the field filling up, her contributions wouldn't be as groundbreaking as her doctoral research. And it might not be a good fit with Incident, but she could apply to other positions at other universities next spring. She just hadn't reckoned on how much she depended on having a good, solid research situation. Without it, she felt adrift.

When she arrived at Carmelita's, she noticed Merilee's car parked in the lot. She hurried inside where she found Merilee seated in a cozy corner. Merilee's face broke into a wide smile when she saw Olivia, and she gave her an enthusiastic wave. Returning her smile and wave, Olivia made her way to the table and leaned down to give her a hug. Merilee liked to scent herself with essential oils, and today she smelled like orange blossoms.

"How lovely of you to suggest lunch, Olivia!" Merilee exclaimed.

Olivia shrugged out of her coat and draped it over her seat, stuffing her cap inside one of the sleeves. "It was a rather good idea, if I do say so," Olivia laughed. "Somehow it doesn't seem right that Jessie isn't here, though."

Merilee nodded. "I'll be sure to take her home a treat." She paused. "So tell me, how is your crowdfunding going? I can't wait to hear!"

Olivia grimaced. "Oh, it's going. I've hit a bit of a plateau. But I'm sure it'll pick up soon." She didn't want Merilee to think that she should donate. "How is your latest craft project going? Carson told me you're working on a quilt?"

"Yes, it's for a baby, actually. But I didn't tell Carson that. I don't want to put any pressure on him."

She gave Olivia a wink, startling her. Why was she telling her this? Was she hoping that she and Carson might get together and have a family? She definitely didn't see that happening, even if Carson weren't in love with someone else. Should she tell Merilee this? It didn't seem right to let her nurture false hopes. But what an awkward conversation to have.

The waitress appeared then to ask her if she wanted anything to drink, giving her a temporary reprieve. As she ordered an horchata, her gaze roamed the room. It was a popular place, despite being out of the way; it was packed. She noticed someone she recognized, so she took a closer look. Why, it was Piper's boyfriend, Axel! But he must not be with Piper, or Merilee would have pointed her out so she could say hello. A tall man was seated in her line of sight so she couldn't see his companion without craning, which she did, curious to see who it was. She was hoping it would be another guy, but it was a woman. An older woman, old enough to be his mother, actually. That must be who it was, she decided. His mom. But then he picked up her hand and kissed it … tenderly, gazing into her eyes with an unmistakable smolder. Her jaw dropped. Was this why Piper said they were going through a rough patch? But if he had Piper, why on Earth would he be with this other woman?

"What is it? Something wrong?" Merilee craned her neck as well, following Olivia's shocked stare.

Olivia immediately turned back around. She didn't want Axel to see her—and Merilee—staring at him. Should she tell Merilee? "I—I'll tell you later. At any rate, back to your quilt. Are you going to sell it or put it in a hope chest?"

Merilee settled back in her chair, her expression a little crestfallen. She must not have missed Olivia's deflection. "I'm not sure. I'm just having fun with it at the moment."

"Well, I love what you do with fabric," Olivia said. "I should commission you to make me a quilt, now that I think about it."

"That would be a blast!" Merilee exclaimed.

"I'm thinking something kind of offbeat, sort of Steampunk."

Merilee nodded eagerly. "I'm already starting to get ideas," she said.

They chattered away for the rest of the meal, which was excellent. Olivia ordered chilaquiles with a side of creamy guacamole, while Merilee had fish tacos with a yummy-looking jicama slaw. Mexican food wasn't all that common back East, and Olivia had always loved it.

Near the end, she noticed Axel leaving with his date. She was relieved to have him gone. His presence was distracting and she was feeling terrible for Piper. Should she tell Piper? Maybe she already knew?

Once home, she followed through on her earlier impulse to call her parents. Her mother answered the phone, sounding distressed. Olivia asked her what was going on.

"Oh, we just can't seem to get your father's blood pressure under control," she said. "The herbalist that you recommended is away on a seminar, and won't be available until after the holidays. And we—we just don't know which of the herbs to take. There are a lot of them, and we don't know about side-effects or interactions. We were thinking that maybe David should get back on his old blood pressure medication." She lowered her voice. "I'm terrified that he might have a stroke or a heart attack."

A shock of electricity stabbed Olivia's heart. "How high is it?" she asked.

"Well, his last reading was 168 over 90."

Olivia let her breath out. "Mom, that's not that high. Over time those readings would be a problem, but in the short term, I don't think he's risking a stroke or anything."

"But our understanding is … after all, they call it the silent killer, right?"

"Listen," Olivia interrupted. "I'm coming home. Tonight."

"What? You don't need to do that, honey."

"Yes," Olivia said firmly. "I do." She walked over to her desk where she had her laptop plugged in and flipped it open. "I actually probably won't get there until tomorrow, but I'm taking the first red eye I can get."

Her mother was silent for a moment. Then Olivia heard a sniffle. "It sure would be great to have you here, sweetheart." Her voice broke on the last word.

"I'll fly into Boston and rent a car. I'll call you back as soon as I know my plans, okay?"

"All right. Thank you so much, honey."

"I love you, Mom. I'll see you soon."

As soon as she hung up, Olivia went to her favorite ticketing service and started scrolling through her options. She would have to drive down to Sacramento to get a flight, and with the sorry state of the airline industry, no way could she get a direct flight from Sacramento to Boston, but it didn't matter. Her parents needed her. And she needed them.

CHAPTER 32

Axel glanced outside as he reviewed his seating chart for lunch reservations, then did a quick double take. Holy fuck, was that Amanda standing outside, scrutinizing the menu? Panicked, he scoured the floor to see which waiters and waitresses were available, settling upon Sharona, who had just delivered her orders to a table of middle-aged matrons. Keeping his back to the door, praying that Amanda wouldn't come barging in before he covered his ass, he motioned Sharona urgently to the wait station.

She followed him there, her eyes questioning.

"Sharona, I need you to cover for me."

"But—I have two extra tables," she said. "Jason didn't show up this morning and we haven't been able to get anyone else to fill in."

Axel raised his fist to his mouth and pretended to gag. "I wouldn't ask except that I seem to be coming down with some kind of horrible stomach bug."

Sharona took a step back. "You do look a little green," she said.

Axel held up his hand and lowered his head, feigning another wave of nausea. "I don't want to give this to everyone in the restaurant," he gasped. "And I sure as hell don't want everyone who might get it assuming that they got food poisoning from Buffington's."

"No, that would be awful," Sharona agreed. She appeared to be holding her breath.

"I'm sorry to ask you to do this when we're shorthanded—"

"No, it's okay," she said quickly, eager to get away from him. "I'll be happy to cover for you. You just take care of yourself, all right?"

Axel gave a dry heave. "Thanks so much, Sharona. I owe you."

"Just … go on home. I'll take care of everything, don't worry."

"O-okay," he quavered, then hurried to the men's room where he produced some wretching sounds, flushed the toilet a couple of times, then washed up. Poking his head out, he scanned the restaurant and saw Amanda talking to Sharona, Sharona shaking her head. Thank God for his alias. Not taking any chances, he slipped out the back as fast as he could. He doubted that she saw his car parked in the lot that the Buffington employees used, as it was behind the restaurant in a lot that also housed a couple of backhoes. But he kept turning his head to make sure no one was following him. Satisfied that he was in the clear, he jumped into his car, started it up, and peeled out of the lot as fast as he could without drawing any attention.

The fucking bitch! What the hell was she doing? Trying to track him down, obviously. She had been pressuring him to come up to Mt Shasta, and when he told her he was too busy right now, she started getting insistent about coming down. Why was it women couldn't take "no" for an answer? Christ, he should have never said he loved her. Big mistake. Hell hath no fury and all that shit.

He was so ready to get out of this crap town. It was starting to get smaller and smaller. Just the other day, when he was with one of his cougars at Carmelita's, he spotted a young woman who had dined at Buffington's not long ago. She wasn't any threat—that he knew of—but it seemed that, at this point, it was impossible to go anywhere without running into someone he knew from the bistro. He had been pleased when he got the job at such an upscale place, but now, given its popularity, it was starting to feel like a liability. He needed to get out of here, the sooner the better.

He parked a block away from his apartment building, just in case Amanda was cruising the town, looking for his car. Very few things pissed him off as much as someone prying into his affairs. He hurried inside and locked the door, pulled down all the shades. He surveyed his living room, which he had already started to pack up. He didn't want to move with any more than he could put in his car, but he was torn about the big screen TV. It was a really nice one, and there was no guarantee that he could get another one for that price. Still, it might have to go. His only option for taking it would involve renting a small trailer, and his plan was to swap his car out at a used car lot in Vacaville, the day he left town. Hooking up the trailer to a new car sounded like too much trouble. Well, one thing he had going for him with the demise of the middle class in America was lots of cheap consumer goods. Thank God for Craigslist and unemployment.

Changing into more comfortable clothes, he settled on his couch and called Piper. She answered right away.

"Axel! Are you at work?"

"No," he said, "I was feeling queasy so I'm taking the rest of the day off."

"Poor baby!" she exclaimed. "Would you like me to come over with some essential oils?"

"Thanks, babe, but I wouldn't want to expose you to this." He didn't want her coming over. She'd notice things missing from around the apartment and wonder why. "You're such a sweetheart to offer, though. How are you?"

"I'm good! I should have a check for you on Monday." She seemed to be holding her breath, waiting for his reaction. He needed to make it a good one.

"Oh, Piper, you sweetheart!" he enthused. "You have totally saved the day, you know that?"

"Have I?"

"Yes! Oh my God, we'll need to celebrate. Monday night. I'm fixing you dinner at your place."

"Okay," she said, giggling. She did that when she was happy.

"And champagne! I'll bring champagne!"

"That sounds wonderful," she said. "I'm so happy I could help you, Axel."

"Well, hopefully you'll be helping both of us," he remarked. "Our future together."

"Yes!" She sounded very relieved.

"Listen, I'm going to sign off for now and try to get some rest," he said. "I love you," he told her, in his sexiest voice.

"I love you," she replied fervently. "If you need anything—anything at all—let me know, okay?"

"I will," he said. "You're the best." He hung up, thinking he should crack open a bottle of champagne right now. Tuesday, he should be able to rent the apartment he had his eye on in Oakland. Thanks to his greedy, piece-of-shit father, he would have to wait until he got the check from Piper. He hoped it didn't get snatched up in the meantime. He'd charmed the landlord, he was pretty sure, and got a quasi-promise that she would hold it for him. Although … there was always Ethel's checking account. He had been leaving it alone to assure her the money she needed to pay for her assisted living while he worked on becoming the beneficiary of her will. But he'd given up on the beneficiary idea. There just wasn't enough time, and once he realized the real gold mine was Piper, he'd slacked off on maintaining that relationship. If he were leaving town, though, neither Ethel nor any of her family would be able to track him, so he didn't see any reason not to clean her out. She was old. She might not die in time to help him out, but she didn't have much time left, and she wasn't exactly in a position to enjoy any of that money.

He glanced at his watch. Ethel's bank closed at noon on Saturday, so he wouldn't be able to get any money—he would have to wait until Monday. He'd write himself a check for cash near closing time so that, if any alarm bells were to go off—say Ethel's rent was due the next day—he'd be gone by then.

Already mourning the loss of his big screen TV, he was about to turn it on when there was a knock at the door. He froze. Could it be Amanda? Could she have followed him somehow? He didn't see how, but … he stayed as still as he could, holding his breath. Another knock, this one louder and more insistent. After a while, whoever it was gave up and went away. He stepped cautiously to his window and peered through the slats of his blinds. When he saw a cop car parked out front, a surge of adrenalin rushed through him, sending his heartbeat into the stratosphere. Had Amanda called the police? Had his dad tipped off the cops up here? As far as he knew, his dad didn't have his address, though he could have figured out how to get it. But that didn't make any sense. Why kill the goose that laid the golden egg?

It must be a coincidence, he thought, trying to calm his racing heart. Maybe there was a sex offender in the neighborhood. Maybe someone lost a valuable dog. Maybe there was a burglary and the cops wanted to know if he had seen or heard anything.

At any rate, it was a warning. Time was drawing short and he needed to get the fuck out of here. Tuesday, he decided. He'd cash Piper's check and hit the road. As for Amanda … well, not only was Eric Johnson gone, Axel Smith would soon be gone, too. And before she had any idea what happened, he'd be setting himself up in San Francisco as the newest, hottest restaurateur. With blond hair. And a hot new goatee.

And the ice blue contact lenses he had ordered online.

As he pondered his makeover, his fright turned into excitement. He loved pulling off a good con. Talk about making a person feel alive! It was almost too easy here in Insipid, but still, it had served him well, all things considered. He headed into his kitchen and pulled a bottle of Dom Perignon from his fridge, one that he had filched from the restaurant before the owners had become more attentive. He grabbed a wine glass and the bottle, reseating himself on his sofa.

"Here's to me," he said, holding his glass aloft. Feeling safe now, he switched on his television and tuned to his favorite show, *Keeping Up with the Kardashians*. He didn't care for those women—they were too fat for his taste—but talk about some successful con artists! They were outstanding. He was always open to learning some new tricks here and there. Too bad he couldn't make a reality TV show out of his own exploits. It would make some damned good television. But as it was, he'd just have to enjoy his conquests in private. He poured himself some more champagne. Soon he would be leaving his detritus behind him. And a new, glorious, cosmopolitan start beckoned.

CHAPTER 33

Buoyed by her conversation with Axel the night before, Piper decided to surprise him by taking Marion and Danny to brunch at Buffington's. Axel had sounded like his old self last night, and she smiled, thinking about their future together: Axel a successful restaurateur, bringing in enough money that she could cut back on her teaching and spend time at home raising their family. She thought two children would probably be just right—a boy and a girl, she hoped. Though she wouldn't mind a third. She hadn't broached the subject of children with Axel yet, of course—they hadn't even discussed marriage, and that came first. She was a traditionalist. But if she knew Axel, she knew he would want to be financially secure before proposing. By loaning him the money he needed to get started, she felt proud and excited that she had contributed so meaningfully to the first, important step.

She was meeting Danny and Marion at the bistro, so she wanted to be sure to get there before they did. She decided to leave a little early. Because she was early, she found a parking place right out front. As she locked her car with her electronic key—also known as a plipper, a delightful fact she had learned from a patient the other day—she noticed a bundled-up woman sitting on the bench outside Buffington's, so swathed in what looked like several coats, a knit watch cap, and a thick wool scarf, that Piper could barely make out two eyes that watched her as she approached. People like this weren't often spotted in Incident, due to the robust social services offered throughout the city. But there were a few. The woman had a coffee can next to her with a sign taped to it that said, "Any little bit helps. God bless."

Piper's heart went out to her, so she rummaged around in her purse and dropped a five-dollar bill into the can. She also made a wish for the woman that she would find comfort and security. The woman nodded in acknowledgement of her donation but seemed a little out of it, her gaze wandering. Piper hoped she would be all right. She went inside and immediately spotted Axel helping to bus one of the tables. That was one of the things she loved about him. Some restaurant managers wouldn't stoop to something as lowly as bussing tables, but not Axel. He pitched in wherever he was needed.

She crept up behind him and tapped him on the shoulder, unable to resist giving him a big hug when he turned around. "Surprise!" she said playfully. She knew that she wasn't supposed to embrace him when he was working, but she couldn't help it. And Incident was a huggy town, after all.

His look of consternation softened as soon as he saw who it was. He leaned down and gave her the briefest of kisses on the lips. "What are you doing here?" he asked, taking her chin between his thumb and forefinger.

"I'm meeting Marion and Danny for brunch," she said. "So you get to meet them!"

Axel gave her a big smile. "That's fantastic, sweethert." He squeezed her arm.

"I'm so glad you're feeling better," she said.

He rolled his eyes in agreement. "No kidding! So, would

you like to go ahead and get seated or wait for your friends?"

Piper started to say that she would wait when she heard the bell on the door jingle. She turned to see Marion and Danny waving at her, headed her way. As soon as they reached Piper and Axel, Piper introduced them. Axel was charming, complimenting Danny on his good taste in women while winking at Marion, and giving Danny a strong, firm handshake.

"Likewise," Danny replied, reaching over to yank a tendril of Piper's hair with an affectionate grin.

"Let's see, the best table in the house," Axel announced, looking around the room, then ushering them to his table of choice. Truth be told, there wasn't really a bad table in the restaurant. As Axel smoothly scooted her chair in, Piper noticed the homeless woman through the front window, turning her head quickly as if she had been peering inside but didn't want to be caught doing so. Piper couldn't imagine how awful it would be to have no home nor money, and to have to watch other people eat delicious food with no hope of enjoying it yourself. She decided to order an extra meal to go so that she could give it to the woman as she left.

After Axel left, Marion leaned over to Piper and squealed softly, "Damn, that's a handsome man!"

Piper nodded happily. "Isn't he?"

"He seems to adore you, Piper," Danny said. "As well he should."

"Thanks, you two!" Piper replied. "He's going to be opening his own restaurant soon."

"In Incident?"

"Yes! Sort of like Chez Panisse, except Incident-style."

"That's great!" Marion said. "We'll be sure to go there every week."

"I'll be supplying the culinary herbs." Piper refrained from telling them that she was going to be loaning him the lion's share of money to get started. She just wasn't sure how they would react, and anyway, it would be a lot more fun to tell them when the restaurant was up and running and a huge success, and Axel had paid her back.

"Even better!" laughed Danny.

Piper steered the conversation away from anything professional Danny might have to share, his last story about the murder suspect having given her nightmares. She knew that a lot of people would find her sensibilities overly fragile and precious, but she couldn't help it. Violence upset her terribly. Even thinking about it disturbed her. She would never understand what drove humans to treat each other so horribly, when being kind to each other made everyone feel so good, giver and receiver alike. And how hard was it, seriously? It was a choice. A choice that anyone could make.

So she focused on their baby, and the preparations that they were making for his or her arrival. They were merging their two home offices into one and turning the other into the baby's room so that they would still have a guest room. Marion was having a ball decorating it, even though they were going to wait until the baby was born to find out the sex. She was using non-gender-oriented colors, a creamy light yellow and a pale, cool green, and she had bought some prints from a local artist who made colorful, stylized linoleum prints of animals and flowers.

"And mobiles, of course!" she said. "And a gorgeous lithophane of a lighthouse for a nightlight."

"So enchanting," Piper murmured, thinking about decorating for her own baby when the time came. She had a room in her house that would be perfect. Would Axel want to move into her house? She hoped so. She loved that house and the gardens. To be honest, she really couldn't imagine living anywhere else, but then, Axel was so loving and accommodating … she couldn't imagine that he would object.

The time passed quickly and Axel stopped by a couple of times to check on them and make sure that everything was just right. Near the end of the meal, Piper motioned the waitress over and ordered a breakfast burrito for the homeless woman outside. When Marion and Danny found out what she was doing, they rolled their eyes and shook their heads. But she could see the fondness in their expressions and knew that, even though they thought she was crazy, they loved this side of her.

"If only everyone in the world could be like you," Marion sighed, reaching over to interlace her fingers with Piper's.

"I'd be out of a job," Danny laughed.

They all laughed at that, and when they left, Axel squeezing Piper's fingers tenderly in farewell, Piper stopped by the bench and held out the bag with the burrito in it to the homeless woman.

"Here," she said. "It's a breakfast burrito, freshly made."

Piper felt taken aback when the woman seemed to gaze at her in dismay. Reluctantly, she took the bag and mumbled thanks. But then she hunched into herself, avoiding any more contact.

Marion caught her eye and shrugged. Danny gave her a kiss on the cheek before they parted. Piper didn't have anywhere to be or anything else to do in town, so she drove back home. She hadn't been there long when she heard her doorbell chime.

Wondering who on earth would be stopping by without notice on a Sunday, she went to the door, perplexed to find an unfamiliar young woman on the stoop. Although, there was something familiar about her, something Piper couldn't place. Maybe a student who dropped one of her classes early on?

"Hi, can I help you?" she said.

"I hope I can help you," the woman replied.

"Help me?"

"Yes, may I come in?"

Piper stepped back and opened the door wider. "Sure," she said. "I was just about to put a kettle on for tea. Would you like some?"

The woman shook her head. Piper led her into the kitchen

anyway and put the kettle on to boil. The woman might change her mind, and she would like a cup herself. As she filled the teapot with tea, she snuck a look at the young woman as she seated herself at the kitchen table. She looked upset, that much she could see. But why had she come to Piper?

"So … what have you come to see me about?" Piper hoped it wasn't a sales pitch or religious crusade.

"Eric Johnson."

Piper regarded her in puzzlement.

"Or, as you probably know him, Axel Smith."

Piper gaped at her, trying make sense of what she just said. "I'm sorry. You're mistaken."

The woman shook her head. "No. I'm positive."

"Look—" Piper set the tea pot down, her hands shaking. "I'm sorry, what's your name?"

"Amanda."

"Amanda, I'm Piper." She took a deep breath. "I find it impossible to believe that Axel is anyone besides who he says he is, but why do you think so? And how do you know Axel?"

"We were dating. I live in Mt. Shasta City but I knew him before, in Sacramento."

Piper felt a surge of panic at the word "dating." But then she came to her senses. Axel had never lived in Sacramento. He had moved to Incident from Santa Rosa. "Wait a minute." A realization dawned on her. "Were you the homeless woman outside Buffington's Bistro?"

Amanda nodded.

Oh, dear. She was a stalker. This wasn't good. She seemed unstable. She must have fixated on Axel at some point—not that she could blame her. Piper felt vulnerable all of a sudden. She didn't think this young woman looked violent, but you never knew.

Piper stood up and said gently, "Amanda, I appreciate your desire to enlighten me, but I need to ask you to leave."

Amanda remained seated. "Piper, you need to listen to me!

He's a two-timing bastard! And—and that might not be all!"

Piper folded her arms. "Amanda, please leave. Now. I won't listen to anything else you have to say."

She jumped up, her expression anguished. "Piper—"

Piper took her elbow and escorted her to the door. "I need you to go," she said. She closed the door firmly behind her. She sank down into the hard-backed chair she had in the foyer and covered her face with her hands. She was tempted to call Axel right away and tell him about what happened.

But as she thought about it, she decided she didn't want to upset him. They had such a wonderful milestone to celebrate tomorrow night, she didn't want to spoil it. She could talk to him about it some other time, and she would. He needed to know that someone was out there, stalking him and spreading lies.

CHAPTER 34

Carson allowed himself the luxury of sleeping in, having performed till late at his gig in Incident last night. Buster had located another bass player to sit in on their sets so that they wouldn't have to cancel. He was fine, but he wasn't Evan. Carson sighed and sat up, tossed the covers back. When he put his feet on the hardwood floor, the shock from the cold woke him up instantly.

He padded into the bathroom and took a long piss. He had drunk quite a few beers last night. Olivia didn't come because she was visiting her family back East; her dad wasn't doing too good. He was worried for her, as he could tell that she had a close relationship to her dad. He sounded like a great guy, actually. And her mom sounded cool, too. He wondered what it would be like to move cross country. Sometimes he felt tempted to go someplace completely new and fresh, where he could start over like Olivia had. But she didn't seem all that happy right now. They had talked on the phone while she was waiting for her plane to take off in Sacramento, and she was feeling some heavy regrets about leaving her family and changing her research direction. She was even talking about moving back, which made him feel sad. Even though they weren't in love, she was starting to feel like the sister he never had. When he was a kid, he thought being an only child was fine. But as an adult, he was thinking it would be cool to have a little sister. Probably not a big one, because then she would want to boss him around. But a little sister … friends of his who had little sisters really enjoyed the relationship. For one thing, their sisters generally adored them and totally looked up to them. He wouldn't mind someone looking up to him right now.

After brushing his teeth, he pulled on a pair of jeans and a long-sleeved T shirt and ambled into the kitchen. There he found his mother frying bacon while Jessie lay next to her on the floor. When he came in, she got up and came over to him for some attention while she nuzzled his leg, tail wagging. God, he loved that dog. He wished people could be more like dogs.

The sound of the sizzling bacon produced a pleasant spritz of orange-pink rods that crisscrossed in different planes in his vision. He gave his mom a peck on the cheek and then poured himself a cup of coffee, settling down at the table to let the caffeine complete the job that the cold floor had started. Pearly winter light streamed in the windows, lighting up the fog of frying grease rising from the skillet.

"Late night?" his mother asked.

"Yeah."

"Are you up for some eggs and bacon?"

"I would kill for some."

Merilee laughed. "No need for any of that! It's free for the taking."

Carson laughed, too. His mom had been in such good spirits lately, it really warmed his heart. He liked it when she kidded around. "I'll make the toast," he said.

"That would be wonderful. Thanks, sweetheart."

Carson took another swallow off his coffee, then got up and cut two slices of bread for toast. As soon as his mom placed the bacon on a paper towel and cracked the eggs into the skillet, he put the bread in the toaster.

Neither one of them spoke much as they ate, even though neither one of them was preoccupied with anything else, a newspaper, an iPad, or a phone. It just felt nice to be quiet. After he finished his breakfast, Carson was contemplating how he wanted to spend the rest of his day when his mom fixed him with a pointed stare. Uh-oh. He knew that look.

"So, tell me, sweetheart, what's your and Olivia's status?" she said.

"Our status?" he repeated. Jesus, she made it sound like some social media cliché, even though he was pretty sure she had never spent a minute on Facebook. She wasn't electronically inclined. And neither was he, really, in terms of how he liked spending his free time. He liked using electronics for his music, but apart from that, he liked hanging out in nature, or with friends who would talk to each other face to face. It made him feel old, but when he went to a taco bar or café and saw a crowd of teenagers sitting at a table, every one of them glued to their phones, some of them probably texting each other, he felt completely baffled. Why wouldn't they just talk to each other? He found the expressiveness of the human face awesome. A text was just a bunch of letters on a tiny screen, everyone's looking alike, more or less, and not only devoid of facial expression, but also body language and tone.

"Yes, are you two serious?"

Carson squirmed in his seat. He didn't really think this was any of her business. But as he studied her face in preparing his reply, he saw hope, fear, longing, and love. She wasn't just being nosy, he saw. She cared about him. She wanted him to be happy. And she wanted to feel close to him, feel like she knew him and what was important to him.

He sighed. "Well, not in the way that you mean, Mom," he said, wincing as her face fell. She liked Olivia a lot, he knew that. "But we're really, really good friends. It's almost like having a sister."

When he said that, her face took on a wistful look.

"What?"

"Oh—it's just that your father and I tried for another child. Tried for years. But we weren't ever able to get pregnant again. Something about my endometriosis. It's a miracle, really, that I was able to have you."

Carson hardly felt like a miracle, but her words touched him unexpectedly. He didn't know what to say.

His mother wiped a tear from her eye and reached over to squeeze his hand. "So, you two are like brother and sister. That's pretty wonderful, really. Is there someone else?"

Carson debated whether to open up about his unrequited crush. Then he figured, what the hell. "Actually—" he hesitated then plowed forward, "there is."

His mother's eyebrows scooched up, encouraging him to continue.

"As a matter of fact, I'm—well, I think I'm in love with Piper."

At first she looked surprised, then something seemed to fall into place. "I see. Well, she is an absolutely beautiful girl, inside and out. You've got great taste, son."

"Yeah, well, she's in love with this total dipshit asshole."

"I'm sorry to hear that. I have to say, I've been surprised throughout my life at how many times a sweetheart ends up paired with a jerk. I was so lucky to find your dad." She gazed sadly at the table for a moment, then looked up. "But it might not last, Carson. Have you let her know how you feel?"

He nodded stiffly.

"I see," she murmured. "Well, there's no telling how things might go in the future. Don't give up hope. And in the meantime, don't stop looking."

He gave her a wry smile. "Don't worry, Mom, I'm pretty sure you have grandchildren in your future."

She balled up her napkin and threw it at him. "I wasn't thinking about myself!" Then she gave a helpless laugh.

"Okay, who am I kidding? I am, yes. I would love to have at least one grandchild. But I want to see you happy," she said. "Like your father and I were."

Yeah, and look at how that turned out, Carson thought. He really had not worked out to his satisfaction whether it was better to love deeply and then lose that person or to protect your heart, not open yourself up to that kind of agony in the first place. And seriously, he didn't know what to think about the fact that Piper couldn't see that jerk restaurant manager for what he was. What did that say about her?

But he voiced none of these thoughts. "Thanks, Mom," he said. "I know you do." He got up and gave her a hug. He thought he would head out to his music studio and finish up the work on his score. He would be flying to LA tomorrow to help synch his soundtrack to the final cut and he had a couple of transition passages to compose before then.

But when he got there, he couldn't stop thinking about his mom, and Piper, and Olivia, and his dad. And he thought about Evan, and how much he missed playing with him, and how sad he felt that they were no longer close. On an impulse, he headed back into the house and grabbed his jacket, shouting to his mom that he was going out and would be back later. He jumped in his car and drove over to Evan's place, a mother-in-law unit that he rented from a couple who were both jazz musicians. It was eleven o'clock; he hoped he wouldn't be too early and wake Evan up. He kept even later hours than Carson did.

When he knocked on the door, however, the length of time it took for Evan to answer let him know he had, in fact, gotten him out of bed. A wave of panic hit him as he considered the possibility that he had intruded on something romantic Evan had going on. But when Evan opened the door, sleepy-eyed and rumpled, he motioned him inside, leaving the door open as he turned his back and headed for the kitchen.

"Coffee?" Evan asked as he filled his coffee pot with water

at the sink.

"Sure, thanks." Nervously, Carson wondered if this was such a good idea. He wasn't sure what he wanted or what he thought he might accomplish.

"'Sup?" Evan mumbled, keeping his back to Carson.

Carson weighed the possibility of some banal reply, but then something made him blurt out, "I guess—I guess I just feel bad that we've grown so far apart, man. I don't really understand how it happened."

Evan turned around then and fixed him with a hard stare. "You don't, huh?"

"Not—not really. I mean, I know I left the band and everything, but—"

"Key words," Evan interrupted; "'and everything.'"

Carson swallowed. "What do you mean?"

Evan's eyes blazed. "I mean you checked out, man! You fucking checked out! Yes, it totally sucked that you left the band. We were good, man! We had a chance of making it, goddamn it! But okay. I got it. Your dad died. I never had the kind of relationship with my old man that you had with yours, but I could see how much you guys dug each other. I probably loved him more than my own dad."

Carson blinked. He had never thought about how his dad's death might have affected Evan.

"But what the fucking hell? You move away, you hardly stay in touch at all. You only came back because your label crashed, and then you waltz in here and think you're just going to take up where you left off? What did you think, that we were all supposed to go into suspended animation and wait for you, the great Carson Duran to make his exalted return?"

Carson didn't know how to respond. All of this was news to him. And yet, as he digested what Evan had to say, he could see the truth in it. His grief had made him blind. Finally, he stammered, "I—I'm sorry, man."

Evan glared at him, then poured the water from the coffee

pot into the coffee maker, sloshing water onto the counter. "Whatever," he muttered, shoving the pot into place.

Carson stood up and took Evan's arm so that he would look him in the eye. "No, I mean it. I'm really sorry. I—I was just … self-centered. You're right."

Evan didn't reply, but Carson thought he saw his gaze soften.

"God, I just—I'm sorry. You were there for me, man. You were. I know. I just—it never occurred to me how my dad's death might affect you."

Evan blinked back tears, wrenching Carson's heart. "I lost you, man. When I lost my favorite father figure, I lost my best friend."

Carson sighed heavily. He sat down in the nearest chair. He wasn't sure how much more of this emotional intensity he could handle. But this was his idea, coming over here.

Finally, he said, "Well, I was wrong. And I was a jerk." He fiddled with the hangnail on his thumb that he had been worrying for weeks now. "I—I don't know how to make it up to you …"

Evan waved off his words.

"But I guess all I can do is be a better friend now."

Hope and doubt chased each other across Evan's face.

"Are we friends?"

Evan ran his hands through his hair and groaned. "Yes, okay. Sure."

"I swear to God, Evan, I want to make this right. You've always been my best friend. I guess I just took it for granted. I've really missed you."

Evan didn't reply for a moment. Then he gave him a mischievous grin. "I thought you didn't believe in God."

Carson laughed. "I don't." He nudged Evan's foot with his. "Don't get all quibbly with me, now."

"Quibbly? What the hell kind of word is that?"

"It's my word. And it's a damned good one." Carson smiled

in relief as they fell into their old habit of bantering. He knew that he had a ways to go before earning Evan's trust again. But he was determined.

He stayed while Evan made himself a piece of toast for breakfast. They chatted about music, and Evan told him about a jazz opera that he was writing; Carson told him about the score he was writing for the documentary. Evan also told him that Zach's recording studio was finally up and running again, but it was too late for Carson to get anything out for Christmas. Still, the hopefulness he felt in taking the first steps in mending his friendship with Evan buoyed him considerably. And when he left, he felt fifty pounds lighter.

CHAPTER 35

Olivia took her time moseying through downtown Amherst, keeping an eye out for Christmas presents for her family in storefront windows. Fluffy snow was falling, adding to the few inches that had accumulated before she arrived, crunching underfoot. Shop owners had dressed up their windows with sprigs of holly, scarlet ribbon, and twinkly lights, giving her a cozy, familiar feeling in the dim afternoon light. This was another thing she hadn't considered about her new home: Christmas was going to not feel like Christmas at all. Incident shops were decorating for the holidays, of course, but with no snow in the forecast—snow was rare in northern California, except for the mountains—it would be hard to get in the mood. Olivia was thinking about coming back during her holiday break, even though that meant she'd be flying back here only a couple of weeks after her return to Incident.

She had arrived in the wee hours of Friday morning, renting a car at the Boston airport and driving home, arriving just in time for breakfast. She had stopped by Piper's house as she left town for Sacramento, for some herbs to give her father, not remembering until she was already halfway to the airport that she had forgotten to bring her own herbs that were helping her to sleep soundly. No nightmares last night, though, for which she was grateful. Perhaps she was past that. It could have been a temporary after-effect of her accident in Pennsylvania on her drive cross country; so maybe she was in the clear. She hoped so.

She saw the latest book by Malcolm Gladwell in the window of the bookstore, which she knew her father would enjoy reading, so she stopped inside to pick up a copy. They often had notecards, too, that her mother liked. And she thought her sister would enjoy Sebastian Barry's novel, *The Secret Scripture*. She had read it on her Kindle on the flight, one of the first novels she had read in years. While she was perusing the stacks, someone tapped her on the shoulder. She turned around to see her high school biology teacher, Mrs. Hardin, beaming at her.

"Olivia!" she exclaimed. "What a pleasure to see you!"

"Likewise," Olivia replied, smiling. Mrs. Hardin had been one of her favorite teachers, one of the reasons Olivia had decided to pursue biology.

"Are you still working on your PhD?" she asked. Olivia had kept in touch with her sporadically.

"No, I graduated last spring," she said, feeling a little guilty that she hadn't let Mrs. Hardin know about that. She would have liked to have known, that she knew. But she wasn't sure that her new research direction would have pleased her.

"So are you teaching at the university? Or are you home for the holidays?"

Olivia took her hat off and stuffed it in her purse. She was starting to feel warm. "I'm teaching at the University of California at Incident," she said, without elaborating.

"How wonderful! I'm sure your parents are very proud.

Olivia nodded. "They are, thanks."

"Now, the last time we spoke, you were working on mapping the three-dimensional structure of the genome." Mrs. Hardin carried several books under her arm; she set them down on the nearest display table.

"That's right."

"How is that going?"

Olivia groaned inwardly, unsure what to say. "Actually, I've changed research direction." Yet, even as she said this, she wondered. If she didn't meet her funding goal on Experiment.com, she wouldn't have the funding she needed to proceed with her research as planned. Her deadline was tomorrow. And if this were the case, she had just about decided to abandon her grandiose plans. She wasn't sure what she had been thinking in the first place.

"Oh?" Mrs. Hardin's quizzical expression was a clear prompt. Olivia searched for the right words.

"Yes, I'm interested, now, in the biophysics of gene expression," she said finally. When she said it like that, it sounded a lot better, she thought. Much more official and less mystical.

Mrs. Hardin shook her head in admiration. "I always said you were the smartest pupil I ever had." She reached over and squeezed Olivia's arm. "I expect great things from you!"

Olivia grinned weakly. "Well, we'll have to see, I guess."

"I am certain of it," Mrs. Hardin said, nodding once for emphasis. "And I wish you the best of luck. Give your parents my best, will you?"

"I sure will. Thanks, Mrs. Hardin." Mrs. Hardin had once told Olivia that, now that she was graduated from high school, she could call her by her first name, Beth. But Olivia couldn't bring herself to do that.

As Mrs. Hardin plucked her books from the table and headed to the cash register, Olivia snuck a quick peek around the bookstore to see if anyone else she knew might be here. She would hate to run into one of her professors from graduate school, or one of her fellow students. Everyone would want to know how her research was going and where she was teaching. Mrs. Hardin might not be familiar with UC

Incident's reputation, but her colleagues would.

She located her purchases and paid for them, deciding that she could finish her Christmas shopping in Incident and bring her presents with her when she came back. She drove home, savoring the picturesque scenery, the thickly frosted roofs of houses, the smooth white comforters of snow that stretched over summer lawns, the twee icicles dripping from eaves, some of them augmented with Christmas lights that caused them to glow in the falling dusk.

When she got to her parents' house, she parked in the driveway in case enough snow accumulated to necessitate plowing overnight, and gathered up her purchases. She scooted up to her room to stash them before coming back downstairs and joining her parents in the living room. Something else that had come up in her research on hypertension was the fact that sleep apnea could be a cause. It made sense: When a person stopped breathing several times an hour, the body became starved for oxygen and raised blood pressure in order to get blood and oxygen to the organs. Her father was a known snorer—her mother often joked about it—so he was scheduled for a sleep study next week. Though apparently, even some non-snorers had sleep apnea.

In the meantime, her father had started taking the herbs that Piper sent along as soon as Olivia arrived; Piper cautioned her that they might take a while before they started working. They weren't like drugs, which often had an immediate effect. But their subtlety was one of the reasons they didn't carry such powerful side-effects. Olivia had talked her parents down from their fears, repeating what Piper had told her: The new guidelines for blood pressure for those over sixty was 150/90, not 120/80, though a number of physicians were sticking to the old ones. Piper believed that blood pressure needed to increase somewhat as a person aged; the new guidelines were based on the fact that a number of elderly with blood pressure 120/80 or lower were not getting enough blood to their brains and were fainting, often breaking bones in the process. And a few decades ago, she said, the systolic recommendation for adults was 100 plus your age. She felt that the blanket 120/80 guidelines were based more on the bottom line for drug companies than the health of the patient.

"It's a sad commentary," she had said, while packaging up the herbs, "that both the editor-in-chief of *The Lancet*, as well as the former editor-in-chief of *The New England Journal of Medicine* have come out on record as saying that current medical studies are compromised by the money to be made, coupled with publish-or-perish."

Olivia knew all about publish-or-perish, that was for sure. She also knew that because so much medical research these days was funded by private pharmaceutical companies, they claimed proprietary interest in the trials and often published only the favorable ones, letting the others sit quietly in the drawer.

Her parents had a fire crackling in the fireplace and cups of mulled cider sitting next to them, filling the room with the scents that Olivia associated with the holidays. She gave both of them a kiss on the cheek and settled down on the sofa, where she slipped off the house shoes she kept in her old room and tucked her feet underneath her.

"Would you like a cup of cider?" her mother asked, glancing at her over her reading glasses, laying her fat hardcover in her lap.

"I'll get one in a minute," Olivia said.

"How was your trip into town?" her father asked.

"Good. I ran into Mrs. Hardin. She said to give you two her best."

"That's awfully nice."

"Yes." Olivia took a strand of hair and wound it around her finger. "By—the way, I wondered what you guys would think if I moved back here?"

"Back … here?" her mother asked surprised. "This house?"

"Well, no, not necessarily. Maybe for a few days or weeks."

Her father laid his paper down. "What's going on, sweetheart?" he asked.

Olivia shrugged, then found tears brimming her eyes. "It's just that—well, things aren't going all that great. I can't get enough funding from traditional sources. I told you about trying crowdfunding, but … it doesn't look like I'm going to meet my goal, which means that I won't get any money. So I'll have to start all over again."

"Is that so bad?' her mother said.

"Well, no, not necessarily, not if I can get something together soon. But … I'm just starting to think that I'm chasing a pipe dream. I mean, honestly, what was I thinking? That I was Madame Curie?" She gave a self-deprecating laugh.

Both of her parents regarded her solemnly. "And what's the matter with that?" her mother asked.

Olivia shook her head, biting her lip to keep her tears from spilling over.

Her father got up and joined her on the couch, reaching over to take her hand. "Honey, we are so proud of you. We know that Incident isn't the most prestigious university, we know that. And we know that the kind of research you want to do is bucking the system. But isn't that what science—true science—is about? Making a difference? Pushing the current boundaries? Gaining new insights?"

His idealism and faith in her pushed her over the edge. Tears splashed down her cheeks.

"Boldly going where no one has ever gone before?" her mother added, causing Olivia to laugh.

They all remained quiet for a few moments. Then her father spoke. "Look, I know how tough it is these days. Academia was a lot easier when I was your age. And the sciences—well, the money required for researching and publishing is pretty overwhelming, I would think. I mean, sure, you could go the safe route. You could go back to doing what you were doing. But it seems to me that now there are plenty of other scientists pursuing that line of thinking. And think about it, what are the applications of that research?"

"Well, it's mainly useful for targeting drugs better, so that they work better."

"What you want to do is so much better, sweetheart," her mother said. "So much more of a boon to humanity."

"If I get any results," she replied. It was honestly feeling hopeless. "If even Rupert has to work so hard for funding, and he has a terrific track record and reputation, what chance do I have? No wonder no one wants to fund my research. Who the hell am I, anyway?"

Her mother took off her glasses and gave Olivia a hard stare. "You're an excellent scientist. You're an honest one. And you care about others."

"Big whoop."

"Big whoop indeed!" Her mother got up and joined her father and Olivia on the couch, squeezing in on her other side and taking her other hand. "Olivia, don't give up, honey. Not yet. We would of course love it if you came back. We miss you! But I don't think you should throw in the towel just yet."

Her father agreed. "Just this experience I had with the blood pressure medicine has got me to rethinking a few things," he said. "The fact is, I had gotten to where I wasn't even ambulatory any more. I was in constant pain. And all my doctor had to tell me was that these drugs didn't do what I was experiencing. Yet, now that I've been off of them for a couple of weeks, the pain is going away, I can walk again, and I'm gaining my strength back. And according to you, I'll have more blood going to my brain. I'm sure your mother thinks that's a good thing." He looked over at her and wrinkled his nose at her. She shook her head and chuckled.

"Absolutely," she said. "Getting old is bad enough without starving our brains of blood!"

Olivia gave her parents' hands a squeeze, then wiped her eyes. "I sure am lucky to have you for my parents," she said.

"We are so lucky to have you," her mother said. She paused, holding Olivia's gaze. "Give it one more semester, how about that?"

"Okay." Olivia reached into her pocket for a tissue and blew her nose. "Thanks for the pep talk."

"Anytime." Her mother got up and stretched. "I'm going to start dinner. Do either one of you want to join me in the kitchen?"

"Sure!" said Olivia's dad.

"I'll be right in," Olivia said.

After they left the room, she decided to pull out her cell phone and check her proposal on Experiment.com. Someone, she saw, had pledged $25. She sighed. Only $24,975 more to go. She felt tears welling up again and blinked them back fiercely. Then she got up and joined her parents in the kitchen.

CHAPTER 36

xel walked briskly into Ethel's bank, wearing his most expensive slacks, shirt, and shoes. He also wore the cashmere coat he had received as a gift. As he waited in line for the next available teller, he looked around the room out of habit, sussing out both individuals and the vibe. It was a local, corn-poney bank, one that would no doubt be easy to knock off if that was his taste. Which it wasn't. The sad attempts at decorating for the holidays were horribly depressing—the dusty, droopy bows hanging in what someone must have deemed strategic locations, the generic tree slimed with fake snow, dotted with scuffed gold baubles, and wrapped with one of those bristling metallic garlands that resembled nothing more than a giant, lurking centipede … And the people, my God. Half of them looked like old Grateful Dead fans, while the other half simply looked dowdy, despite their clownish insistence on garishly bright colors. The guy in front of him was actually wearing a purple canvas kilt. Truth be told, Ethel had more class than 98% of the inhabitants of this hick town.

He waited until he was in front of the teller before writing his check, finding that this always inspired confidence. He had transferred all but $500 from Ethel's savings account into her checking account online; he would write a check for all but $200 in her checking. So he wasn't leaving her with zero cash; besides, she still had her portfolio.

"Good afternoon, sir," the teller greeted him, with a friendly tilt of her head. "How can I help you today?"

He flashed her a smile, then dropped his gaze to the checkbook and wrote out the amount with a flourish. "I'll need you to cash this check for me," he said. He was thankful that he had gotten Ethel to order checks with his name on them when she added him as a signatory to the account. He tore the check off and handed it to her.

"I'll need to see some ID, please, sir."

"Of course." He extracted his Axel Smith driver's license and laid it on the counter. The teller examined it and handed it back to him with a flirtatious smile.

"Thank you, sir."

As she counted out the bills, Axel felt a rising excitement. He could practically taste his new freedom and impending good fortune: financial freedom, a severing of his relationship with his parents, a new identity, a new life. The amount made for quite a nice bundle, which he tucked into the inside pocket of his coat. He bade the teller a Merry Christmas, "Or a happy holiday, whichever you prefer," he quipped, with a rakish grin, eliciting a giggle from her.

Then he strode to his car, his feeling of triumph so giddy, even the cold drizzle didn't dampen his spirits. He had decided to go ahead and trade in his Mercedes at a used car dealer in Corning yesterday afternoon. It would be easier not to make the transaction while he was on the run and have to move all his belongings from his old car to his new one. Good thing, too. He had seen a cop checking out cars parked in the neighborhood when he returned home. It probably had nothing to do with him, but he congratulated himself on listening to his intuition, in case it did. So he was now the proud owner of a 2002 PT Cruiser. A dorky car if there ever was one, but it did have a lot of room.

Driving over to his bank, he deposited half the cash into his checking account, keeping the other half for contingencies. On his way home, he mentally ran over his list of things to do before moving out tomorrow, gratified to note how little there was left. He called the Oakland apartment manager as soon as he got to his apartment and offered to send her the first and last months' rent plus the security deposit via Paypal, which she accepted. He put the transaction through, using the new account that he had established with his alias, then went into his bedroom to pack up his personal items apart from the toiletries he would need tonight and in the morning. He didn't plan to change for his dinner with Piper, but he selected his clothes for his exit with care. In the morning, he would dye his hair.

He sighed happily. Everything was falling into place.

Before leaving for Piper's, he snatched up the red roses he had purchased from Safeway earlier and the bottle of champagne he had filched from Buffington's yesterday. He figured even if they did notice it missing and they suspected him, it wouldn't matter because he would be gone and impossible to find. Besides, he wasn't going to get his final paycheck; they owed him.

Pulling up to Piper's house, he parked in such a way that the car wouldn't be all that visible from her doorstep. But if she did notice it, he had a story ready. He saw that she had decorated tastefully and botanically for the holidays, with pots of berried holly crowding the stoop, graceful branches of fir and juniper framing the door and windows. Around and through them all, she had woven soft, pearly lights that were no doubt composed of some kind of energy efficient bulbs. As he rang the bell, he looked up and noticed sprigs of mistletoe dangling from the crown of the door. Such a romantic, he thought, shaking his head.

As she opened the door, warm light and tempting scents spilled out into the damp fog. She looked a vision in an ivory and deep green dress decorated with crimson ribbons. It was really kind of a shame that she ended up being the main con here in Incident. Under other circumstances, he could imagine actually pairing up with her. Someone as naïve and trusting as she was made for a great cover. And he felt certain that he could fool around all he wanted on the side with a woman like Piper and she would never suspect. If she found out, he was sure he could get her to believe it was her fault.

But alas, that was not to be. And there were plenty of other fish out there for a guy like him.

"Axel!" she exclaimed, drawing him inside where she wrapped her arms around him in a passionate hug.

"Hey there, angel," he said, burying his nose in her hair and inhaling deeply. She not only looked good, she smelled good, he had to admit. She smelled like the outdoors, like roses, like something more intangible but womanly.

She looked past him; he followed her gaze and saw the nose of his car poking out past the hedge that lined one side of the driveway. Damn it. She gave him a puzzled look. "New car?"

"Oh, no, it's a rental," he said. "My Mercedes is in the shop."

"Nothing serious, I hope."

"No, I think it's just that the starter is beginning to wear out."

"That's good." She grabbed his hand and led him into the kitchen.

The aroma of roasting beef was unmistakable. Even though he had offered to cook dinner tonight, he'd subsequently made a big deal of how busy he was, and Piper predictably took the bait. She had a standing rib roast in the oven, she said, with Yorkshire pudding. On the counter he noted a large salad that included dried cranberries. She accepted the bouquet of roses with obvious pleasure and put them in a crystal vase with some water. Then she took two champagne glasses down from the cabinet and placed them on the breakfast bar.

"First things first," Axel declared, seizing her in a passionate embrace, leaning her back, and kissing her with all the gallantry of a pirate. Piper giggled during the kiss, spoiling the effect, but … whatever. Afterward, she straightened up and fanned herself, smiling at him.

"Will you do the honors?" she asked.

"With pleasure," he replied. He popped the cork on the champagne and poured it so generously that it spilled over the sides. He thought that created a nice impression of exuberance. Raising his glass aloft, he held Piper's gaze and said solemnly, "To us." Then he wound his arm around Piper's, and they each drank from each other's glass.

They sipped the champagne with the appetizers that Piper had prepared: leek tarts with gruyere and fresh sage. For dinner, she opened an expensive Burgundy. "Danny helped me pick this out," she told him, as she filled his glass. They chatted about his restaurant, Axel dropping plenty of hints about the married life with children he envisioned before them. Piper asked him about his Christmas plans, and he said that he didn't have any—what were hers? She told him that she usually spent them with Marion and Danny and wondered if he might like to join them this year. He said he couldn't think of anything more delightful.

After dessert, a flourless chocolate cake with crème fraiche and raspberries, she excused herself, then returned to the table with an envelope. Bless her, the envelope was lavender.

She sat down and handed it to him. He leaned across the table and kissed her lingeringly on the lips, then opened the envelope and extracted the check. His heart rate went up went he saw the amount—even more than he had hoped! And, good girl, it was a cashier's check.

He looked up at her, his expression solemn. "Oh, darling,"

he said. "You're my angel, my guardian angel, you know that?"

Piper glowed, clasping his hand tight. "I'm so glad I could do this for you!"

"Well, you won't be sorry, I can guarantee that."

"I know I won't." Piper continued to smile at him, then some thought seemed to cloud her expression.

"Anything wrong, darling?" he asked.

Piper shrugged. "Oh, I've—I've been trying to decide whether to even bother you with this, but … I think you should know."

Axel tensed but made an effort to appear at ease. "Whatever you need to tell me, I want to hear, sweetheart."

She exhaled heavily. "Well, okay. Yesterday, this woman came by, and I—I think she's stalking you."

"Good lord!" he exclaimed. "What was her name?"

"Amanda. I didn't get her last name."

Axel said nothing for a beat, wondering which tack to take. Should he pretend he didn't know who she was, that she was some stranger who had fixated on him? Or should he play it with a half-truth, admit that he knew her, but leave it at that? "What did she say to you? I hope she didn't threaten you."

"Oh no! Nothing like that." Piper was now twisting her napkin in her hands. "She … claimed, actually, that you were really someone named Eric Johnson."

Axel shook his head in apparent confusion. "I'm sorry—who?"

"Eric Johnson."

Axel pretended to think.

"Maybe Aaron?"

He continued to feign confusion, but inside he was boiling. That fucking bitch Amanda! What the hell did she think she was doing? Axel forced a smile and laid his hand on Piper's wrist, assuming a concerned, benevolent expression. "Well, poor dear. I don't think she's dangerous to you. But if she contacts you again, be sure to let me know right away."

"I will." Piper continued to look troubled. "How do you know her, anyway?"

"Oh—" Axel waved his hand dismissively in the air. "She came into the bistro a couple of times."

"Why—why do you think she said she thought you were this Johnson guy?"

Axel wagged his head in utter bemusement. "It's impossible to make sense out of a disturbed mind," he said. Axel fastened his most adoring gaze on Piper. "But let's not waste a minute more talking about poor, disturbed Amanda. We've got so much to look forward to."

Piper smiled and seemed to relax. The rest of the evening went well, and he made sure to put on a virtuoso performance in bed. He begged off staying the night, saying that he needed to go in early to work the next morning. She said that she understood, but there was something off in her goodnight kiss, something hesitant and reserved, which put him on guard.

He drove home thoughtfully, wondering if he needed to worry about Piper as well as Amanda, whom he now suspected of being behind the cop checking out cars in his neighborhood. Was Piper being straight with him that she didn't know who Eric Johnson was? Surely. She wouldn't have wanted him to stay the night if she thought he was somehow involved in a murder. He knew that she didn't read the news—too much negativity, she always said. Still … he might need to worry, he decided. He just might. He would need to keep his antennae up. He was far too close to success to let anything get in the way now.

CHAPTER 37

Piper awoke feeling uneasy. She had a nagging feeling that she had made a mistake by giving Axel her savings. He had explained everything with Amanda, of course, so that it all made sense … but her radar was pinging. She rolled over on her side, balling the covers in her fists, her stomach knotted. She was always telling her patients that they should never ignore their intuition.

She glanced at her clock and saw that it was only 6:30. Too early to call anyone, really. And besides, Marion and Danny were gone for a few days, staying at a hot springs resort that was off the grid and had no Internet nor cell phone service. She had been so glad for them when they told her about their plans—both of them had been working extra hard lately and she thought it a great idea to have some relaxed time with no distractions to prepare for their baby's arrival. But she would have given anything to be able to call them right now.

She decided to try anyway, fetching her cell phone from her dresser, then scooting back under the covers. Both their phones went straight to voice mail. Olivia was out of town. Piper hadn't made much time for other friends right now, so she didn't feel that she could call anyone in her women's group. And if she called her parents, they would just be angry with her and tell her how foolish she had been. A tear ran down her cheek.

But was he really Eric Johnson? She was having a hard time wrapping her mind around that possibility. And everything Axel said made perfect sense. And yet … when she first brought up Amanda, it seemed like he waited a fraction of a second too long to answer, as if he were weighing his options. And when she brought up Amanda's accusation that he was somebody else, his reaction seemed off, somehow. But maybe not.

Worries and second-guesses had kept her up most of the night. Now there was no way she was getting back to sleep, even though the sun had not yet risen and the room was dark and cold.

How could he have not stayed with me last night? she brooded, as she stepped into her slippers and slipped on her robe. How could anything be more important than what she had done for him? She had given him all her money! He couldn't make a little extra time for her in his busy schedule?

She shambled anxiously into the kitchen to put her kettle on for tea. This would be a great time to have a dog, she thought, wondering if she could call Carson and Merilee and ask to borrow Jessie for the day. As she sat at her table, waiting for the water to boil, she pondered what she should do. How could she find out the truth? She had no way of getting back in touch with Amanda to ask her more questions. She regretted shooing her away now. She drummed the table with her fingers, trying to think if she had any options. She couldn't cancel the check. It was a cashier's check, as good as cash. *Dummy*, she scolded herself savagely, hurting her feelings and making herself feel even worse.

Her kettle came to a boil, but she felt too wound up to do anything as leisurely as brew a cup of tea. She tried to call Axel and tell him she needed to come over and talk to him. When he didn't pick up, she decided to go over to his apartment. He might be angry if she showed up unannounced and so early, but for Pete's sake, considering what she had just done for him, it seemed the least he could do was reassure her.

As she drove over to his apartment, she shivered from the cold. It took a while for her car to get warmed up enough for the heater to work. Some people had left their Christmas lights burning all night, but oddly, instead of cheering her, they looked ghostly and forlorn, shrouded in mist. Axel's apartment complex had no designated parking, so everyone parked on the street, making it difficult to find parking this time of day. There was nothing on his block, so she widened her search to the next block and as she was pulling into a spot near the corner, she saw someone exiting his building. The guy had platinum blond hair, which looked a little bizarre, especially in the dim light. It was practically glowing. Then she did a double take. Axel? Why had he bleached his hair?

This made her feel even more uneasy. She decided not to approach him right now. She needed some time to think. She waited for him to get in his car and drive off, but he opened the door and tossed something inside and returned to his apartment building. She sat and fretted. The fact that he had a different car and a new hair color didn't bode well, given Amanda's accusations that he was not who he claimed to be. She tried calling Marion and Danny again, but their phones once again went straight to voice mail. She could hardly bear the thought that Axel not only didn't love her, not only wasn't her soul mate, but was also a con artist who had just stolen her life's savings. She could try confronting him, but she shrank at the thought.

Then she remembered the place that Axel had shown her that he wanted to buy for his restaurant. She should go by there and see if it was no longer for sale, maybe call the real estate agent and see if Axel had put down the earnest money she had given him earlier. If he had, then she probably didn't need to worry.

If he hadn't … well, she would cross that bridge when she came to it.

She started up her Beetle and headed for the venue Axel had shown her as the site for his new restaurant. As she drove, she tried to give Axel the benefit of the doubt and not look at everything so suspiciously: Axel's car was in the shop, so of course he needed to rent another car. And maybe he was trying out a new look for his new restaurant and he wanted to surprise her. The fact that he hadn't wanted to stay the night was disappointing, but not catastrophic. He had a lot on his mind with his mother's stroke and a lot of work to do getting his restaurant up and running. As she ran these explanations through her mind, she relaxed. It was probably silly not to have just run up to him for a hug when she saw him.

Before she knew it, she had reached her destination. She parked out front. The "For Sale or Lease" sign was still in the window, with no "Sold" sticker. Well, that might not mean anything. Maybe it was in escrow. She glanced at her car clock and saw that it was now 7:30. A weak sun was just starting to straggle over the Cascades. She couldn't wait any longer, so she got out of the car and walked up to the sign where the agent's number was listed. She retrieved her cell phone from her pocket and dialed. Thankfully, the agent answered.

"Hello, Mr. Thoroughgood?" she said.

"Yes. Who's speaking?"

"Piper. Piper Fairchild. I'm calling about the property on Sycamore." She leaned back and read the number above the door. "2714 Sycamore."

"Why, yes! What can I tell you about it?"

"Is it still available?"

"Absolutely."

"No—no one has made an offer or given you earnest money?"

"They haven't."

"I see." Piper's throat closed up. "Well, thanks for the information," she choked. "I'll be back in touch." She hung up before the agent could ask her any more questions. Dear God. She leaned weakly against the storefront window, dismay chasing despair.

After a while, she got back in her car, wondering what to do next. Should she go to the police? The thing was, the fact that he lied about the property didn't automatically make him a con artist. Maybe there was a perfectly reasonable explanation. Maybe he had thought at first that he would give the agent the earnest money, but he had decided to wait until he was sure he would have the money for the down payment so he wouldn't lose the earnest money if things fell through.

It would be terrible if she got Axel involved with the police and it all turned out to be an error. Could he forgive her if she did that? She tried to clear her head by shaking it. This was all so confusing and disorienting and distressing. Part of her was tempted to call Axel, just to hear his voice and reassure herself that he was the man she thought he was. Another part of her recoiled at the idea. As she sat in her Beetle, she suddenly realized that she had class in twenty minutes. With everything else going on, she had completely forgotten.

She started up her car and raced over to the university. She did her best to conduct a decent class, but she had no memory of it afterward. Two students stayed to talk to her about their final projects; she hoped she gave them some decent advice and information. Her afternoon free, she drove back home, her land line ringing as she came in the back door. Hoping against hope it might be someone who could help her, she rushed to pick it up. It was her landlady, Margaret.

"Piper! So glad to have caught you, dear."

"Merry Christmas, Margaret," Pipe said warmly. "What's up?"

"Well, it turns out that someone has offered to buy our house—the one you're renting."

"They have? But—"

"Don't worry, dear. We told them that you had a lease option to buy."

Piper relaxed momentarily, but she could tell that wasn't the whole story.

"The—thing is, dear, Frank has been diagnosed with lymphoma. And Medicare won't cover all the costs of treatment. We need the money now, or I wouldn't be putting any pressure on you. But we thought perhaps you could go ahead and start the purchase, give us whatever you have for a down payment and that will be fine, I'm sure."

"Oh no, Margaret, that's terrible news about Frank! I am so sorry."

"Thank you, Piper."

Piper fought back a wave of nausea as she realized she had no money to give them. She should tell them that, but she just couldn't make herself. The thought of losing her home on top of everything else was just more than she could bear. Maybe she could borrow some money from her parents. Maybe she could get a loan from the bank. She couldn't just give up without trying. "Okay, well, thanks so much for telling me," she said finally. "I'll see what I can get together and I'll call you back, all right?"

"Of course, sweetie."

"And—and I'll stop by later with some herbs for Frank."

Margaret thanked her and hung up. Piper sat staring out her window, feeling utterly overwhelmed. She had never felt so scattered or helpless. As she sat, gathering her strength, the forest beyond the window beckoned. She decided that the best thing she could do was to take a walk in her beloved woods.

She grabbed her cloak and pulled on her Wellingtons. It had been raining and off and on for the past couple of days, though today was merely overcast. Still, the trails would be muddy. As she tramped through her back yard, her devas came out in full force to show her affection, their frazzled energy state reflecting her own. *Thank you*, she told them mentally as they buzzed frantically around her; *I'll be okay, don't worry.*

As she made her way into the forest, lost in thought, a ragged man scared her half to death when he bounded out of the brush. "Oh my goodness!" she cried. He wore at first what she thought was a hat with furry earflaps, but then she realized that the flaps were matted hair. His face was streaked with dirt but his eyes looked oddly bright in the gloom. He had bundled up with several coats and taped his shoes together with duct tape.

"Beware!" he shouted.

"S–sorry?" she stammered. He looked vaguely familiar.

"There are people!" he said.

"People?" Now she placed him. He was the homeless man she had seen trudging along the road when she drove over to Marion and Danny's the other night. And no doubt the same man she had surprised in her back yard that time.

"People in the forest!"

She nodded. "Okay. Thank you."

"People in the forest!"

"Got it. I'll be careful."

He glared at her.

"Oh—do you mean me?" she said, wondering if he thought she was trespassing on his territory.

He shook his head and then ran off. Into the forest, she noticed, not out of it. Was he trying to warn her about a homeless camp? Or some kind of meth operation? People had been known to set up temporary camps to cook meth, and they didn't take kindly to strangers.

She hesitated, thinking maybe it would be safer to go home. But the thought of just whiling away the hours all alone, wondering what was going on with Axel didn't appeal at all. The forest devas were now hibernating, as they usually did this time of year; so they weren't there to reassure her. But for now, the innocence of the forest comforted her. She decided to go deeper. And to search for solace in in the spare beauty of the winter woods.

CHAPTER 38

arson sat slouched in a chair at his boarding gate, stiff from a night spent at the airport. Fog in San Francisco had canceled his flight home last night, and the earliest he could get on another one that connected to Incident was this morning. Even so, he was in terrific spirits. His synching session with the film's editors went great. He really liked the director and producer of the film he was working on, and they were thrilled with the score he had written. They told him that they would definitely want more music from him in the future. Not only that, they had passed his name along to a couple of other filmmakers. For the first time in years, things were looking up in his career.

Which made the gnawing unease he felt quite puzzling. He didn't mind flying, so it wasn't phobia-based. He didn't have any commitments until tomorrow, so that wasn't a problem. He had checked in with his mom, and everything was okay at home. Maybe he had a block against success? Was that what was troubling him? He had never had any problems before, but maybe his experience with failure had introduced an element of fear that hadn't been there previously.

Whatever was going on, he decided to ignore it, focus

on something else. He had texted Olivia to let her know his session had gone well, but had not yet heard back from her. He thought that perhaps she was traveling today as well, so she could be in the air.

He thought he might just go ahead and record his CD at Zach's rebuilt studio when he got home. He could at least give a few copies as late Christmas presents. With his scoring work providing him with some good money, that took a little pressure off his recording career.

He watched as an airline representative changed the departure time at the gate and groaned. Another hour's delay, which would make his connection in San Francisco tight. Well, nothing he could do but hope for the best. He got up and ambled over to a nearby Mexican food stall and ordered a breakfast burrito.

When he finally boarded, he found himself oddly anxious to get home. He felt tense until he arrived at SFO, then he made a mad dash to the terminal that housed flights undertaken by small planes. He made it just in time, but then the plane ended up sitting on the tarmac for a half-hour because of congestion. He relaxed a little when they became airborne, the loud droning of the aircraft's motor filling his vision with vibrating brown-green noodles. But upon landing, he felt fidgety as they went through all the procedures necessary to debark the passenger's. Fortunately, he had only a carry-on, so he hustled out to long-term parking to jump in his car.

What on Earth was going on? he wondered. This was crazy. Was he developing some kind of anxiety disorder? The only thing he could think was that he was worried about how his score would be received by the industry when the film came out. Now that he had something worth losing, he cared a lot more. Still, this seemed like an odd response. Maybe he ate something last night at the airport that had him feeling off. Sometimes stomach upset could feel similar to anxiety.

Once home, he found his mom's car missing from the driveway. She had probably gone to work. It was damp and chilly, so she had left Jessie inside, evidently. She was waiting for him at the door, crowding him so frantically that he could hardly get the door open.

"Hey, Jessie. Hey, girl. What's up?" he said, dropping to a crouch so that he could give her a full body-rub. She whined, sending tendrils of violet and fuchsia through his vision, and licked him in the face. When he stood up, she danced in place, then nudged the door with her nose.

Oh! He got it. She had to pee. "Here you go," he said, opening the door and standing aside to let her out. But she stopped and sat down, looking up at him expectantly.

"What?" he said. She whined again. "You want to go for a walk?"

She sprang to all fours.

Carson looked out the door. "I don't know, girl, it's kinda nasty out. It's cold and wet … I just got home and need to get settled. How about later?"

Jessie looked so distraught that it pierced his heart. He couldn't say no to a face like that. He had no idea what was going on—she wasn't one to chase deer or other wild animals—but he figured, what the hell. He grabbed his rain jacket from its hook and closed the door behind him. Jessie scampered to the forest so fast that Carson had to jog to keep her in sight.

"Hey! Slow down!" he shouted. But it was as if she didn't hear him. In fact, pretty soon, he could no longer see her white-tipped tail swishing in the air as she rocketed up the mist-shrouded path.

This did concern him, as he was now starting to suspect that she was on some animal's trail. And it was possible that it could be an animal that could hurt her. "Jessie!" he called. "Jessie, come!" He increased his pace, thinking that he should probably get more aerobic exercise. He was starting to get winded.

"Jessie!" he called, then stopped and listened for her bark. Nothing.

This was so unlike her. And that feeling of anxiety he had been feeling all morning … it was getting worse. He shivered. He hoped that what he was experiencing wasn't some foreboding about something terrible happening to Jessie.

"Jessie!" he called again. But all he heard was a gust of wind rattling the bare limbs of the winter oaks. And the sound of his own labored breath.

CHAPTER 39

Olivia drove along the Mass Pike in a happy daze, despite the traffic, despite the messy driving conditions. A slushy snow was pelting down, and semis were throwing sheets of sludge across her windshield. But when she had checked on her crowdfunding status for her research this morning, she found that an anonymous donor had put her over the top. Just in the nick of time! She was so delighted she couldn't stop smiling at breakfast, which cheered her parents no end. And they had told her that they would pay for her trip back for the holidays as her Christmas present.

She had given herself plenty of time to get to the airport, turn in her car, and go through security. And she was full of plans on how to get started setting up her research after winter break. With this vote of confidence from the universe, and the fact that her parents seemed to be in good shape, both physically and psychologically, the thought of continuing to establish her career and home in Incident seemed more appealing, especially if she could travel to Massachusetts a couple of times a year. Emily and her family had stopped by yesterday afternoon, and they had had a good visit. Emily was grateful for Olivia's intervention, and they were feeling closer than they ever had. Maybe the distance made them both realize how lucky they were to have family. For some reason, Piper came into her mind. Olivia knew that she was estranged from her parents and her brother, and she thought how sad that would be. It was hard to understand, as lovely a person as Piper was.

Something nudged at her thoughts then, some scrap of a dream that might have involved Piper. She tried to chase it down and call it up, but she didn't have much luck. Oh well. She noticed a flutter of anxiety in her stomach and squelched it. She wasn't particularly keen on flying, and she hated the whole security theater that air travel involved these days. Nor was she looking forward to sitting in a cramped, uncomfortable seat for however many hours it was going to take, with a change of planes in Chicago.

After she returned her car to the rental agency, she took the shuttle to Logan airport. The van was crowded with students whose winter break started early, she guessed, and other holiday travelers. One woman was wearing a green headband that had felt antlers attached to them, an oddly playful contrast to her grim, bulldoggy expression.

As she entered the terminal, she looked up her flight on the video display, not surprised to see that her flight was delayed. She was just glad it wasn't canceled, like the ones to Buffalo and Rochester, and she would still have plenty of time for her connection. She went through security to get it out of the way, and stopped at a Starbucks to buy a chocolate croissant and cup of coffee. Then she got settled in a seat at the gate. She had waited to send Carson a text from her phone about her funding earlier, given the three-hour time difference. So she sent him one now, perplexed when it wouldn't go through. Maybe because of the weather. She saved it in her outbox, then pulled out her Kindle to while away the time before she boarded. She wouldn't be able to relax until she was on the plane. She'd had flights canceled out from under her before, and the snow was supposed to get heavier as the day progressed.

Finally, they boarded, though not without some shenanigans involving overhead luggage space. Olivia had ended up with a seat in the middle of the row, given her last minute travel plans, but given the fact that her seat was over the wing, she wouldn't be able to see much out the window anyway. A heavily perfumed woman took the window seat while a handsome thirty-something guy took the aisle. He reminded her of Axel, Piper' boyfriend, and as she made that association, her dream came flooding back to her.

The dream took place in a forest, a shadowy, misty forest. Piper was walking along in her cloak, the one that reminded Olivia of Little Red Riding Hood, not a very auspicious metaphor. Axel was stalking her, lurking behind trees and thick bushes. Olivia was watching them both from some kind of omniscient point of view, as if she hovered above them in some disembodied state. Piper came to a small clearing and paused. Axel circled her, hidden by the thick brush, then aimed a revolver at her and shot her in the back of the head. She crumpled to the ground with the softest of cries, her blood mingling with the red of her hood. Olivia felt certain that this was no ordinary dream. Damn it, if only she hadn't repressed her dreams before now! She might have gotten a warning sooner. Frantically, she dug her cell phone out of her purse and called Piper to warn her. But still no luck in her calls going through.

Soon, the announcement came over the PA system to turn off all cell phones. The phones that used to be in the backs of plane seats were no longer available. She tried to read during the flight to Chicago, but she was so distraught and worried that she couldn't concentrate. She tried to convince herself that this wasn't a prescient dream, that it was simply symbolic of her fears for Piper now that she knew Axel was unfaithful. But as soon as the plane landed in Chicago, she tried calling again. This time, her call went through.

"Pick up, Piper. Pick up, pick up," she muttered. No answer, and now everyone was getting up and shuffling off the plane. As soon as she got off the jetway, though, she tried again. Nothing. She wouldn't stop calling, she resolved, until she reached her. If it were true that people could be connected by a morphic field as Rupert believed, every quantum in her field was thrumming.

CHAPTER 40

overing inside the foyer to his apartment building, Axel peered out the window, making sure to stay out of sight. As he had ferried his dop kit to his PT Cruiser, his sixth sense kicked in. Someone was watching him. He had learned never to discount this feeling, so, without letting on in any way whatsoever, he scanned the street. At first he didn't see anything, but then … bingo. He spotted Piper's green Beetle parked on the next block. His eyes narrowed. Casually, he completed his errand, then retreated to the foyer to see if she came to see him. When she didn't, he got his keys ready and waited for her next move. Soon, she started up and drove past. He didn't think she could see him, but he leaned back even so, counted to ten, and sprinted out to his car.

The metallic green of her VW stood out in the early dawn, picking up every bit of ambient light. He had no problem catching up to her, but he hung back, fuming as he drove. He had spent a restless night. He tossed and turned until dawn, trying to decide whether Piper was a threat. Fucking Amanda, that nosy bitch! Wouldn't you know she'd do something like stalk him! He wouldn't mind putting a bullet in her head, actually. But doing anything about her would create a complication that he didn't need.

He had bleached his hair last night when he got home so that he wouldn't have to do it in the morning. He liked the look a lot, a Billy Idol bad-ass look. With the new ice-blue contact lenses, he thought the combination striking enough that no one looking for Axel Smith would take a second glance at him. Piper's check rested snugly in his breast pocket, and his wallet was fat with cash.

He honestly didn't want to kill Piper. The idea was repugnant, in fact. But he didn't want her screwing up his plans. If she were as passive and ashamed—and therefore quiet—as he imagined she would be when she finally realized that he had skipped town with her savings, he could probably leave her alone. She'd never find him. Probably wouldn't even look for him. And by shedding Axel Smith, he'd also be shedding Eric Johnson. All in all, leaving her alone was the easiest path and the one he preferred.

But he needed to know if she might pose a threat to his flight. At this point, she knew what car he was driving and she had glimpsed his new hair color. His heart sank when he realized where she was headed: the commercial property he had claimed he was going to buy.

She parked out in front; he parked around the corner where he had a good view of her. She sat in her car for a few minutes and then got out. He watched her make a call on her cell phone while she kept her eyes on the sign that had the real estate agent's contact information. It was a brief conversation and then … she was covering her face with her hands and slumping against the side of the building. Not good. Not good.

He tensed, waiting for her to call him, to clear things up. When she didn't, he didn't think that was a good sign, either. The danger level just ratcheted up considerably. He needed to know if she was going to get in touch with the police. Actually, even better, he needed to prevent her from ever calling the police. If she was checking up on him, she might not be as passive as he thought.

She started up her car and backed out of her parking place. Fortunately, she turned the opposite way; he followed. She appeared to be heading to the University, which caused him to relax a little. He had some time. But he needed to keep close tabs on her. She could and probably would call the police or that asshole DA she had for a friend at any time. So he parked in the visitor lot while she went to faculty parking, donned his Kangol cap, and waited until he saw her walk past, blending into a wad of students making their way to class. He halted when she stopped outside of what was evidently her classroom, one of her students engaging her in conversation. He took out his cell phone and pretended to compose a long text until she went inside and closed the door behind her. Then he sauntered over to the student center where he bought a cup of coffee to nurse until the end of her class. Whenever that was. He realized he didn't know. He looked around and spotted two pretty young women sharing a bagel at an adjacent table and asked them when this period's classes were over. They were only too happy to tell him. He was right—this new look of his was sick.

Ten minutes before her class was over, Axel strolled back to the building where she taught. He found a bulletin board down the hall from her classroom and pretended to study it intently when class let out. She didn't come out for the longest time, probably earnestly talking about plants to her dorky botany students, and when she did emerge, the expression on her face worried him. Much to his relief, she headed straight home. There he parked in a hiding place near the entrance to her driveway, a small pull-out partially overgrown with buck brush and manzanita bushes, and opened his glove compartment. This is where he kept the revolver his dad had given him on his eighteenth birthday. "Stolen and never traced!" he dad had crowed when he gave it to him. "Registered to some asshole in Idaho." He had never used it except for target practice, but he was glad he had it now. He didn't quite have his plan worked out, but something would occur to him, he felt sure. He crept up to her house, gun in hand. Better safe than sorry.

He skulked up to the side of the house where she kept a window cracked for fresh air, as quietly as he could, and planted himself underneath it. His heart nearly stopped when he realized that she was talking on the phone. He strained to hear her conversation, holding his breath, resenting the way the blood was pounding in his ears.

She was exclaiming over somebody named Frank—so not her DA friend, and not the police. She was talking to some acquaintance. Something about herbs. Finally, she hung up. He risked sticking his head up enough to get a glimpse of her. She appeared to be thinking. Should he just waste her right now? She had no nearby neighbors. Even if someone heard the shot, they might not think anything of it. In a rural area, people shot guns off all the time. He swallowed, slid the safety off, raised his head carefully once again, then cursed as she moved out of view.

He ducked back down, crouched among her azaleas, wondering how he should proceed when he heard her back door slam. His heartbeat quickened. If he were in any luck at all, she would be heading into that forest of hers that she loved to prattle on about so much. Cautiously, he peeked around the corner as her red cape disappeared into the forest gloom. He had trained his gun on her when some crazy homeless guy popped out of the bushes and started raving at her. This was getting better all the time! If she were found dead in the forest, the blame would undoubtedly fall on somebody like this guy. And by the time her body was discovered, he himself would be comfortably established in his new location with his new identity, having left no tracks whatsoever.

The concept of leaving no tracks amused him as he jogged noiselessly into the forest, once the homeless guy ran off and

Piper continued deeper into the woods. Mist clouded the trail and the winter woods that lined it, but her cape glowed like an ember, making her easy to follow without getting close enough to tip her off. Evergreen California holly bushes towered overhead, providing some good cover should he need it, along with more thick, bristling buck brush and dense manzanita.

He contemplated trying to get ahead of her along the edge of the trail, but that might prove difficult without making a racket. And he had dressed in his getaway clothes; he didn't want them to get dirty or torn. He was considering getting close enough to shoot her in the back on the trail when she suddenly stopped. Warily, he melted into the brush and made his way forward on what seemed like a game trail that paralleled the main trail. Soon, he had reached the spot where she had halted; a small glade. He then saw what had captured her attention: a crude lean-to made out of branches and small trees. Perfect! If he shot her here, some meth cook would be the first suspect.

Very, very carefully, he circled around her so that he could shoot from the direction of the lean-to. He almost stumbled over the lip of a bluff that the mist concealed until he was right on top of it. His pulse hammering from adrenalin, he forced himself to calm down as he picked his spot to make his kill. Piper's back was toward him, so that was convenient. He had just lifted his gun and steadied his wrist with his other hand when her fucking cell phone went off. She answered, and he let his arm drop, silently cursing whomever had called her. He didn't want the person on the other end to hear any commotion or think that something had happened to her.

He was close enough to hear her, but he was so keyed up, his mind wasn't making much sense of her words, which seemed to be mainly along the lines of distressed exclamations. Maybe there wasn't much sense to be made. Finally, she ended the call and turned around, looking wildly around her.

Isn't gonna help you, he thought, as he raised his gun once more and aimed it at her head. Just as he was about to squeeze the trigger, however, some crazy-assed animal came out of fucking nowhere and attacked him. God, what the fuck was it? A wolf? A coyote? It was on him, growling and biting—too close to shoot, so he clubbed it in the head with his gun and it fell to the ground. What the hell? It was a fucking dog??

He glanced up and saw Piper gazing at him in horror, the ruckus having exposed his hiding place. He expected her to run, but she seemed paralyzed from shock, her eyes enormous. He needed to shoot now, before she bolted, but then next thing he knew, someone was rushing into the glade, calling for the dog he had just clubbed. Jesus Christ, it was that dipshit musician! What the hell was he doing here?

Piper screamed at him to leave, to get away, but he didn't. He stood perplexed, trying to take in the situation. Axel decided it was time to take control. He stepped out from the bushes and whipped his gun back and forth between them.

"Axel, don't do this!" Piper begged.

"Fucking shut up!"

"What the hell is going on?" demanded the dipshit musician.

"None of your business," Axel snarled. "Shut the fuck up!" He could tell that the guy was thinking about charging him. He should shoot him first. Even if Piper came after him, he felt confident he could dispatch with her in short order. If she tried to run, he could nail her before she got very far.

"Axel, no!" Piper sobbed. "You've got the money—just take it and go!" She should know that sniveling never got anyone anything. He would have thought she could face this moment with more dignity.

At this moment, everything slowed. It was just like the time he had taken Kristy down. It was as if every droplet of mist became suspended in the air, as if every single sound in the universe went still. He trained his gun on the musician, aware of each nanogram and increment of pressure as he squeezed the trigger, the shock on the kid's face assuming a comical look. But just as he took his shot, a giant beast came barreling out of the forest. Axel felt a strange reverberation in his chest, as if a phantom train were rumbling past, but of course, that was crazy. Terror seized him, loosing his bowels and bladder. What the freaking fuck was this thing? What the freaking fucking hell??

His legs took on a life of their own as they began churning in instinctive flight from the monster, a monster that shouldn't exist. He ran blindly, every single intelligible thought blotted out by abject horror. When he found himself careening off the bluff he had identified only moments earlier, he felt a vast and irrational relief. That relief turned to dismay when he felt first a stabbing, tearing pain in his back; and when he hit bottom, the leg that crumpled underneath him snapped.

And that was the last thing he registered before everything went black.

CHAPTER 41

iper sat quietly in a beanbag chair in Merilee and Carson's family room, Jessie nestled beside her, her head in Piper's lap. Jessie seemed to be fully recovered from the concussion Axel had given her, and Piper took comfort in her presence. She had been spending time with Jessie every day the past week, ever since Jessie had risked her life to save Piper's.

Carson and Merilee left her alone to have her time with Jessie; they had both been so incredibly kind. Fortunately, when Axel shot Carson, the creature that had come hurtling out of the forest threw his aim off, and the bullet had ended up only grazing Carson's arm. She was still trying to process that. Sasquatch, as best she could tell. Hairy and huge and smelly and terrifying, biological, corporeal, and real.

Things had happened so quickly and the entire scene was so surreal that Piper couldn't take it in at the time. She had had a week to process it, but she knew it was going to take a lot longer than that to get over the shock and the trauma. In fact, she had made an appointment to see a therapist who specialized in traumatic stress; she would have her first visit tomorrow.

The Sasquatch had seemed enraged, and Piper was afraid that after Axel ran off, he might turn his attention to her and Carson. She gathered that the lean-to belonged to him, and they were invading his territory. And she knew that this creature was capable of tearing them limb from limb. But the next thing she knew, she found herself surrounded by a cloud of what at first seemed like fireflies, but which she soon realized were devas. Some had wings, some didn't, but they all swarmed around her, enveloping her in their radiant embrace. Even more surprisingly, the Bigfoot appeared to recoil from them. He glared at her, looking spookily human yet jarringly feral, and vanished back into the forest. Maybe it was the presence of the gun that angered him so much, she thought numbly, the force of his heavy footsteps vibrating the forest floor; she remembered that Halil had told her that they hated guns.

Both Piper and Carson had frozen during the split-second altercation between Axel and the Forest Dweller. But as soon as they were both gone, Carson rushed over to where Jessie lay limp. Piper feared the worst, and so did Carson, but shortly after Carson gathered her into his lap, she stirred and gave him a lick. The devas drifted to Jessie and seemed to caress her before they melted into the forest, their lights reflecting on the slick, wet branches until they winked out one by one. Thank God Jessie was okay. Piper didn't think she could have handled it if Axel had killed her. That was when Piper noticed the blood dripping down Carson's arm. She ripped some fabric from her blouse to bind it, and called 911 on her cell phone. It was amazing that she had a signal as deep in the forest as they were. She noticed later that she had six missed calls from Olivia before the last one finally went through, alerting her to the danger she was in. So the coverage must have been some odd trick of the towers in the area combined with the terrain. So many things had come together to spare her life, she felt humbled and awed.

Once Piper had tended to his wound, Carson decided to scout for Axel, to see what had happened to him and make sure he wasn't still a threat. Piper stayed with Jessie, stroking her and soothing her. Carson found him at the bottom of a bluff, with an obvious serious injury and either unconscious or dead. When help arrived, they treated Carson and told him he would be fine. He then took them to Axel's location, where they determined that he was still alive and sent a helicopter to get him out of the gulch and transport him to the hospital. As soon as they could move him, they were going to send him to Sacramento where he would be charged with the murder of Kristy Holloway. Piper had since found out who Eric Johnson was. After that, Axel would return to Incident to face charges of assault, attempted murder, and anything else they could come up with. Danny was determined to make sure he stayed in jail for the rest of his life.

And Danny, that sweetheart, had found a way to cancel her cashier's check while keeping it as evidence so that Piper could access her funds. She had told him and Marion everything when they got home, of course, including the situation with her home and her landlords. She was now in escrow to buy her home, and for that, she was incredibly grateful.

But trauma, she was learning, scored a person deeply, and she was having a hard time taking much joy or pleasure in anything, including her lovely devas, who had gone out of their way to comfort her the past week. They had even gotten one of her rose bushes to produce a rare winter bloom. Everyone's kindness was so very moving. But she grieved the loss of her innocence and the brutal end to the relationship she thought she had.

She heard a soft knock and looked up to see Carson standing at the entrance to the family room. In his arms, he held an adorable, fluffy puppy. "Can I come in?" he asked.

Jessie raised her head at the scent and sight of the puppy. She gave a brief woof, which Piper wasn't sure how to interpret. "Of course," she said. "Who's that you've got there with you?"

Carson sat down on the floor cross-legged, and handed her the puppy. Jessie got up with a snort and resettled nearby. "You were talking about getting a dog the other day," he said, "and a little girl was giving these puppies away in front of the co-op. If you don't want her, we'll keep her." At that, Jessie gave a low moan. "But she just seemed to call out to me and tell me that you were meant for each other."

Piper cradled the puppy in her lap while the pup frantically licked her hands, her stubby tail wagging ferociously. "She's beautiful," she said. "What kind of puppy is she?"

"A cross between a chocolate lab and a poodle," he said. "So I guess that makes her a labradoodle."

Piper smiled. "I love that word."

"I do, too." Carson smiled back.

Piper's heart swelled at the wiggly, furry warmth of the sweet creature in her lap; this was the strongest emotion she had felt in a week. She had expected to sob her heart out when she finally got home after the shooting, alone with her grief and shock; but instead, she had felt numb and empty. She hadn't shed a tear. She didn't even know what to feel about Axel and their relationship—although, that seemed a euphemism for what had existed between them. Danny had explained to her that individuals like Axel lacked empathy. They didn't feel the same emotions that most people did. "They can have keen insight into their targets' psychology," he told her. "But whereas sensing someone's vulnerability would arouse your or my compassion, all it does is excite their predatory instincts." She had shuddered at the word "predatory." He was a predator. To him, she was prey.

"How are you doing?" Carson asked gently.

"I don't know," she said, her voice sounding dull and flat. "I'm trying to figure out where I went wrong. Marion always told me I had terrible taste in men. Why can she see it but I can't?"

Carson shrugged. "I think it's a lot easier to see other people's foibles than our own."

"Well, you're nice to say so." The puppy snuggled even deeper into her lap and began to doze. She felt grateful for its trusting innocence. "You know, my friend Danny tells me that Axel's a sociopath. And that sociopaths often target people who are innocent and kind."

Carson sighed. "I can see that."

"So … does that mean I should be less innocent, less kind?"

Carson gazed at her with such depth of emotion that she found herself trembling. "Well, less naïve, maybe. I guess. But honestly, Piper, I love the fact that you're so kind. I love your innocence. It's refreshing. It's really … beautiful."

For some reason, these words ruptured the dam that held back her tears. They streamed down her face. "I don't feel beautiful," she sobbed. "I feel foolish and stupid."

"Oh, hey," he murmured. He hesitated, then got up and wedged himself next to her on the bean bag chair and put his arms around her. "Is this okay?" he asked.

She nodded, unable to speak. Jessie got up then and flopped down on the other side of her, nudging her with her nose. Piper reached out to acknowledge her; the puppy stirred, but didn't awaken. Carson brushed her tears away with his thumbs and held her while she cried. When she was finally spent, she thanked him for his kindness.

"You're welcome," he said. "Any time. And I mean that."

She heaved a shaky breath.

"Seriously, Piper, you're anything but foolish. Don't let that bastard make you doubt yourself. Yes, you probably need to get your radar in better shape. And yes, you should probably make people earn your trust." He paused. "I've had to learn that lesson myself. But even though you might want to guard your heart a little better, please don't let this harden it. Don't."

She pondered his words, wondering how much control

she had over something like that. Right now, her heart felt anything but hard. It felt crushed to a leaky pulp. A movement in the corner of the room caught her eye, and she noticed a shy deva peeking out from the shamrock Merilee had placed by the north window. He blew her a kiss, which Piper felt physically, as if a tiny, silver minnow had burrowed inside of her and inoculated her with a sliver of hope.

She would take it, she decided. Even if it was just a sliver. Hope was the one thing that the ancient Greeks felt could sustain mankind in the face of the evil that someone like Axel represented. It was the only antidote for despair.

"I'm going to keep the puppy," she said finally. "And I'm going to name her Hope."

AFTERWORD

While I hope that this novel provides a good read and an entertaining one, of course, the message I want to convey with these pages is anything but entertaining. It's possible that some readers might think that the character of Axel is over the top, but in fact, he is based on extensive research on the topic of sociopathy.

People who have not personally been targeted by a sociopath nor read the literature, often think that they are all serial killers, like Hannibal Lector, like Axel was shaping up to be. However, most sociopaths are unrecognized as they go about leaving a wake of destroyed lives, looted companies, and stolen dreams. The high-functioning ones are often lauded as captains of industry, charismatic leaders, and pillars of society. The low-functioning ones are generally lotharios, small-time grifters, and entitled abusers. Rarely are their actions illegal. Instead, they usually con people into giving them what they want voluntarily, such as gigolos who attach themselves romantically to someone forty years their senior and are rewarded with the inheritance that should have gone to family, bully or trick them, or skirt the edge of legality.

Once you accept the fact that 4% of the population are sociopaths, however, and you know the characteristics of a sociopath—which are surprisingly uniform across the disorder—they become obvious. Psychologist Robert Hare pioneered the sociopath checklist of traits that are present in this disorder. Axel presented almost all of them:

> Sociopaths can be charismatic and charming. I wouldn't go so far as to say that everyone who is charismatic is a sociopath, but when you encounter someone who is

extremely charismatic, it pays to be wary and to look for other red flags before giving this person your trust, your money, your affections, or your vote.

Generally, sociopaths like to use a sob story in order to garner unearned sympathy right off the bat. It throws their targets off guard and makes them ignore many of the other red flags.

They are pathological liars. They lie constantly, even when they don't need to lie, although they will of course lie to get what they want and to protect their identity and motives. They are excellent liars and can even pass lie detectors tests. They can fool lawyers, judges, juries, and therapists.

They tend to be voracious sexually and many victims say that the sex they had with a sociopath was some of the best they've ever had.

They have no empathy. None. They might be able to fake it, but often they can't, especially if you scrutinize them carefully. They are shrewd judges of character, though, which they use in order to exploit weakness and manipulate.

They possess no remorse nor guilt and have no trouble whatsoever looking at themselves in the mirror or sleeping at night, no matter how atrocious their actions might be. Instead, they derive a great amount of enjoyment in conning people, viewing their targets with contempt for being so easy to con.

They often portray or even view themselves as the victim, even as they are ruthlessly victimizing others.

They seek power, dominance, money, and status. That is all they care about. They are incapable of true affection or love. They are predators.

They usually "love-bomb" their targets, presenting themselves as the man or woman of the target's dreams, seeming too good to be true. Once they are certain that the target is firmly in their grasp, Mr. Hyde emerges.

They isolate their target from former friends and family members. Once the person is isolated, they have no one else to turn to as the relationship becomes increasingly abusive, either physically, emotionally, psychologically, and/or financially.

They often operate romantically, but they also use their skills to dupe and take advantage of people financially, politically, professionally, and/or spiritually. They are often vague about their background and history so that you can fill in the blanks and they can shape their history to seem as if you're soul mates or they're the perfect business partner.

They get bored easily and are constantly looking for excitement. Conning people provides them a lot of excitement.

They "gaslight" their targets, strenuously and convincingly rewriting history, causing their targets to doubt their own instincts and sometimes their own eyes. In addition, they subtly and skillfully call the sanity or credibility of their target to others so that no one will believe them if they try to blow the whistle. They can be truly, amazingly convincing.

> They excel at crocodile tears.
>
> They feel completely entitled to whatever it is they want, no matter how unreasonable, unattainable, or abhorrent.
>
> They think the rules don't apply to them.

If you think you recognize anyone you know or anyone in a leadership position from this list of red flags, pay very close attention to how they act from the moment the light bulb goes off. If they continue to behave in this way (and you need to pay attention to their actions, not what they say, because they will always tell you what you want to hear and/or lie to suit their purposes), you need to face reality. Most people don't want to believe that sociopaths exist, or that they're as common as they are (14 million in the United States, as an estimate), or that the charming person you find so engaging could be one.

Therapy is of no use in trying to get a sociopath to behave like a compassionate, empathetic, ethical human being. They are perfectly happy with who they are and see no need to change. They often end up using what they learn in therapy as a way to better manipulate their targets, or they con the therapist. The only thing we can do in the face of a threat like sociopathy is to recognize the warning signals and heed them, listen to any gut misgivings we might have, avoid the sociopath, and most importantly, refrain from enabling them. As master manipulators, they tend to be quite good at getting people to enable them.

Piper is the perfect target for someone like Axel. Sociopaths often target healers, the innocent and guileless, the selfless, the vulnerable— those who trust unconditionally, make constant excuses for bad behavior, give people too many "second" chances, and always put others' needs before their own. Sociopaths often strike when a target is at his or her most vulnerable: after a divorce or breakup, loss of job or company, a health crisis, or major life disappointment. If you found yourself gnashing your teeth at all the times that Piper ignored red flags, made excuses for Axel, and downplayed her intuition, know that this is par for the course for those mesmerized and groomed by a sociopath.

My hope is to raise awareness of this pathology so that we, as individuals and a society, will stop enabling sociopaths. So many of them rise to the top of their profession because they are willing to do whatever it takes to get there, much to the detriment of whatever system they're conning. But they couldn't do it without our help. They represent only 4% of the population. We can't change sociopaths, but we can change our response to them. One thing that concerns me is Americans' insistence on "charisma" for their political leaders. Yes, we want someone who can inspire, but charisma is something that we need to approach warily. It is often a red flag, not a reason by itself to support someone. Instead, we need to look at their record in terms of how they have treated constituents, coworkers, colleagues, customers, vendors, and family. We need to judge them on their experience, their policies, their proposals, and integrity.

Sociopaths in powerful positions can wreak enormous havoc. It is possible that almost all the wars that have taken place in human history have at least one sociopath at their core. They may lurk at the center of the majority of human-caused disasters, economic depressions and recessions, mishandled pandemics, genocide, and climate change. But they can do it only with our help.

Most people are good people. They have a conscience;

they have a moral compass. They are capable of empathy and compassion. But good people can be only too easily manipulated by a sociopath if they don't realize who and what they're dealing with. If you're interested in learning more about sociopathy and ways in which you can protect yourself, your loved ones, and your community, there are ample resources available online and in book form. And they make for compelling reading.

P.S. If you suffer from hypertension with no known cause, I urge you to get a sleep study to check for apnea, if you haven't already. You can have apnea even if you don't snore.

www.ingramcontent.com/pod-product-compliance
Lightning Source LLC
Chambersburg PA
CBHW020253200626
46816CB00001BA/274